'TIS THE SEASON

to embrace the wonder, indulge in the passion and
surrender to the love that the holidays awaken

Charming Christmas romances
by three unforgettable

Natalie Anderson

Carole Mortimer

Alison Roberts

Natalie Anderson

'TIS THE SEASON

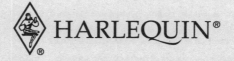

HARLEQUIN®

TORONTO • NEW YORK • LONDON
AMSTERDAM • PARIS • SYDNEY • HAMBURG
STOCKHOLM • ATHENS • TOKYO • MILAN • MADRID
PRAGUE • WARSAW • BUDAPEST • AUCKLAND

ISBN-13: 978-0-373-83741-0

'TIS THE SEASON

Copyright © 2010 by Harlequin Books S.A.

The publisher acknowledges the copyright holders of the individual works as follows:

SNOWBOUND WITH THE BILLIONAIRE
Copyright © 2009 by Carole Mortimer

TWINS FOR CHRISTMAS
Copyright © 2009 by Alison Roberts

THE MILLIONAIRE'S MISTLETOE MISTRESS
Copyright © 2009 by Natalie Anderson

Recycling programs for this product may not exist in your area.

CONTENTS

SNOWBOUND WITH THE BILLIONAIRE 7
Carole Mortimer

TWINS FOR CHRISTMAS   101
Alison Roberts

THE MILLIONAIRE'S   203
  MISTLETOE MISTRESS
Natalie Anderson

For Peter,
who makes every day feel like Christmas!

SNOWBOUND WITH THE BILLIONAIRE

Carole Mortimer

Dear Reader,

It's that time of year again!

Christmas is a special time, for family and for friends, and my own family is no different. All our sons come home for the holidays, and my parents come to stay, too, and for days the house is full of warmth and love and laughter.

I hope that my love of Christmas is shared with all of you when you read my Christmas stories.

Happy Christmas!

Carole Mortimer

CHAPTER ONE

CARO'S SEARCHING GAZE swept over the sea of happy faces as she left the baggage area at Heathrow Airport, looking for her brother Gavin. It was the day before Christmas Eve, and there were dozens of people waiting expectantly for family and friends to arrive for the holidays. Caro wasn't in the least surprised when Gavin didn't appear to be one of them; her absent-minded brother had probably forgotten she was arriving today!

'I'll take it from here, thanks.'

Caro froze the second she heard that arrogantly forceful voice behind her, the colour fading from her cheeks, the blood in her veins turning to ice, and her excitement at being back in England again turning to cold dread.

No!

It couldn't be...

Not here. Not now!

She had been in Majorca for over a year—

'Have a good Christmas!' called out the man, who had very kindly offered to push Caro's luggage trolley through for her, happily as he hastened away to be greeted by a pretty blonde woman and two young children.

'Could you get a move on, Caro?' rasped that all-too-familiar voice. 'We're holding everyone up.'

Caro turned sharply, eyes wide, feeling numb with disbelief as she looked up at the man who had now taken charge of the trolley and her luggage. It really *was* Jake! She took in everything about his face in that single glance. Aged in his mid-thirties, Jake had dark hair, green eyes—angrily accusing!—high cheekbones either side of an arrogant slash of a nose, and sculptured lips that at the moment were thinned with displeasure. His firm jaw was tightly clenched.

Jake Montgomery.

Caro's estranged husband…

Jake gave Caro a steely look—long enough to register the fact that, at ten years his junior, she was as beautiful as ever—before turning his hungry gaze to the baby she carried in her arms.

The baby's hair was the same red-gold as Caro's, but eyes the same emerald-green as his own stared back at him with guileless curiosity. The nose was small and snub, and the mouth a perfect bow in a chubby face warmly golden from the Majorcan sun.

Magdalena. His six-month-old daughter that Jake hadn't even known existed until a few hours ago.

The six-month-old daughter who had absolutely no idea that Jake was her father!

Jake's instinct—*need*—was to snatch the baby from Caro and hold her in his arms for the very first time. To bury his face in the baby's silky red-gold curls. To breathe in the essence of her. To feel the solidity of her very existence.

That was Jake's instinct. Logic told him he couldn't do that—that he was a stranger to Magdalena and she would probably scream the place down if he were to try and take her from the comfort and safety of her mother's arms.

Jake's mouth thinned grimly as he thought of Caro's year-long deception that had made him a stranger to his own daughter, and he clenched his fingers tightly about the handle of the trolley to stop himself from giving in to the temptation to reach out and shake Caro where she stood.

'Let's get out of here.'

'I'm not going anywhere with you, Jake!' Caro's sky-blue eyes glittered with determination, her cheeks aflame with colour now as she stood her ground with her arms protectively about the baby.

'Oh, yes, Caro, you most certainly are,' Jake contradicted her, his long-held patience finally at breaking point. 'Unless, that is, you would prefer to stand here in front of all these people and tell me the reason you didn't inform me of the existence of my own daughter?' he added with pointed challenge.

What Caro wanted to do was to sit down and cry. Or scream and shout. But most of all she wanted Jake to just disappear. To not be here at all. 'We have nothing to discuss,' she told him firmly, unhappily aware that he easily towered over her five-feet-four-inch height as she attempted to take charge of the trolley herself.

And failed miserably.

'I really don't advise that we have this conversation here, Caro,' Jake reiterated before he strode off, pushing the trolley in front of him.

Leaving Caro no choice but to follow him. All of Magdalena's food, clothes and other baby needs were in that trolley—as was the suitcase she had packed for their week-long seasonal stay.

Caro almost had to run to keep up with Jake's much longer strides as he headed towards one of the exits, and she was not in the least surprised when people moved aside to make a path before him—like Moses parting the Red Sea!

What was Jake doing here? How could he possibly

have known Caro would be on that particular flight from Majorca?

Gavin!

She ground her teeth in exasperation. Her totally brilliant but equally impossible and absent-minded younger brother was noticeably absent!

Caro hadn't even wanted to make this trip to England, but Gavin had talked her into it with the claim that with their parents both dead they were now the only family each of them had, and that Christmas was a time for families to be together.

Maybe all with the intention of Jake being the one to meet her at the airport instead of her brother...?

No, Gavin was absent-minded—rarely knew what time it was, let alone which day of the week—but still Caro didn't believe he would have deliberately put her in this awkward position.

'Where's Gavin?' Caro asked as she unwillingly followed Jake outside into the icily cold wind.

Snow had been forecast in England for Christmas, and Caro had dressed both Magdalena and herself accordingly, the two of them wearing jeans and heavy sweaters beneath their warm coats. Nevertheless, she pulled up the hood of Magdalena's pink coat to keep off most of the biting chill.

Jake turned to look at his wife and daughter, a fist clenching in his chest as he was once again hit with the likeness between them.

Caro's long hair was that same unusual shade of red-gold, her skin tanned with the same golden hue, her nose slightly upturned, her mouth a full pouting bow, and her chin small and stubbornly pointed. But her eyes were a clear sky-blue, and surrounded by the thickest, darkest lashes Jake had ever seen. Caro was undeniably still the most beautiful woman he had ever seen.

She was also—no matter how much she might wish it were otherwise!—still his wife.

As Magdalena was undoubtedly his daughter...

'Will you please tell me where Gavin is?' Caro prompted again impatiently.

A satisfied smile curved Jake's mouth. 'When I last saw him?'

He quirked dark brows. 'He was grappling with a particularly troublesome glitch in the program for the new security system he's in the middle of developing for Montgomery Software.'

'Your doing?'

'Yes, as a matter of fact...' Jake drawled unapologetically.

Caro gave a pained grimace as she closed her eyes. Her younger brother was currently, and probably always would be, one of the most brilliant computer programmers in the world. He was also one of the most single-minded. Nothing penetrated his concentration once he was caught up in one of his beloved computer programs. That single-mindedness was the very reason Jake Montgomery had employed Gavin at Montgomery Software two and a half years ago, after he'd left university.

It was that employment that had led to Caro meeting and falling in love with Jake only weeks later...

None of which was of the least help now, with the awkward situation she found herself in!

She attempted a conciliatory smile. 'It was very kind of you to meet us, Jake, but—'

'Believe me, Caro, kindness didn't enter into my emotions at all when I learnt that Gavin had taken the unprecedented step of taking the afternoon off on the day before Christmas Eve because he had to go to the airport to pick up a relative. As you're the only relative Gavin has…' He shrugged. 'I cashed in a few favours with a friend who owns one of the airlines, and he managed to ascertain that a Caroline Montgomery was arriving on a flight from Majorca. Along with her *six-month-old baby daughter*—Magdalena Montgomery,' Jake gritted.

Caro eyed him warily, noticing as she did so the lines of grimness beside Jake's eyes and mouth, the touches of grey in the darkness of the hair at his temples. Neither of which had been there when she had seen him a little over a year ago.

Not that Caro thought for a moment that it had been her walking out of their marriage that had brought about those changes in Jake. As she knew only too well, he simply hadn't cared enough about her or their marriage for that to be the case. He'd found someone new to occupy his time with, and she hadn't been able to bear that.

'It was easy enough after that to come up with something that would distract Gavin so that he totally forgot he was going anywhere this afternoon,' Jake added with an evil smile. 'Don't worry—I've left a message with my secretary to assure him of your safety once he does emerge from his programming trance.'

Gavin was now the least of her worries. 'Jake—'

'I don't intend continuing this conversation now, Caro,' he stated.

'When, then?' She stubbornly stood her ground.

'When I'm good and ready!' His eyes glittered dangerously.

'I hate to burst your bubble, Jake, but I no longer give a damn— Where are you going with my luggage?' Caro demanded as Jake turned away to push the trolley across the road.

He didn't even glance back as he answered her. 'Wherever it is I'm going, I would advise that you follow me!'

'I— But— Jake!' Caro protested, making no effort to follow him—her days of following where Jake led were long over!

Jake drew in a deep controlling breath as he came to an abrupt halt on the island in the middle of the road, appreciating the fact that if he did follow his instinct to shake Caro right here and now there were enough policemen and women milling about the airport to arrest him on the spot!

How could she have done this to him? No matter what their differences were, how could she have kept her pregnancy from him—let alone the birth of their daughter six months ago? Did Caro really hate him *that* much...?

Jake had been asking himself those same questions for the last three hours—since learning of Caro and Magdalena's imminent arrival in England. Since he had learnt of his daughter's existence...

He still had no answers to those questions.

But Caro did. And before this day was out she was going to give Jake those answers. Just not here. And certainly not now.

He turned slowly, steeling himself not to be affected by how young and defenceless she suddenly looked, with her hair flowing about her shoulders and her coat buttoned up against the cold. Fitted jeans emphasised her slenderness, and her expression was once again defensive as she held Magdalena to her tightly.

Caro was wise to feel apprehension! 'My car is parked over here,' Jake informed her abruptly.

'Your car?' Caro shook her head, her expression becoming stubborn. 'Magdalena and I can easily get a taxi to Gavin's apartment.'

Jake's eyes narrowed. 'You and I both know there is no way I'm going to let you go anywhere until the two of us have had a chance to talk.'

She swallowed hard. 'You can't stop me—'

'No?' Jake challenged softly.

Caro felt a shiver of apprehension run down the length of her spine as she saw the cold and ruthless determination on Jake's handsome face.

A face she had fallen instantly in love with over two years ago…

But she hadn't fallen in love with just his face, Caro accepted heavily. She had fallen in love with the whole package. The self-assurance that bordered on arrogance. The air of power that his incredible wealth gave him. The athletic fitness of his six-foot-two-inch frame. The experienced and mesmerising lover who had held Caro so totally in his thrall that she hadn't even noticed that Jake had never, ever—not even during the height of passion—told her that he loved her.

No, she wouldn't even go there!

She *couldn't* go there.

It would remind her all too painfully of how her father had damaged their whole family with his fickle behaviour…

'I'm not about to argue with you on this point, Caro,' Jake bit out as he saw stubborn resolve return to her expression. 'You're going to come to my car with me. Then I'm going to drive us somewhere private, so that we can talk about this like two rational human beings.'

Sky-blue eyes warred with his for several long seconds as Jake waited for Caro to capitulate to his demand. And she *would* capitulate. Jake simply wouldn't accept any other outcome to this conversation.

Yes, Jake wanted answers from his wife. Explanations for what she had done—if she had any! But he also wanted to sit somewhere quietly and hold his daughter in his arms for the first time. To familiarise himself with the weight and feel of her. To check all of her fingers and toes. To see her smile—

Damn it—Caro had better have a really good explanation for denying him knowledge of his own daughter for all these months.

'Well?' he pressed. 'What's it going to be? A slanging match here? Or a more civilised conversation somewhere less public?' He gave a pointed glance at the stream of people constantly leaving the airport building, several of them shooting curious looks their way as they obviously sensed the tension of their exchange.

Caro's earlier sense of dread returned with a vengeance. She knew that Jake was more than capable of carrying out his threat. That he was more than capable of simply picking up both her and Magdalena and carrying them to his car if necessary.

Her chin rose as she met the challenge in that emerald-green gaze. 'Very well. But wherever we go I'm only staying long enough so that we can sort this situation out.'

'Whatever.' Mocking humour darkened glittering green eyes.

After all, Jake mused wickedly as Caro finally fell into step beside him to walk across to the car park, she hadn't specified exactly to whose satisfaction the situation had to be sorted out...

CHAPTER TWO

'HOW DID YOU MANAGE that so quickly?' Caro stared in surprise at the baby-seat that had obviously been professionally fitted into the back of the sleek dark green car that Jake had unlocked, before opening the door so that she could strap the now dozing Magdalena safely inside.

Jake mouth twisted humourlessly. 'It's amazing what can be achieved in just the few hours I've known of Magdalena's existence.'

Caro knew it wasn't so amazing when you were multi-multi-millionaire Jake Montgomery!

She straightened after securing the sleeping Magdalena into her seat, realising as she turned that Jake was standing far too close to her. Far too close for comfort. For *her* comfort, anyway!

Jake looked down at Caro through narrowed lids, taking his time as he noted the subtle changes in her. Her hair was longer. The lines of tension that had been beside her eyes and mouth a year ago when she'd walked out on him and their marriage were no longer there. Instead her make-up-less face was tanned a deep, healthy gold, her eyes were a clear blue.

He couldn't resist reaching out to touch the softness of her tanned cheek. 'Motherhood suits you, Caro...'

'Don't!' She shied away from that reaching hand.

Jake's mouth tightened as he allowed his hand to drop

back to his side. 'You never used to complain about my touching you,' he said dryly.

Caro was finding it increasingly difficult to deny the memories of Jake that she had managed to keep at bay for at least six months of the last year.

It hadn't been so easy to do during the long months of her pregnancy, but since Magdalena's birth Caro had been kept too busy caring for her baby daughter to allow thoughts of Jake to disrupt her increasingly calm existence.

Any existence would be calm after living in the maelstrom that was Jake Montgomery's life and consequently had become Caro's own for the year she had been his wife.

She had been physically and emotionally drained when she'd arrived in Majorca, but the much more relaxed lifestyle on the island, and the friendliness of the people, had eventually acted as a balm to those broken emotions.

A balm that had swiftly disappeared a few minutes ago at the first sound of Jake's arrogant voice!

She shot him a narrow-eyed stare before climbing into the front passenger seat of the car. 'Motherhood isn't the only reason for the changes in me, Jake.'

Cold anger blazed in the depths of his green eyes. 'You—'

'Could we just go, and get this over with?' Caro interrupted wearily. 'I've been travelling since early this morning, and what I need more than anything is a hot bath and something decent to eat.' She leant her head back against the seat, her eyes closing.

Jake continued to look down at her for several long seconds, his jaw clenching as he recalled the way Caro had flinched away from him just now. As if she found his slightest touch distasteful.

What had he ever done to Caro to make her feel that way…?

Jake's inner frustration with the situation filled him with a need to *make* Caro talk to him and tell him what was wrong.

But the obvious exhaustion on her face told him that she really was tired, that it hadn't been at all easy travelling with a six-month-old baby.

Not that Jake would know anything about that, of course, never having been allowed to travel with his baby daughter!

Jake slammed Caro's door, his expression stony as he strode round the car to get in behind the wheel, his movements automatic as he backed the car out of the parking space to drive towards the airport exit.

They drove in complete silence for several minutes, but it was a silence Caro found oppressive rather than restful.

'Jake—'

'It's the day before Christmas Eve, Caro, and the traffic on roads is insane. With you and Magdalena in the car, I really would prefer to concentrate on my driving,' Jake cut in quietly.

Caro gave a sceptical snort, knowing that Jake was perfectly capable of driving and talking at the same time. That he was more than capable of doing any damn thing he chose. In this case he simply chose not to.

Her own tension from the situation was increasing by the second, and a single glance at Jake's rigidly set face was enough to intensify that fluttering of unease in her chest. That Jake was coldly furious under his façade of icy calm she had no doubts. That the fury was directed towards her was also in no doubt.

Because of Magdalena.

Because Caro hadn't chosen to tell Jake she was pregnant, let alone that he had a six-month-old daughter!

No matter what Jake might be thinking to the contrary, that hadn't been an easy decision to make. But, remembering her own incredibly difficult relationship with her father, she'd thought she was doing the right thing...

'She's beautiful.'

Caro turned sharply to look at Jake, her expression becoming pained as she saw the hunger in his gaze as he shot a glance at Magdalena's reflection in his mirror before returning his attention back to the busy road.

Caro looked at her daughter. Magdalena was fast asleep now, her lashes long and dark against her rosily chubby cheeks, her red-gold hair in wispy curls about her face. 'Yes, she is,' Caro acknowledged huskily, and she turned back to look sightlessly out of the front window, her hands clenched so tightly her nails were digging into her palms.

'Why Majorca, Caro?' Jake suddenly asked as his hands tightly gripped the steering wheel.

His emotions were in turmoil, Jake acknowledged wryly. And not just because he had met his daughter for the very first time...

Being with Caro again, recognising the bloom motherhood had given to her beauty, being able to smell the perfume she always wore—which Jake knew he would associate with Caro until the day he died—was churning up his memories as much as he was sure his own presence was churning up Caro's...if for a completely different reason.

And not good memories, either, going by her recent reaction to him!

'Why not Majorca?' Caro countered guardedly.

Jake sighed heavily. 'Did you go there because you

knew it was the very last place I would think of looking for you?'

Caro shot him a surprised look. 'It never even occurred to me that you would *want* to look for me.'

His mouth compressed. 'Don't be so naïve, Caro. Once I had calmed down enough to be able to think straight, of *course* I looked for you.'

Her frown was pained. 'I can't imagine why...'

'Can't you?' Jake grated.

Caro's face was very pale. 'Gavin knew where I could be reached—'

'And no amount of cajoling, persuasion or even threats of outright violence would make him tell me where that was,' Jake revealed, his expression tight as he recalled his brother-in-law's refusal to even discuss Caro, let alone tell Jake where she was.

Even the threat of being sacked hadn't shifted Gavin's loyalty to Caro—probably because Gavin, although in a world of his own most of the time, was well aware of his own value in the world of computer software! Whatever the reason, nothing Jake had done or said had managed to shake the younger man's resolve not to reveal his sister's whereabouts.

Jake could still remember the knife-thrust of Gavin's last comment on the subject. 'If Caro had wanted you to find her, then she would have made sure you could do so by now.' The truth of that statement had been undisputable. And painfully final...

'I'm sure that Gavin would have forwarded any correspondence to me, if you had asked him to.'

'I didn't want to write you a *letter,* Caro!' Jake exclaimed.

'I was referring to the divorce papers.'

'There isn't going to be any divorce,' he said definitely.

'Not a year ago, and certainly not now.' He gave a pointed look in the mirror at Magdalena.

Caro had been afraid this was going to be Jake's reaction to knowing he had a daughter. Afraid and not a little apprehensive. She knew Jake well enough to know that once he was set on a course of action nothing deterred him from achieving his goal.

In the same way Jake had decided two years ago— once he'd realised that Caro simply wasn't the type of woman to have affairs—that she would have to marry him instead...

The only problem with that, of course, had been that once Jake had physically tired of her she had still been his wife!

And after growing up experiencing her father's numerous affairs, not the type of wife to meekly sit back and tolerate Jake behaving in the same way...

She drew in a determined breath. 'Jake, I have no intention— This isn't the way into central London!' Caro said, as she realised Jake was driving in the opposite direction from the one she wanted to go.

He gave a terse inclination of his head. 'That's because we aren't going into the City.'

Caro felt a shiver go down her spine. 'Then where are we going?'

Jake shrugged. 'I own a house in the country.'

She blinked. 'You do?' When Caro had married Jake she had simply moved into his penthouse apartment in Mayfair with him. Much as Caro would have preferred it, there had never been any suggestion of them moving out of London. 'Why?'

Jake raised dark brows. 'Are you asking as my wife, or just out of idle curiosity?' he taunted.

'Neither!' Caro snapped. 'I...' She moistened dry lips.

'I'm just surprised that you've moved out of London, that's all.'

'I said I have a house in the country, Caro, not that I actually live there,' Jake answered coolly.

'Oh.' She gave a knowing nod. 'Then the house is just a business investment?'

'Something like that,' he said.

Caro eyed him warily. 'And that's where we're going?'

He raised a dark eyebrow. 'Do you have a problem with that?'

Now that her initial shock had worn off, Caro had a problem being there with Jake at all!

Much as she wished it wasn't so, Caro was totally aware of her husband as he sat beside her, wearing a casual black cashmere sweater with faded jeans. So much so that she could almost feel the lean sensuality of his hands and fingers on the steering wheel. Was totally attuned to the width of his shoulders. His muscled chest. His taut stomach. His powerful thighs and legs.

Caro was aware of all of those things from the top of her head to the tips of her toes!

It had been this way from the beginning, of course. Caro had been completely bowled off her feet the moment she was introduced to Jake, when she'd accompanied Gavin to a summer party at Montgomery Software.

At the time the attraction had appeared to be mutual.

No, it *had* been mutual! Whatever had followed, Caro had absolutely no doubts that Jake had initially wanted her physically. Enough to marry her, at least...

She gave a weary sigh. 'I can't see that the two of us

talking now is going to resolve anything, Jake. It never did in the past.'

His jaw tightened, a nerve pulsing in his cheek. 'You must realise the situation has now changed, Caro.'

She closed her eyes briefly. 'Because of Magdalena?' She was going to *kill* her little brother when she finally managed to drag him away from his computer. Hang, draw and quarter him!

'Of *course* because of Magdalena!' Jake rasped his impatience. 'You've obviously done a fantastic job with her so far—'

'How kind!'

Jake eyes glittered warningly as he heard the heavy sarcasm in her tone. 'Where do you live in Majorca? How do you work to support yourself when you have a young baby to care for?'

Her cheeks were flushed. 'I don't think that's any of your business, do you?'

'I'm *making* it my business!'

She shrugged slender shoulders. 'I had some money of my own saved when we separated a year ago—'

'When you walked out on me, you mean,' Jake corrected her harshly.

Caro stared at him for several long seconds. 'Whatever,' she finally dismissed. 'There was enough money to enable me to buy a small *finca* in a village on the west coast of the island. It's nothing grand, but it's perfectly adequate for the two of us.'

Jake didn't want just 'adequate' for his wife and daughter! 'That doesn't answer my question as to how you have continued to support yourself and Magdalena.'

Caro's eyes flashed. 'How do you *imagine* I support myself, Jake? By taking a paying lover every night?'

Jake's mouth went completely dry at the thought of

her taking even one lover, let alone a different one every night. Caro was his. She had always been his. Would always *be* his!

To his surprise—and pleasure—Jake had been Caro's first lover. He had every intention of being her last one, too...

'I was a journalist when we met, Jake, and I'm still a journalist. I write some freelance pieces for the English newspaper on the island, and I have some money left in reserve from my savings,' she explained. 'I'm also thinking of writing a book. *An Englishwoman in Majorca.* What do you think?' she couldn't help asking naughtily.

Jake scowled. 'You really want to know?'

'Probably not.' She sighed heavily.

'I think that you have a husband, Caro, and that *he* should be the one providing for you and Magdalena.'

Caro eyed him mockingly. 'To keep me living in the privileged lifestyle to which I had become accustomed?' She shook her head. 'I don't need or want that lifestyle, Jake. I never did.'

Jake's money, and the power that went along with his wealth, had never interested Caro. All she had ever wanted was Jake's undivided love. Something Caro knew, after learning of his affair with another woman, that Jake was incapable of giving her...

'Nevertheless—'

'There is no nevertheless,' Caro interrupted him firmly. 'I've managed perfectly well on my own so far, and I have every intention of continuing to do so.'

Jake frowned heavily. 'We'll talk about this further when we reach the house.'

'Anything to do with giving me any of your money, for any reason, is non-negotiable, Jake.'

'*I'll* decide what is or isn't negotiable.'

'No,' Caro argued shakily. 'No, Jake, you *won't*,' she repeated more decisively. 'I wasn't interested in your money two years ago, and I'm not interested in it now, either.'

Jake fingers were now clasped so tightly about the steering wheel that his knuckles showed white. 'Then what *does* interest you, Caro? Damn it, I've never understood what it is you want from me!'

Caro was all too aware of that.

She had been too much in love with Jake during those first few months of their marriage to realise that he had never indicated verbally that he returned the emotion. To realise that the only time Jake let down the tight control he had over his emotions was when they were in bed together.

Caro realised now that her lack of insight was probably because for the first few months of their marriage that was exactly where they had spent most of their time together!

Sex—even the incredible, mind-blowing sex she and Jake had shared—wasn't enough to keep a marriage together. Especially after Caro had learnt even that wasn't exclusive! After growing up with a constantly straying father and a thoroughly humiliated mother, she had sworn she'd never repeat their mistakes and remain in a miserable, faithless marriage. So when she'd learnt about Jake's infidelity she'd left him immediately.

'Nothing, Jake,' Caro told him flatly now. 'There's absolutely *nothing* you have that I could possibly want.'

They would see about that, Jake decided grimly.

Because he had absolutely no intention of letting Caro leave his life for a second time...

CHAPTER THREE

'LET ME,' JAKE INSISTED, as Caro would have unstrapped Magdalena from the baby-seat before lifting her out of the car.

Magdalena had woken up the moment Jake parked the car in front of a mellow stone manor house, and the deep green of her eyes was now fixed steadily on Jake as Caro reluctantly stepped aside to allow him to take their daughter from the back seat.

A lump caught and held in Jake's throat as one of Magdalena's tiny starfish hands came to rest on the broadness of his shoulder as he straightened with her in his arms. She was heavier than he had expected, but warm, and her gaze was so trusting and open as she looked at him—in a way so reminiscent of the way Caro had once looked at him—that Jake just wanted to bury his face in the softness of her red-gold curls. To at last hold his daughter close and never let her go.

'We should get this conversation over with—snow is forecast for later today,' Caro reminded him huskily, after a brief glance at the grey and overcast sky.

Jake straightened, his gaze completely unreadable as he turned to watch her take Magdalena's changing bag from the boot of the car. 'I'll get the rest of your luggage later.'

'We won't be staying long enough to need any of the

other luggage,' Caro insisted quickly as she slung the bag over her shoulder.

Jake gave her a pitying glance before striding off towards the house with Magdalena still in his arms.

Caro's unease returned with a vengeance as she hurried to follow him up the stone steps to the huge oak door. But she was prevented from questioning him about that pitying look as the door was immediately opened by a beaming middle-aged woman.

'Mr Montgomery!' the woman, obviously the housekeeper, greeted him cordially as the three of them stepped inside the warmth of the house. 'And this must be Mrs Montgomery.' Her smile widened to encompass Caro. 'And little Magdalena.' The woman's face softened completely as she looked at the baby Jake held so confidently in his arms.

Caro felt her trepidation deepen as she realised that the older woman had obviously been expecting her and Magdalena to arrive here with Jake this afternoon...

What had he told the housekeeper about them? What possible explanation could Jake have given for the sudden arrival of his wife and baby daughter?

Although, knowing Jake's arrogance, he probably hadn't bothered to give an explanation at all!

Besides which, he had told Caro that he didn't actually live here...

So what were they doing here now? Why had Jake brought them all the way out here to—wherever—when it would have been so much easier for them to have talked in London?

The housekeeper's next comment answered some of those questions. 'The linen and the cot have been delivered, and the cot's already made up in Magdalena's room,' she told Jake. 'I've put the highchair in the dining room, and the other things you ordered to be delivered are in the drawing room.'

Caro's eyes were wide as she turned to look at Jake. He'd had a cot, a highchair and 'other things' delivered here since speaking to Gavin earlier this morning and learning of Magdalena's existence…?

'Thanks, Mrs Weaver,' he answered the housekeeper briskly. 'I'm sure Mrs Montgomery would appreciate a cup of tea, if it's not too much trouble?'

'Of course.' The housekeeper gave Caro another beaming smile. 'I won't be long.' She bustled off towards the back of the house, where the kitchen was obviously situated.

Caro waited only long enough for the plump and motherly woman to disappear through the door at the end of the hallway before speaking. 'Jake, what's going on?'

'I'm sure we'll be more comfortable in the drawing room, Caro,' he evaded, before striding off to enter a room to the right of the spacious entrance hall.

Caro followed more reluctantly, curious about the 'other things' that awaited them in the drawing room, and at the same time very wary about the fact that Jake had ordered any of those things to be delivered at all. Plus there was the highchair, of course. And the cot was most worrying of all! That meant Jake intended them to stay here overnight…

All this coupled with that pitying look Jake had given her a few minutes ago, and Caro knew she was right to feel apprehensive.

Jake, having sat down on the carpeted floor to take off Magdalena's coat and interest her in the numerous toys there, glanced up as Caro entered the drawing room, and was struck once again by her almost ethereal beauty.

Two years ago Caro had been exquisitely lovely. So much so that Jake had been knocked off his feet the first time he'd looked at that cloud of red-gold hair, those deep blue eyes and the sensuously kissable mouth, the delectable curves of her slender body that had been clearly outlined in the red sun-dress she had been wearing.

But now, at twenty-six and also a mother, Caro possessed something much more elusive. A serenity, perhaps? An inner peace both with herself and the life she had chosen?

A life Caro had *chosen*, Jake recalled with a scowl, and that totally excluded him.

'Take your coat off and stay a while, Caro,' he offered as she made no effort to come farther into the room.

'It's how long you expect me to *stay* that concerns me!' Her eyes flashed deeply blue. 'Especially as you appear to have a cot upstairs for Magdalena to sleep in!'

Jake gave a wicked smile. 'Don't worry. I'm sure a bed can be found for you to sleep in, too.'

An angry flush darkened the paleness of her cheeks. 'No doubt Mrs Weaver has already assumed that as your wife I will be sharing yours!'

'No doubt,' Jake acknowledged casually.

Caro gave a firm shake of her head as she crossed the room to stand over him and Magdalena. 'Neither Magdalena nor I will be staying long enough to need a bed of any kind.'

His mouth tightened. 'Oh, I think that you will.'

'We're spending Christmas with Gavin!'

Jake gave an unconcerned shrug. 'Your brother is quite welcome to join us here if he wishes to. Although, knowing Gavin, he's probably forgotten that it *is* Christmas.'

Caro knew Gavin better than Jake did—and she was

also pretty sure her brother had forgotten it was the holiday season! Focused didn't even begin to describe Gavin when he was working on a problem with a computer program; obsessive probably more aptly described it. Gavin probably wouldn't emerge from his programming fog until the New Year! Unless he was given a very firm nudge...

Caro's mouth firmed. 'I need to call him.'

'Go ahead,' Jake invited, with a gesture towards a telephone on the table near the window that looked out into a walled garden. 'I'm sure Magdalena and I can manage to amuse each other for a few minutes.'

Caro was sure they could, too—with the amount of toys that literally covered half the carpet!

At only six months old Magdalena wouldn't even know what to do with most of them. At the moment she was really only interested in toys she could put in her mouth and chew in an effort to alleviate the discomfort of teething.

'I would rather be alone when I speak to Gavin,' Caro pointed out, having every intention of telling her brother exactly what she thought of him for so thoughtlessly landing her in this awkward situation.

Leaving Jake at all, when Caro had been still in love with him, had been difficult enough, and that difficulty had been added to by the fact that she had known he would never have allowed her to leave if he had known she was pregnant.

As he had no intention of allowing her to leave now...?

Jake could almost see the thoughts going through Caro's mind, and knew the exact moment when it dawned on her that he really wasn't going to let her to leave here any time soon. Her cheeks lost their healthy colour. There was an apprehensive tremble to those pouting, kissable lips. Her eyes clouded with apprehension and she looked across at him warily.

It made Jake want to stand up and grasp her firmly by the arms, before berating her soundly and condemning her for leaving him—especially for keeping Magdalena's existence a secret from him all these months.

But most of all Jake knew that he wanted to kiss that trembling from her lips. To kiss her until she didn't have the strength or the will to leave him again!

Jake had been so angry with Caro when she'd left him just over a year ago. Both before, during and after the business trip that had necessitated him going to the States for six days. Jake had been angry before he went away because Caro had originally intended going with him, but a political scandal had broken and she had chosen to remain in England to cover that story instead.

Jake had been so annoyed with her for making that choice that through sheer bloody-mindedness he hadn't even called her while he was away. To make matters worse, his PA had taken to her bed with a very bad cold within a day of their arrival in New York, unexpectedly delaying Jake's return.

Caro's reaction to that delay had been unexpected and completely baffling.

As soon as Jake had let himself into their penthouse apartment he had been confronted by a stony-faced Caro, telling him she was leaving him, that her bags were already packed and waiting in her car in the car park beneath the building.

There had been no explanation, no real argument, just a totally unreachable Caro, insisting that their marriage was at an end.

Jake had thought it was an aberration at the time—that she was just annoyed with him because he hadn't called her while he was away, and upset because his day's delay had meant he hadn't got back in time for their first wedding anniversary. He had fully expected to be able to sort out the problem with Caro once she had calmed down.

Instead of which she had chosen to completely disappear.

The suddenness of her decision to end their marriage hadn't made any sense to him a year ago and it made even less sense now, when it was obvious that Caro must have already known of her pregnancy when she'd made her decision to leave him.

'By all means use the telephone in my study to call Gavin,' Jake told her now. 'But when you do be sure and tell him that you won't be joining him in London for Christmas after all.'

Caro eyed Jake in frustration, knowing by the open challenge she could see in those chilling green eyes that he meant exactly what he said.

There was no way Jake could make her stay here.

No—she knew better than that, Caro instantly chided herself. Jake could do anything he wanted. He always had!

She ran a weary hand through her travel-mussed hair. 'I can't believe you want to spend the Christmas holiday with me any more than I want to spend it with you.'

'Then you are wrong, Caro,' he said simply.

Caro gave him a searching look, but she could read nothing from his expression except a determination that warned her of the futility of even trying to argue with him.

It was something Caro knew she had to do, but was no longer sure that she could. She had managed to walk out on Jake once; she wasn't sure she had the strength to do it again!

She couldn't still be in love with him, could she…?

How could she possibly be? Jake had married her because it had been the only way he could get her into his bed, not because he was in love with her. It had been a marriage he had completely ignored, along with the vows he had made, when he'd chosen to take his mistress with him to New York instead of Caro.

No, of *course* she didn't still love Jake!

Her gaze rose to meet the challenge in his. 'Fortunately, Jake, what *you* want is no longer of any importance to me.'

His eyes glittered dangerously. 'I think you should go and make your phone call to Gavin, Caro,' he warned softly. 'Before I'm tempted to stand up and show you exactly what it is I *do* want!'

Caro wanted to continue arguing the point—but at the same time she simply wanted to gather Magdalena up into her arms and make a run for it!

Which she already knew would be totally futile.

Jake might have ceased wanting her a long time ago, but she only had to see his gentleness with Magdalena, to watch the way his expression softened with wonder every time he so much as looked at his daughter, to know that there was no way he was going to let her leave here with their baby.

Just as Caro would never leave without her…

CHAPTER FOUR

'How was Gavin?' Jake asked wryly when Caro returned to the drawing room after making her telephone call, knowing by the frustrated impatience of her expression that her brother must have been his usual exasperating self.

She gave a dismissive shake of her head as she moved absently to pour them both a cup of tea from the pot Mrs Weaver had delivered in her absence. 'He said "great" a lot.' She grimaced. 'Which normally means he isn't listening to a word that's being said to him!'

Jake raised mocking brows. 'Looks like you're stuck here with me for the holidays, then, doesn't it?'

Her mouth firmed as she distractedly placed his cup of tea safely out of Magdalena's way before taking a sip from her own cup. 'It's my intention to go to Montgomery Software and drag Gavin from the building kicking and screaming, if necessary—'

'Caro,' Jake interrupted softly, 'this is Magdalena's first Christmas. Don't you think she should spend it with both her mother *and* her father?'

She eyed him scathingly. 'Considering how well that worked for *you*?'

Jake's mouth tightened at this reference to his own childhood Christmases, with divorced parents who had only spent the holiday season together 'for Jake's sake'. By the time he was nine he had known exactly what was going on, and would have preferred it if they had just not bothered and as a result stopped hurting each other. And him...

He scowled. 'It's hardly the same, is it?'

'Close enough,' Caro bit out tightly.

Jake looked at her searchingly for several long seconds before his attention was drawn back to Magdalena, as she banged a coloured brick on the carpeted floor. His expression gentled as he looked at his young daughter. And he finally understood what his parents had at least tried to do for him when he was a child—even if they had failed miserably...

Despite the fact that he and Caro had married, Jake had never envisaged, let alone considered, that he might one day have a child of his own. But as he looked at Magdalena, as love for his baby daughter filled his heart, Jake at last realised why his parents had tried so hard for all those years to give him the kind of magical Christmas every child deserved but so sadly didn't always have.

It was too late to tell his parents that, of course; they had both died five years ago—within months of each other. Neither of them had ever remarried, and after years of continuing arguments and bitterness between them it had almost been as if one couldn't survive without that conflict with the other...

'At least my parents only attempted to be civilised with each other at Christmas,' he said, knowing that Caro's own parents had stayed together for the sake of the children—and made Caro and Gavin's childhoods hell as a result. 'And there's the added fact that I don't think the two of us actually hate each other as your own parents did!'

Caro felt a jolt in her chest where she knew her heart to be. No, despite everything, she didn't *hate* Jake...

How could she possibly hate someone she had once

loved so deeply? How could she possibly hate Jake when she had only to look at Magdalena, her beloved daughter, and see her likeness to him?

Magdalena had Caro's own hair colour, of course, but it had been obvious within weeks of Magdalena's birth that she was going to have Jake's emerald-coloured eyes. As she had his facial structure. His height. His determination!

Although she was generally quite placid, Magdalena's will could become intractable if she was determined on something.

Just like Jake's…

Caro gave a rueful smile. 'I'm sure that it's nice to think we don't actually hate each other, Jake—'

'Nice?' he repeated dryly, the expression in his eyes having nothing to do with 'nice' and everything to do with—

Caro broke abruptly away from the mesmerising sensuality of Jake's gaze. It had been losing herself in that gaze and having no will to resist it that had persuaded her into marrying Jake in the first place!

'It's time to give Magdalena her tea,' she said briskly as she bent to scoop her daughter up into her arms.

Magdalena gave her a beaming smile, as if she sensed that food might be on the agenda.

Jake drew in a sharp breath. 'She has two teeth!'

Caro felt emotion catch at the back of her throat as she saw the love blazing in the depths of Jake's eyes as he stared in wonder at his baby daughter—Magdalena's smile having revealed the two tiny white teeth in her lower gum.

Jake looked at Magdalena in a way he never had, nor ever would, look at Caro…

'Given the opportunity, she'll bite you with them, too,' Caro warned huskily as she turned away to pick up

Magdalena's changing bag. 'Will Mrs Weaver mind if I invade her kitchen to make up Magdalena's food?'

'That would be *my* kitchen, Caro,' Jake said. 'Or yours, if you should decide to live in this house,' he added.

Caro looked at him sharply, but could read nothing from Jake's suddenly closed expression. 'I'm not staying on in England at all after the holidays.'

'You will,' he bit out uncompromisingly.

Caro frowned with deepening frustration at his arrogance. 'Somehow I don't think so!'

His smile was completely lacking in humour. 'You know me better than to believe that, Caro.'

She shook her head. 'I'm not sure that I ever knew you, Jake.'

His mouth tightened. 'You knew me, all right. And you still know me well enough to realise that there is no way I'm going to allow you and our baby to return to Majorca,' he added bluntly.

Blue eyes warred with emerald-green for several long seconds. Caro was finally the one to look away first. 'You obviously don't know *me* at all if *you* believe that,' she countered, before turning to stride purposefully from the room.

Jake watched her go, admiring the way her hair moved silkily over her shoulders and halfway down the length of her spine. The stirring, the hardening of his thighs as his gaze moved down to where her hips and the rounded firmness of her bottom were clearly outlined against the snugness of her jeans, told Jake that he still wanted his wife as badly as he had the first time he'd looked at her.

'COME AND HELP ME decorate the tree, Caro,' Jake invited as he stood beside the tree he'd had delivered earlier that day, along with everything else he had thought the three of them would need to enable them to spend Christmas here. 'We had fun decorating the tree together two years ago—remember?' he added, as Caro remained stubbornly unmoving beside the fireplace.

What Jake most remembered about that day in December, only weeks after they had married, was the way he and Caro had made love beneath the tree instead of decorating it.

She gave him a scorching glance. 'I have a much more vivid memory of us *not* decorating the tree together last year!'

Jake's mouth compressed as he recalled the bleakness of the Christmas he had been forced to spend alone the previous year. Caro had left him only days earlier, and had already all but disappeared off the face of the earth. Had arrived on the island of Majorca, as he now knew.

'That was *your* choice, Caro, not mine!'

Yes, it had been, Caro acknowledged with an inward sigh. But at the time it hadn't seemed like a choice, merely the inevitable conclusion of the end of her marriage.

She and Jake should never have married each other. If she had only been agreeable to a brief affair, then she knew they wouldn't have done. With the example of his parents' stormy marriage, getting married himself had never been a part of Jake's plans for his future.

She had been a fool, Caro told herself for what had to be the hundredth time. A naïve fool who had believed that the love she felt for Jake and the desire he felt for her— that she had stupidly mistaken for love!—was enough to make a marriage between them work.

And Jake was being naïve if he thought she would

consider—even for a moment—any idea of resuming that marriage just because of Magdalena.

Caro had left Jake because of his involvement with another woman and because she had no intention of living in the kind of loveless marriage her parents had had for so many years. She wasn't about to let him bully her into reconsidering that decision.

Although glancing at Jake's face now, recognising the growing desire gleaming in the emerald depths of his eyes as he looked steadily back at her, was enough to tell Caro that bullying her wasn't on Jake's agenda at this precise moment!

She straightened hastily. 'I think I'll go up and check on Magdalena.' Her daughter had been sleepy enough after eating her tea to need a short nap.

In the cot Jake had arranged to be delivered that morning, once he had learnt of Magdalena's existence...

'We'll hear her when she wakes up.' Jake gave a pointed glance at the baby-listening device plugged into the wall socket even as he took the step that blocked her exit from the room.

Caro looked up at him warily, her breathing becoming shallow, almost non-existent, as she saw the way Jake's gaze lingered on her parted lips. It was as tangible as a light brushing of his own lips against hers...

Caro's legs felt weak, and an insidious warmth was moving up her limbs to between her thighs, and then higher, into her breasts, the nipples hardening and tingling with an awareness Caro had tried so hard this last year to banish even from her thoughts.

She nervously moistened her lips with the tip of her tongue, and at once realised her mistake as Jake's darkened gaze followed the movement. One of his hands moved up, as if to encircle her nape beneath the heavy thickness of her hair, causing Caro to twist sharply away. 'Don't—'

'That's the second time today you've flinched away from me!' Jake growled, his clenched jaw as inflexible as the fingers that now encircled her nape.

'Let go of me, Jake,' she ordered, even as her legs began to shake in reaction to his touch.

The intensity of his gaze held hers captive as he slowly shook his head. 'I can't do that, Caro.'

She swallowed hard, her eyes wide. 'Can't…?'

'Can't,' Jake echoed gruffly.

It was true! Touching Caro again, feeling the silkiness of her skin beneath his fingers, there was no way Jake could just let her go. Not without first tasting her…

Caro trembled, her eyes deep blue pools in the pallor of her face. 'You've always been able to do anything you want, Jake, so don't say you can't let me go…'

'Not this time,' he breathed, his gaze holding hers as his head lowered and his mouth captured hers. Not gently or tentatively, but more like a thirsty man in a desert being offered his first drink of water in a very long time.

In complete contrast to her struggles against the restraint of his hand against her nape, her lips were soft and warm beneath his, and they tasted of the sweetness of honey. Honey that Jake wanted to drink, to drown in.

And he had every intention of drinking from her until he had ensured Caro wanted this as much as he did!

He kissed Caro deeply, hungrily, his arms about her now as he held her captive, one hand against her back and the other against the base of her spine. He pressed the slenderness of her hips against the arousal of his thighs, letting her know without words exactly how she affected him.

Caro gasped, her hands moving up to grasp Jake's

shoulders as she felt the hard intimacy of his thighs pressed against the soft swell of her abdomen. Jake at once took advantage of her softly parted lips to run the silkiness of his tongue along the pout of her lower lip.

She gave an aching groan, having no will left with which to fight as Jake plundered the softness of her mouth, his tongue a warm and silky invasion, teasing, duelling with hers, playing with all of her senses. That tongue plunged and claimed, and then plunged and claimed again and again, in an ever-arousing rhythm.

Caro moaned low in her throat as both Jake's hands lowered to cup the soft curve of her bottom, to hold her against him as he moved the hardness of his arousal against her in the same erotic rhythm as his lips and tongue continued to claim, to lay siege to hers.

She forgot everyone and everything in the wild rush of her own desire. She was so hot, consumed with the sensual need of her heated senses, as aroused now as Jake obviously was as she feverishly returned the demand of his kisses.

Caro shivered as she felt the coolness of Jake's hand against the heat of her flesh beneath her sweater, her protest becoming another aching groan as that hand cupped her breast, the soft pad of his thumb moving unerringly across the hardened bud of her nipple through the thin material of her bra. Stroking softly. Rhythmically. Pleasure was pulsing, dampening between Caro's thighs as she felt the aching need for Jake to fill them.

It had been so long—too long!—since Caro had been aroused like this. She knew that Jake would only have to touch her between her thighs, just a single touch of his finger against that pulsing nub, and she would explode into climax. A climax she now needed so badly that her body actually throbbed with a pleasure that bordered on pain.

The sudden sound of Magdalena's gurgling and incomprehensible talking as she awakened came over the baby-listening device, causing Caro to freeze in Jake's arms before she pulled away to stare up at him in horrified disbelief.

Jake drew in a deeply controlling breath, and a nerve pulsed in his tightly clenched jaw as he saw the unmistakable look of horror on Caro's face before she pushed completely away from him, immediately averting her face so that Jake could no longer see or read her expression.

'Damn it, Caro—'

'Don't say anything, Jake!' she warned shakily. 'That was— I have no idea what just happened.' The tone of her voice was obviously one of self-disgust.

'You know *exactly* what happened—'

'I know *what* happened—I'm trying to tell you it won't happen again!' Caro cried, and her spine straightened before she turned to give him a fiercely challenging look.

Jake studied her through narrowed lids, knowing by the flush to her cheeks, the brightness to her eyes, the slight shaking of her hands, that he hadn't imagined Caro's arousal just now. That, despite her denials, she was still aroused.

'Are you so sure of that?' He softly returned that challenge.

'Yes!' she insisted. 'I'm going upstairs to get Magdalena now, and once she's changed and fed I'm going to order a taxi to take me back into London.'

Jake hands clenched at his sides. 'You're not going anywhere, Caro.'

The colour that suffused her cheeks now was due to

outraged anger. 'I really don't advise that you even *think* about trying to stop me from leaving, Jake!'

'You and I both know that I would do it if I had to,' he grated harshly.

She gave him a scathing glance. 'Still as arrogant as ever, I see.'

He smiled grimly. 'Luckily for you, this time I don't have to be,' he said. 'Take a look out of the window, Caro,' Jake advised, as she stared at him blankly.

A frown appeared between her brows as she stepped back to the window, that frown turning to a look of dismay as Caro looked out at what Jake must have already seen.

Snow.

Thick heavy flakes of it were falling steadily outside the window. And, from the look of the accumulation of snow on the lawn and flowerbeds in the garden, it had been falling completely unnoticed by either of them for some time.

Long enough and heavy enough, Jake noted with intense satisfaction, for Caro not to be able to go *anywhere* this evening...

CHAPTER FIVE

HANGING, DRAWING AND quartering was too good for Gavin, Caro decided furiously as she impatiently paced the bedroom next to Magdalena's. Mrs Weaver had brought Caro here so that she could bathe and change before dinner. It was a beautiful high-ceilinged bedroom, decorated in pale lemons and golds, and looking out over the long driveway at the front of the house.

A driveway that was now covered in at least three inches of completely non-negotiable snow!

Non-negotiable because she had the safety of her six-month-old baby to think of...

Caro was totally unable to shut from her mind the memories of once again being in Jake's arms, of responding to his kisses and caresses. If she'd only had herself to consider then Caro knew she would have risked trying to walk out of here.

Magdalena was downstairs with Jake right now, having been bathed and fed. Father and daughter were both lying on the carpeted floor, playing with Magdalena's new toys. Caro had left them a few minutes ago to come upstairs with the housekeeper.

How *could* she have allowed Jake to kiss and touch her in that way?

How could she have stopped him when her resistance had melted at the first touch of his lips against hers...?

'Perhaps you would like me to run your bath for you, like I used to?'

Caro turned sharply to find Jake leaning against the open bedroom doorway, her cheeks becoming hot as that green gaze moved over and down her body with slow deliberation. Heatedly reminding her of the times Jake *had* run a bath for her in the past—before joining her there!

'No, thank you,' she snapped irritably. 'Where's Magdalena?'

'Apparently, Mrs Weaver has always wanted to be a grandmother,' Jake divulged as he strode farther into the bedroom and deposited Caro's suitcase on the bed. 'She offered to show Magdalena the sweet delights of the icing on the Christmas cookies while I went outside and collected your case from the car,' he added dryly as Caro raised a questioning eyebrow at his initial reply. 'Do you have everything you need?'

What Caro needed most of all, after what had happened between them earlier, was to get out of here! An impossibility for the foreseeable future, when the snow continued to fall so relentlessly...

'I do now,' Caro muttered awkwardly. 'I—thank you for bringing in my suitcase,' she added uncomfortably.

Jake raised teasing brows. 'Did that hurt?'

Her smile was rueful as she sat down on the side of the bed. 'Not too much—considering that *you* were the one who had to go outside into the cold snow!' Caro hadn't missed that Jake's hair was still slightly wet from his venture outside, the dampness causing it to curl slightly about his ears and nape.

Nor had she forgotten how soft and silky that hair had felt a short time ago, when her fingers had become entangled in its dark richness...

Jake frowned. 'We could use these few minutes alone to talk, Caro.'

'About what?' she asked sharply, her gaze wary.

Jake gave a shrug. 'Perhaps a good place for us to start would be for me to ask whether or not there's anyone else in your life at the moment?' He deliberately kept his tone light—when in reality even the thought of Caro in another man's arms made him feel positively violent!

Her eyelashes flickered down, concealing her expression from him. 'Besides Magdalena, you mean?'

'Don't be obtuse, Caro,' he rapped out curtly.

'Is that what I'm being?' she asked a little sadly, rising to her feet to stand in front of the window, looking out at the still heavily falling snow. 'There really isn't a lot of time left for anything or anyone else in your life when you have a young baby to care for.'

Which didn't exactly answer his question... 'Are you emotionally or physically involved with anyone else?' he repeated.

She turned suddenly, challenge in the deep blue of her eyes. 'Are *you*?'

Jake easily met that challenge. 'No.'

'Oh.' She seemed momentarily nonplussed by the bluntness of his reply. 'I somehow never imagined you would be spending Christmas on your own...'

'Frankly, I'm surprised that you've bothered to wonder about how I would spend *any* of my time, let alone Christmas,' Jake said bitterly. 'As far as I can tell you haven't given our marriage or me a single thought this last year!'

'Not a positive one, at least,' she confirmed hard-heartedly.

Jake drew in a frustrated breath; Caro still hadn't answered his question as to whether or not there was a man in her life.

He had no idea whether to take that as an indication that there *was* another man or that there wasn't...

Either way, he intended making sure there would be no other men in Caro's future! 'Are you sure you wouldn't like some help with your bath...?' he offered sardonically.

'Positive,' Caro snapped.

'Pity,' Jake taunted.

Caro felt the warmth of the blush in her cheeks. 'Look, we're obviously stuck here together until this weather breaks, but let's not either of us imagine this is anything more than that—Jake...?' Her eyes had widened in alarm as Jake strolled unhurriedly across the bedroom until he stood only inches away from her.

So close that Caro could once more see those grey flecks in the darkness of the hair at his temples, the lines beside his nose and mouth that hadn't been there a year ago, either. Just as she could see the gold flecks in the deep green of Jake's eyes. And feel the heat emanating from his body...

'Just an observation, Caro—but I don't believe either of us was even aware that it was snowing earlier,' he murmured.

That was true, of course. But it didn't alter the fact that Caro didn't want even the possibility of a repeat of their earlier intimacy. She dared not risk a repeat! Being in Jake's arms again, being kissed by him, kissing him in return as his hands caressed the length of her body, the warmth of her bare flesh, had shown Caro just how dangerous that closeness could be.

She squared her shoulders defiantly. 'I'm out of here as soon as the weather improves.'

Jake glanced briefly out of the window, his gaze once again challenging as it returned to meet Caro's. 'Don't wish the snow away, Caro,' he chided. 'I'm sure you wouldn't want to deny all those thousands of children the fun of a white Christmas. Building a snowman. Snowball fights. Making snow angels.'

'Perhaps next year…' Caro responded sarcastically.

His gaze was openly amused now. 'I hate to disappoint you, Caro, but I turned on the television just now to check the weather forecast, and they're expecting this snow to continue on through tonight and tomorrow at least.'

Caro's heart sank at the thought of being snowed in here with Jake for days rather than the hours she had been hoping for.

'Then I'll just have to wish very hard that "they" are wrong, won't I?' she said stubbornly.

Jake gave an appreciative chuckle at her vehemence, his laughter instantly making him look younger and less grim. More like the Jake that Caro had met and fallen in love with two years ago…

That man hadn't been real, Caro reminded herself fiercely. The man she had loved, the man she had thought she'd married, had been a figment of her imagination. The real Jake Montgomery wasn't the man Caro had believed was as much in love with her as she was with him.

No, the real Jake Montgomery was faithless, selfish, ruthless and totally incapable of feeling love for any woman—least of all his wife.

And Caro intended to keep reminding herself of that fact—often!—for however long the two of them were forced to stay here together.

Jake's gaze moved restlessly over Caro's face. He could almost see her mentally rebuilding her barriers against him. Barriers he had no time or patience for. She wasn't

only the mother of his daughter, she was still his wife—
and the sooner she accepted that fact the better it would
be for all of them.

Caro turned away to move to the bed, to unfasten her
suitcase and look down frowningly at its contents. 'I hope
you don't expect me to dress for dinner.'

'Well, I'm not going to complain if you come downstairs naked, but Mrs Weaver may be a little shocked.'

'Very funny!' Caro turned to glare at him. 'As I was
spending the week with Gavin—whose only concession
to going out for the evening is to change into a clean
T-shirt—I didn't bring any clothes with me but another
pair of jeans and some sweaters,' she explained impatiently.

'I really don't give a damn what you do or don't wear
for dinner, Caro,' Jake dismissed. Considering the effect
her tight-fitting jeans had had on him earlier, Jake had
absolutely no problem with Caro continuing to wear them.
Or not...

When he'd held Caro in his arms earlier, kissed her,
touched her, caressed her, it had been as if the last year had
never happened. All the physical desire Jake had always
felt for her had returned with a vengeance. Jake was sure
the two of them would have made love if Magdalena
hadn't woken up when she had.

Magdalena...

Jake still felt completely awed by the existence of his
daughter. She was totally enchanting. Beautiful. A tiny,
perfect, unique human being that he and Caro had created
together.

Jake's heart turned to ice as he thought of the months
of Magdalena's life that Caro had deliberately, wilfully,
denied him. Months—over a year, if he included Caro's
pregnancy—that could never be recaptured. He didn't

intend being denied or excluded from another day, an hour, even a minute of his young daughter's life!

He looked at Caro coldly. 'Let's just try and make the best of our present situation, hmm?'

'As long as it's understood that I'm leaving here as soon as the weather permits, and taking the first available flight back to Majorca.'

'Is there nothing you miss about living in England, Caro? Such as seeing your friends? Spending time with Gavin?' Jake added unfairly, knowing that the bond between brother and sister was all the stronger because of the unhappiness of their childhood.

'Well, of course I miss all of those things, Jake,' Caro answered coolly.

'Just not enough to live in England?' he guessed, wondering more and more if there wasn't another pull that drew Caro back to Majorca...

'No,' she confirmed huskily.

'Could that be because I live here?' He saw the answer to that question in the set of Caro's mouth. 'Damn it, Caro—'

'Jake, I really would like to take a bath now.' Caro turned away deliberately, not sure how much more of this her battered emotions could take.

Seeing Jake again so unexpectedly at the airport earlier had been bad enough. Being here in this house with him—kissing him and being kissed by him earlier!—was shredding the barriers Caro had managed to gather about her emotions this past year.

Being in this house with him? Hold on a moment...

Her gaze was narrowed as she turned to look at him. 'How long have you owned this house, Jake?'

He eyed her, frowning. 'Why?'

Her expression remained wary. 'I'm just curious.

I don't remember you ever expressing any interest in buying a house in the country. It just seems a strange thing for you to do, when all of your business interests are in London...'

Jake's eyes had narrowed to steely slits. 'As you suggested earlier, it's a business investment.'

Was Jake telling the truth?

Or was this house something else entirely?

Caro had been so upset when Jake had left for that business trip to New York after the two of them had argued because she hadn't been able to accompany him as originally planned. After two days of absolute silence from him she had decided to join Jake in New York for their wedding anniversary. The gift she had for him—her confirmed pregnancy—was something she had wanted to share with him in person.

Caro had been so excited at the idea of surprising Jake by arriving unexpectedly, being able to tell him of the baby they were expecting. She had actually been in the process of packing her suitcase for her trip to New York later that afternoon when she'd answered the telephone call from an estate agent, concerning the house Mr Montgomery was purchasing in Surrey...

This house, perhaps?

A house she'd had no knowledge of at all until the agent had telephoned to say the sale had been completed.

A house Caro had seen absolutely no reason for Jake not to have told her about unless he had deliberately wanted to keep its existence a secret from her.

As he had also no doubt wanted to keep it a secret that another woman had accompanied him to New York.

And he would have succeeded in doing just that if

the other woman hadn't answered Caro's telephone call to Jake's hotel suite in New York that agonising day a year ago…

CHAPTER SIX

JAKE WAS INSTANTLY concerned as he saw all the colour drain from Caro's face and her eyes become dark pools of pain.

What had he said? What was she thinking about that could have caused this reaction in her?

They had been talking about his reason for buying this house, that was all. And, okay, it hadn't been something he had shared with Caro a year ago. But there had been a really good reason why he hadn't.

Damn it, she hadn't stayed around long enough for Jake to tell her *anything* when he'd got back from New York; she had just packed her bags and left!

All the time knowing that she carried his child…

He scowled. 'I'm going back downstairs to be with Magdalena. Join us when you're ready.' He turned sharply on his heel and strode forcefully from the bedroom.

Before he did or said something he would regret. Before he did or said something they would *both* regret!

Caro felt numbed as she watched Jake leave the bedroom, her memories of the past having opened up wounds that hadn't even begun to heal, but which she had forced to the back of her mind in an effort to not let them hurt her any more.

She'd had no idea how long Jake had been involved with the other woman—long enough, it seemed, for him to have decided to purchase a house in which she could live, where Jake might visit her in complete privacy.

This house!

The more Caro thought about it the more convinced she became that she was right. Jake had brought her to the house he had initially bought for his mistress. Worse, he had brought Magdalena to the house in which his mistress had lived for the duration of their affair!

How could he?

How *dared* he?

WHATEVER HAD UPSET Caro about their conversation earlier, Jake could see by the determined sparkle of her eyes when she rejoined him and Magdalena in the sitting room an hour or so later, to find him holding the baby while he finished decorating the tree, that she was completely over it.

Caro's hair had been freshly washed and dried to become a wild cascade of red-gold curls down the length of her spine. She had added only a peach lipgloss to the glowing beauty of her face, and her lashes were naturally long and dark against the bright blue of her eyes. Black jeans now fitted snugly to Caro's lean hips and legs, and the blue of her sweater was an exact match for the colour of her eyes.

She looked utterly, absolutely beautiful—and hardly old enough to be mother to a six-month-old baby.

Jake felt a now familiar clenching in his gut as he looked across the room. Anger and desire warred inside him. Anger because Caro had not only left him, but had also denied him knowledge of Magdalena until today. Desire because Jake only had to look at her to want to make love with her.

This last agonising year of complete silence from Caro should have cured him of the desire he had once felt for her. It *should* have. But Jake knew only too well that it *hadn't*. That he wanted her still.

'Better late than never, I suppose,' he said pointedly as Caro strolled over to join them.

She frowned. 'I'm sure you and Magdalena have had fun decorating the Christmas tree together.'

'The first of many such experiences,' Jake assured her.

Caro eyed him warily as she heard the underlying anger in Jake's tone. 'We didn't see that many Christmas trees in Majorca...'

Jake's eyes glittered with the hardness of the emeralds they resembled. 'Magdalena will never be in Majorca for Christmas,' he stated grimly.

Caro blinked. Magdalena would *never* be in Majorca for Christmas?

She swallowed hard, her chin rising to meet the challenge in Jake's eyes. She took the reaching Magdalena into her arms. 'I realise that we will now have to—to come to some sort of agreement concerning your visiting rights to Magdalena, but I very much doubt it will include her spending all of her Christmases in England with you.' Caro felt better just to have the warmth, the tangible solidness of Magdalena back in her own arms.

She had delayed coming downstairs for as long as possible, taking her time over her bath and washing her hair, before unpacking her own clothes and Magdalena's into several of the empty drawers in the dressing table.

That delay hadn't lessened the obvious strain between herself and Jake by one iota!

Neither had it made her immune to how devastatingly attractive he looked this evening, in tailored black trousers and a dark green cashmere sweater.

'Oh, you can be *sure* we'll be coming to some sort of agreement concerning Magdalena, Caro,' Jake said.

Caro heard the obvious threat behind his words and she looked up at him searchingly. Jake always had been one of the most arrestingly compelling men she had ever met, but there was an edge of danger to him now that she had never encountered before.

Of *course* Caro had never seen that edge of danger during their marriage—she had never attempted to thwart Jake until this last year!

The day she had left him didn't count; Jake had been too stunned at the time—and sure that her leaving him was only a brief glitch in their marriage simply because his delay in returning from his business trip on time had caused him to miss their first wedding anniversary—for him to have reacted with anything more than impatient indulgence.

Learning that Caro had kept her pregnancy and Magdalena's birth from him had changed that indulgence to a cold fury.

A cold fury that was a little scary to say the least!

'I don't think now is the right time for us to discuss this, do you?' Caro murmured quietly as Mrs Weaver appeared in the doorway to tell them that dinner was ready to be served.

'We'll find a right time later,' he agreed as they walked through to the dining room.

The menace behind Jake's words was enough to rob Caro of any appetite she might have had, and she picked listlessly at the delicious food Mrs Weaver had prepared for their dinner. The fact that Magdalena sat at the table with them, chewing on a teething ring, should have eased the tension slightly, but Caro was too aware of Jake as he sat broodingly, darkly silent across the table from her to be able to relax her guard for a moment.

This was all so different from what Caro had imagined when she had agreed to spend Christmas in England with Gavin. So different that Caro could feel slight hysteria building inside her as the meal progressed. Hysteria that was sure to increase even further once Magdalena had gone to bed for the night, leaving the two of them alone together...

'BRANDY?' JAKE OFFERED tersely, once he and Caro had returned to the drawing room after putting Magdalena into her cot for the night.

The baby had fallen asleep almost instantly, looking incredibly angelic as she lay there with her red-gold curls framing the smooth beauty of her face, dark lashes resting on cheeks that were rosily healthy.

His daughter.

That realisation still almost brought Jake to his knees!

Caro stood hesitantly just inside the doorway of the drawing room. 'I think I might just go up to bed myself—'

'I think not, Caro,' Jake said, strolling across the room to thrust a brandy glass into her hand. 'Drink that. It might help settle your nerves,' he added.

'I'm not nervous,' she denied, even as her fingers curled firmly about the glass.

'Then perhaps you should be,' he advised softly.

Caro's eyes were deep blue pools of uncertainty as she looked up at him. 'Stop trying to bully me, Jake,' she said.

'I hope I'm succeeding rather than just *trying*!' he said

cruelly. 'Do you have any idea of the sheer effort of will I've been exerting all day, just in an effort not to reach out and strangle you?'

The throat he was threatening to throttle moved convulsively, but to Caro's credit she stood her ground. 'Am I supposed to feel grateful for your self-control?' she snapped.

Jake's mouth curved into a humourless smile. 'Gratitude might be a start.' He took a much needed swallow of his own brandy, welcoming the burning feel of the alcohol as it slid down his throat.

Caro frowned. 'I doubt that your getting drunk is going to help the situation!'

'I very much doubt that *anything* is going to help your present situation,' Jake snarled.

'*My* situation?'

'Tell me why you did it, Caro,' he demanded. 'Tell me with what right, what justification, you denied me knowledge of my own daughter!'

The conversation they had been skirting around all day had finally arrived, Caro realised heavily. Along with a deepening of that danger Caro had sensed in Jake earlier.

She took an involuntary step back from him before answering. 'Our marriage was over.'

'By whose definition?'

'By *our* definition!' she cried. 'Jake, please don't bring all of this up again now,' she added pleadingly. 'It's too late. Can't you see that?' Her voice broke emotionally.

Jake looked grim. 'The only thing I can see at the moment is my daughter. The daughter who is as much mine as she is yours. The daughter *you* chose to deny me!'

'At the time I didn't feel I had any choice at all other than to do what I did.'

'What did I ever do to you, Caro?' Jake asked. 'What could I possibly have done to make you behave so—so cruelly? Damn it, Caro, *talk* to me!' he demanded fiercely as she continued to stare at him. 'Explain it to me so that I can at least understand, if not forgive, why you felt justified in doing something so calculating and callous?'

Jake had been battling with this dilemma all day. He simply couldn't believe that the Caro he had thought he knew, the loving and passionate Caro who had been his wife for a year, the same passionate Caro who had responded when he'd held her in his arms earlier today, was capable of doing something so heartless. And yet the evidence—Magdalena's existence, the fact that she was undoubtedly his daughter—proved otherwise.

Caro had known earlier today that this conversation was inevitable—as soon as Jake and not Gavin had been the one to meet her at Heathrow Airport. As inevitable as it was painful.

She couldn't even feel angry with Gavin any more for being the absent-minded instigator of this confrontation with Jake. She knew it would have eventually happened at some time, so why not now? She certainly couldn't have kept Magdalena's existence a secret from Jake for ever. Especially not once Magdalena herself became old enough to ask the inevitable questions about her father's identity...

Better that it should happen now, while Magdalena was still too young to be seriously affected by the changes that were sure to occur in her life once Caro and Jake had sorted out some sort of visiting rights.

Caro gave a heavy sigh. 'Let's sit down, Jake.'

'I'd rather stand, thanks,' he came back stiffly.

Caro sat down anyway—mainly because she wasn't absolutely sure her legs would continue to support her when this promised to be the most difficult conversation of her life.

'I never meant to be callous or cruel, Jake.' She took a shuddering breath. 'And my actions certainly weren't calculated, either. At the time I felt my decisions were limited—'

'Limited by *what*?' he exclaimed.

Even thinking about Jake's affair with another woman was enough to bring the tears to Caro's eyes. She had loved him so much, so completely, that learning how he had betrayed her—in the same way her father had betrayed her mother, time and time again—had literally broken Caro's heart into little pieces. Pieces that loving Magdalena had partially healed, but had never completely fused back together. Perhaps they never would…

'I'm going quietly insane here, Caro,' Jake said tautly.

'I'm trying, Jake,' she assured him shakily.

'Try harder,' he pressed.

'It isn't that easy…'

'I'm not asking for easy, Caro—I just want the truth, damn it!' He glared across the room at her.

Caro could see Jake's tension in the dark frown between the hard green eyes, the lines that had deepened beside his nose and mouth and the clenched line of his jaw. But the discovery of his affair had shocked her so deeply that she hadn't even been able to confront Jake with it—and doing so now was proving harder than she could ever have imagined. As if talking about it, putting it into actual words, would make it even more real than it already was.

As if it would shatter her heart all over again…

She stared down at the swirling pattern on the gold-coloured carpet and moistened her lips with the tip of her tongue, still not knowing quite where to begin.

Jake's gaze was hungry as it followed the provocative movement of Caro's tongue across her lips. His thighs hardened in immediate response as he imagined that tongue sweeping moistly over a certain part of his anatomy.

Hell, even in the midst of this mess, and feeling this frustrated anger towards her, his body still betrayed the desire for her that was never far beneath the surface of his emotions.

'You may as well just spit it out, Caro,' he rasped, his anger all the more harsh because of that desire. 'I assure you, nothing you have to say now can hurt me any more than you have already!'

'*I* hurt *you*?' She looked slightly bewildered by the accusation.

Jake scowled darkly. 'What did you imagine, Caro? That I didn't have any feelings that could be hurt?'

That was exactly what Caro had thought!

And so far today that belief had proved true. Jake had been angry when he'd met her at the airport, coldly so, and nothing he had said or done since that time had shown her that he felt anything but anger towards her.

A nagging little voice spoke inside her head. Except the desire she had sensed when he'd kissed her earlier. A desire Caro had more than reciprocated!

That didn't mean anything, she assured herself firmly. It had simply been the last remnants of the desire they had felt for each other during the year of their marriage.

'Jake—' Caro broke off abruptly, her expression panicked as the sound of Magdalena screaming could clearly be heard over the intercom.

Caro didn't hesitate—didn't even spare Jake a second glance as she ran from the room and up the stairs to her daughter's bedroom.

CHAPTER SEVEN

'WHAT'S WRONG WITH HER?' Jake couldn't keep the anxiety out of his voice as he hovered over Caro in the semi-darkened bedroom.

Caro sat down on the bed to cradle the obviously distressed Magdalena against her. Jake's heart had literally stopped when he'd heard Magdalena scream, and he had only been one step behind Caro as they both ran up the stairs, Caro reaching the cot first, to snatch their red-faced daughter up into her arms.

'More teeth on the way, probably,' she answered distractedly, even as she put a hand against Magdalena's obviously heated brow. 'I have some gel to rub on her gums—if you wouldn't mind getting it from the changing-bag for me?' She nodded in the direction of the temporary changing area she had set up earlier on the dressing table.

Jake located the gel easily, his gaze still fixed on Magdalena as he handed the tube to Caro after removing the top. The baby was very red in the face. Her cheeks were wet with tears, and her eyes—the same green as his own—had darkened with distress or pain. Jake couldn't decide which. Whichever it was, he knew couldn't bear to see Magdalena this way.

'Should we call a doctor?' he prompted gruffly, even as he reached out compulsively to touch the dampness of his baby daughter's curls.

Caro shook her head. 'Let's see if the gel does any good first.'

'But—'

Caro's expression was sympathetic as she looked up at him. 'I know just how useless you feel, seeing her like this, Jake,' she assured him gently. 'But just give it a minute or so, hmm?'

This last desolate year aside, that 'minute or so' had to be the longest Jake had ever suffered through, as he sat down abruptly beside Caro on the bed and anxiously watched Magdalena's face for any sign of improvement.

The changes were subtle at first. A slight lessening in the baby's hiccuping sobs. An easing of the shuddering of her tiny body. A little less redness to her cheeks. Until finally her eyelids began to droop tiredly and her head dropped down onto Caro's shoulder. She fell back to sleep as if the last ten minutes of trauma had never happened.

Madonna and child...

Jake wasn't even sure where that unbidden thought had come from. Maybe because tomorrow was Christmas Eve? All he knew was that as he looked at Caro and Magdalena together the anger he had been feeling towards Caro all day died as suddenly as it had flared into life, and he knew that the two of them were as precious to him as that other mother and child had been to the world two thousand years ago.

Caro was his Madonna.

Magdalena his child.

They both belonged to him. Belonged *with* him. Whether Caro accepted that yet or not.

It was up to Jake to ensure that she did...

CARO STRAIGHTENED slowly from carefully placing the sleeping Magdalena back in her cot, aware that there had been a sudden shift of emotions in the last few minutes as she and Jake sat together in silence and waited to see if the gel on the baby's gums would have the desired effect.

Their relief had been tangible as, obviously no longer in pain, Magdalena had begun to fall back to sleep.

And not just their relief, Caro acknowledged with an increase of the fluttering sensation in the pit of her stomach as she turned slowly to look at Jake and found his darkened gaze fixed on her hungrily. But also the same hunger that had been building inside her for the last few minutes!

Jake gave a rueful shake of his head. 'Was it like this when her first two teeth came through?'

'Worse,' Caro admitted with a smile. 'I had no idea what was happening the first time, and I'm afraid I panicked completely. I drove hell-for-leather to the doctor's clinic in the next village.' She laughed quietly at the memory. 'I felt a little foolish once he had made his diagnosis.'

Jake sighed. 'I would have done exactly the same.'

She blinked. 'You would?'

He nodded, his expression pained. 'It's hard to see her like that, isn't it?'

Caro drew in a ragged breath. 'You love Magdalena already, don't you?'

'From the moment I first set eyes on her,' Jake confirmed without the slightest hesitation, that dark gaze never leaving her face.

Caro felt her heart sink at the stark honesty of Jake's admission. They had never discussed having children during their brief year of marriage, and Caro's pregnancy had been completely unplanned. But she had always wanted to have children with Jake some day, and that desire had become increasingly more apparent to her as their marriage had progressed. However, she had been concerned that Jake would only care for any children they had in the same offhand manner with which he'd cared for her.

The absolute adoration she saw in his gaze every time he looked at Magdalena clearly showed her that his manner was nothing so lukewarm as offhand for their baby. He already loved their daughter as deeply as Caro did.

She swallowed hard. 'Jake—'

'Let's not talk any more tonight, Caro,' he murmured, even as he held out his open hand to her, to encourage her to place hers inside it. 'Talking isn't what we do best,' he added ruefully as she still hesitated.

Talking was what they should have done more of. Both before and after they were married. Especially before they were married. Then Caro might have at least been pre-warned—might have guarded against the possibility, the pain of Jake's interest turning to other women as her father's had done.

'You're thinking too much,' Jake reproved huskily when he saw the increasing unease in her shadowed blue eyes. 'I promise we'll talk again in the morning.'

Her eyes widened. 'But—'

'No more talk, Caro.' Jake placed soft, silencing fingertips against her lips and moved so that only the barest whisper of air separated their two bodies.

He could smell her softly elusive perfume now, and the tang of lemon shampoo she must have used on her hair. Her skin had taken on the tone of honey in the soft glow of the bedside lamp, and her eyes were as clear and blue as a summer sky as she stared up at him. Wide, heavily lashed eyes that a man could drown in if he gazed into those sky-blue depths for long enough.

Her cheek felt soft and silky as Jake's hand moved to cup the side of her face. Her lips, so full and inviting, were slightly parted as she breathed softly, that breath warm against the palm of his hand.

Dear God, how he had ached to taste those lips again! To sip and taste them before crushing and parting them beneath his own and claiming the hot sweetness within.

Caro had been lost the moment Jake placed his fingertips against her lips. Even the softness of that caress was enough to cause a tingling in her body, creating an ache inside her that went bone-deep and then deeper still. She felt her breasts swell and her nipples harden as heat suffused between her thighs.

As she gazed up at Jake she could see naked hunger in the dark green depths of his eyes, and his breath was released in a fierce hiss as he read that same desire reflected back at him in her candid blue gaze.

She gave a half-protesting shake of her head. 'Jake...'

'Caro...' he groaned throatily, even as his head lowered and his mouth captured hers.

Dear God!

Caro had no defence against the heat, the sweet, aching joy of Jake's lips parting hers as he deepened the kiss. His arms moved about her like steel bands as he pulled her body in close to his, moulding her soft curves to his much harder ones from breast to thigh.

Her arms moved up of their own volition as his mouth continued to plunder, to claim hers, and her fingers became entangled in the dark thickness of hair at his nape as she surrendered, gave herself to that claim.

Tomorrow. They would talk tomorrow. At this moment in time Caro didn't care if tomorrow never came. She just wanted Jake. Wanted him to make love to her as much as she ached to make love to him…!

Jake's arms tightened about Caro. She tasted even sweeter than he remembered, her lips full and responsive against his as he continued to kiss her hungrily, fiercely. His hands moved beneath the soft wool of her sweater and he touched the smooth silkiness of her curvaceous back.

Her skin had always been as smooth and soft as satin, her breasts so perfect and round as they fitted neatly into the palms of Jake's hands.

Those breasts felt slightly fuller than Jake remembered as his hand moved to cup that softness, to caress. The nipples hardened as he ran the soft pad of his thumb against them, causing Caro to groan low in her throat and her thighs to press more urgently against his.

Jake wondered what other changes pregnancy and childbirth had made in the delicious body that he knew better than he did his own.

He had to know. To touch. To see.

His mouth continued to plunder hers even as he bent to lift her up into his arms, before turning towards the open doorway to the adjoining bedroom.

Reality pushed through the fierce desire that was fogging Caro's brain—a totally disorientating feeling much like not having her feet on the ground. She pulled sharply back from Jake to look dazedly about her, realising she really didn't have her feet on the ground—that Jake had lifted her up into his arms and was now carrying her.

'Don't worry—we'll leave the door open between the bedrooms so that we can hear Magdalena,' Jake assured her gruffly as he placed her down on the bed before joining her there, his chiselled features all light and shadow from the moon reflecting on the snow outside and coming in through the window.

Caro knew she should stop this. *Now.* That to allow this to go any further than it already had would be a big mistake on her part.

But as Jake gently pushed her sweater aside to bare her breasts to the heat of his gaze, his hand cupping her softness as he slowly lowered his head and claimed one hardened nipple between his parted lips, drawing it into the heated cavern of his mouth, Caro knew she had no will left with which to fight him. Or the desire blazing completely out of control through the whole of her body.

Instead her fingers once again became entangled in the thickness of Jake's hair and she held him to her, the sensation of his lips and mouth drawing on her nipple like nothing else she had ever known. Her back arched as she urged him on, crying out her pleasure as his hand claimed her other breast, the dual assault upon her senses driving her ever nearer to release.

A release that Caro craved, ached for, needed as much as she did air to breathe…!

Jake's mouth came down on hers once more as their clothes, the last barrier between them, disappeared quickly—thrown without care onto the carpeted floor beside the bed.

Flesh against flesh. Shoulders, breasts, thighs, ankles. Their legs tangled together as they sought even closer contact, and Caro felt the pulse of Jake's hard arousal against her thigh.

It was a hardness she wanted inside her, thrusting deep, again and again, as the two of them pleasured each other.

She moved, rolling slightly so that he was now the one lying back against the pillows, her gaze briefly holding his before she slid slowly, leisurely, down the length of his chest, lips kissing, teeth gently biting as she familiarised herself with all the pleasure spots she knew so well.

The hard tip of his nipple. The flatness of his muscled abdomen. The well of his navel. The dip where his legs joined his hips.

Jake's breath caught in a hiss, his fingers clenching in the sheet beneath him as he felt Caro's lips and tongue against him, sliding the length of his arousal, that teasing tongue not quite touching the sensitive tip before she began the caress all over again. Again. And again. Every time without quite going far enough.

'Caro—please!' Jake begged, raising his head slightly to look down at her.

Just the sight of her red-gold hair cascading over his thighs as she knelt between his legs was enough to increase his need. Then he finally felt her take him inside the heated silkiness of her pleasure-giving mouth.

'Oh, yes…!' he groaned achingly, his head falling back onto the pillows as he felt the flick of her tongue against the tip of his swollen shaft. 'Don't stop, Caro. For God's sake, don't stop!'

Caro could sense Jake's imminent release as she ran her tongue slowly, leisurely, over his arousal, her own thighs clenching as they pulsed with the same need.

'I want to be inside you, Caro,' Jake muttered fiercely. 'I need to be inside you!' He reached out to grasp her arms and lifted her over and above him.

The feel of his hardness against her own swollen arousal was almost more than Caro could stand, and she rubbed herself slowly against the long length of him. Again and again as the pleasure built up inside her.

'I need to be inside you *now*,' Jake repeated feverishly as he looked up at her, his eyes dark with desperation in the moonlight.

Her gaze held his as she moved up onto her knees and her hand moved down to encircle him, to guide him into her. She could feel each and every inner convulsion as she took him inside her, inch by slow inch, until she cried out as he touched the deepest heart of her.

'Am I hurting you?' It took every ounce of Jake's considerable will-power to remain still beneath her, to keep from thrusting even more deeply inside her. Caro had been pregnant, had given birth since they'd last made love, and he had no idea whether or not she had suffered any repercussions from that. 'Caro—' He broke off, his concern fading to pleasure as he felt her inner convulsions as she climaxed around his increasingly hardening shaft.

Jake gritted his teeth in an effort to stop those convulsions from driving him over the same precipice. He intended making love with her until they were both satiated. Until they were too exhausted to do any more than fall asleep in each other's arms.

More than anything else Jake had missed holding his wife in his arms as they slept...

CHAPTER EIGHT

IT WAS JUST BEGINNING to get light, and Jake lay looking at the woman who still slept in the bed beside him, face-down on the bed, her hair a silken red-gold curtain across the pillow beneath her, her arms up beside her head, the sheet having fallen back to reveal the bareness of her curvaceous back.

Not that he was surprised that Caro still slept. After that first needy, uncontrollable lovemaking the two of them had made love for a second time. Slowly. Leisurely. Pleasurably. Finally falling asleep in each other's arms, as Jake had hoped that they would, some time in the early hours of this morning.

Jake's world had never felt more perfect.

Caro was once again at his side.

His daughter was sleeping peacefully and obviously free from pain when he had checked on her a short time ago in the adjoining bedroom.

Snow still blanketed the ground outside.

And today was Christmas Eve.

The eve of a new beginning for him and Caro, he hoped.

Yes, Jake could honestly claim that his world had never been more perfect.

Now all he had to do was convince her to remain a part of that perfect world...

CARO FELT SLIGHTLY disorientated as she woke to muted silence rather than to the usual sounds of the village wakening: women talking loudly together as they made their early-morning visit to the bakery for bread and pastries to give to the men before they left for work; children chattering happily as they waited for the bus that would take them to school in the next village; car horns tooting; garage doors closing; dogs barking—

Oh, dear God!

The reason Caro couldn't hear any of those things was because she wasn't in Majorca! She was in England. With Jake. And last night—

Caro lifted panicked lids—and quickly closed them again as she saw Jake lying in bed beside her, already awake and leaning up on one elbow to look down at her with an expression of complete satisfaction.

Last night they had—

Most of the night they had—

Caro's hands clenched in the pillow and her lids squeezed tightly closed as she tried to shut out the memories of what she and Jake had done last night. Impossible!

Now that she was fully awake those memories were too vivid to be denied. She could remember every kiss. Each caress. Every moment of pleasure—and there had been many!—was clearly etched on her brain.

And she could still feel the raw sensuality of Jake's body beneath, above, inside her own...

Caro didn't care if there had been a blizzard in the night. Even if the snow was now two feet deep outside she was leaving here today! Now! Immediately—

'I know you're awake, Caro.' A finger caressed lightly down the length of her bared spine to accompany that indulgent observation.

'Don't do that!' she snapped fiercely, and she opened her eyes to glare at Jake in warning, at the same time pulling the sheet up over her nakedness and turning on her side. 'And stop looking at me like that, too,' she ordered.

Jake gave a lazy smile. 'Exactly how *am* I looking at you, Caro…?'

'Like a cat contemplating a tasty bowl of cream!'

Jake chuckled. 'More like a cat that would like to lick you all over,' he corrected ruefully, as he picked up a long strand of her hair and began to play with it.

Caro felt the colour warm her cheeks at the vivid images that instantly flooded her mind. Not imagined ones either. Jake had indeed licked her all over the night before…

She drew in a sharp breath and knocked his hand away from her hair. 'Last night was—'

'Beautiful,' Jake put in softly.

Well…yes, it had certainly been that.

But she wasn't about to be seduced into thinking last night had been any more than a physical manifestation of circumstances. A typical example of two people who had once been married to each other indulging in a little curiosity as to whether or not they were still physically attracted to each other. Which she and Jake undoubtedly were!

To allow herself to believe that last night had been anything more than that would be madness on her part.

They had both been worried about Magdalena. Emotions had been running high. That was all it had been.

If only Jake didn't look so *good* this morning, with his hair slightly mussed and falling endearingly across his brow, his expression one of relaxed indulgence, with all the harshness of yesterday smoothed away from the chiselled ruggedness of his face.

Caro didn't dare even let her gaze wander any lower. She already knew what she would see: wide shoulders, a muscled chest covered in a light dusting of dark hair, a stomach flat and smooth—

Stop it, Caro, she instructed herself firmly. So Jake was still the most physically beautiful man she had ever seen—that certainly didn't nullify the fact that he was also one of the most unfaithful!

Her mouth tightened determinedly. 'If you wouldn't mind, Jake, I would like to get up now and take a shower before Magdalena wakes up wanting her breakfast.'

'Are you sure?' Jake's gaze warmly ran the length of her body. 'Wouldn't you rather—?'

'All I want right now, Jake, is to take a shower!' she insisted firmly.

'Pity,' he drawled as he lay back on his pillows, arms behind his head as he contemplated her through narrowed lids.

Her face was flushed and beautiful, her lips slightly swollen from the force of their lovemaking, and her hair was a red-gold tangle about her shoulders. Bare shoulders showed slight signs of the rasp of the stubble on his chin as he'd kissed every inch of her body.

Making Jake wonder if Caro had other, more intimate signs of their lovemaking…

'I would prefer it if you left my bedroom before I get out of bed,' she said.

Jake gave an unconcerned shrug. 'That would actually be *our* bedroom, Caro.'

'Our—?' She blinked. 'What do you mean…?'

'Obviously you didn't check the wardrobe when you unpacked yesterday. If you had,' he continued mockingly as Caro continued to stare at him, 'you would have seen my clothes hanging up in there.'

There had been no reason for Caro to look in the wardrobe when she'd unpacked last night; jeans and jumpers didn't need to be hung up. 'You mean this is your bedroom?'

'*Our* bedroom,' he repeated lightly.

'I— But—'

'We are still married,' he reminded her dryly.

'Technically, yes,' she conceded with a frown.

'In *every* way, Caro,' Jake corrected as he reached out to lift her left hand. 'You still wear my ring.' The gold band on her third finger glittered in the early-morning light.

After Jake's betrayal a year ago Caro had wanted to rip that plain gold band from her finger and toss it into the Mediterranean Sea! She had wanted to. But she hadn't been able to.

'Only because Majorca is a mainly Catholic island,' she defended in a panic. 'I didn't think the locals in the village would be too impressed with a very pregnant unmarried woman moving into their midst!'

Jake's eyes narrowed to glittering green slits. 'Are you deliberately trying to create an argument with me?'

Her expression was challenging. 'Am I succeeding?'

'Getting there,' he admitted through gritted teeth.

'Good,' she said with satisfaction.

'We still need to talk, Caro, not argue—'

'I don't have anything to say to you, Jake,' she cut in defiantly. 'Now, would you mind kindly removing yourself from your bed so that I can get up and go to the bathroom?'

'As a matter of fact, I do mind.' He scowled blackly.

'I can't get out of bed until you leave,' she snapped exasperatedly.

He raised disbelieving brows. 'You aren't trying to

tell me that after last night you're actually feeling *shy* at the idea of my seeing you naked?'

It did seem a little ridiculous—more than a little—after the intimacies they had shared during the night. But that was exactly what Caro was feeling!

Last night it had been dark, with only the moonlight reflecting on the snow outside to lighten the room, and that pale reflection had cast their bodies mainly into shadow. But it was completely daylight now, and Caro was completely aware of the fact that she had been pregnant since Jake had last seen her naked in the daylight. The necessary swelling of her body had left its mark on her. No amount of oil or lotions rubbed into her skin had prevented those tell-tale stretch marks of pregnancy…

She drew in a ragged breath. 'Are you deliberately trying to embarrass me?'

Jake gave a rueful shake of his head as he sat up. 'I'm trying—and obviously not succeeding—to tell you that I *like* the changes to your body.'

She blinked. 'You do?'

He nodded. 'Your breasts are fuller, more responsive than ever. And you have those deliciously enticing marks on your stomach that I can trace right down to your—'

'That's enough!' Caro squeaked.

'Not nearly enough,' Jake murmured, and he moved so that the length of his body was only inches away from hers. 'Having a child has only made you more beautiful. Last night was wonderful.' His voice lowered huskily. 'Deliciously erotic…'

'Stop it, Jake!' she protested desperately, his words swiftly bringing back the memory of how his lips had travelled the length of her body before he had— 'You really do have to stop talking like this,' she repeated weakly.

'No, I really don't, Caro,' he insisted firmly, reaching

out to grasp her arm as she would have thrown back the covers and turned to get out of bed. 'We can build on last night,' he insisted. 'We can make something of our marriage again—'

'No!' Caro wrenched her arm out of his grasp, her eyes glittering fiercely now. 'I don't want to talk about any of this.'

'Well, tough—because I do.'

'I don't *care*, Jake,' she almost wailed. 'It's enough for me to tell you I will never be married to you again. *Never!*' she repeated vehemently, and she t urned to throw back the bedclothes to get out of bed and march across the room towards the bathroom.

Initially she gave Jake an entirely enticing view of the fullness of her breasts, before she turned and showed him an even more provocative view of her bottom...

Until the bathroom door slammed behind her and closed off his line of sight, that was.

Jake lay back on the pillows, his hands once again behind his head, his expression grim as he stared up at the ceiling unseeingly.

As much as Caro might want to forget last night had ever happened, Jake knew that he never would...

CHAPTER NINE

'GAVIN RANG WHILE you were in the shower.' Jake turned to inform Caro as she entered the dining room half an hour or so later. He sat eating his breakfast with Magdalena, her happy smile showing she was none the worse for her upset last night.

Caro had been disconcerted when she'd gone through to collect Magdalena from her cot and found her gone, but it hadn't been too difficult to guess exactly who she had gone with.

And she was disconcerted now by this scene of domesticity...

She had initially gone to the kitchen to prepare Magdalena's breakfast, but to her surprise Mrs Weaver had informed her that Jake had already fed the baby and was now in the dining room eating his own breakfast.

Jake seemed to be taking his newly acquired paternal role far too seriously for her liking...

'Gavin seemed a little concerned that his absent-mindedness had resulted in my learning of Magdalena's existence,' Jake continued sarcastically, as Caro bent down to kiss the baby good morning.

Caro straightened slowly; her brother was going to be more than 'a little concerned' when she next saw him. If Gavin had paid more attention to what was happening, then none of the last twenty-four hours would have happened.

But that wasn't entirely true, was it? Her confrontation with Jake *would* have happened—if not now, then at some time in the future, she acknowledged once again.

She turned away to the side-dresser to help herself to a cup of coffee from the pot and a piece of toast she wasn't sure she was going to be able to eat. How could she possibly swallow when her mouth was completely dry and her stomach churned into knots?

Worse, one glance out of the window had shown her that more snow had fallen in the night. Far too much for her to be able to leave, as she had decided she would when she'd woken up this morning.

'Is this not talking to me to be my punishment for last night?' Jake asked impatiently at her continued silence.

Caro's cheeks flushed a fiery red. 'Don't be ridiculous,' she snapped as she sat down next to Magdalena and tried to ignore how relaxed and attractive Jake looked this morning in faded blue jeans and a form-fitting black sweater.

His mouth firmed. 'So you *are* talking to me?'

'On certain subjects, yes,' she conceded tersely.

Jake gave a teasing smile. 'I can easily guess which subjects you consider taboo.'

'Good—then you'll know which ones to avoid, won't you?' Caro gave him a hard glance over the rim of her cup as she took a much needed sip of her coffee.

Unfortunately her shower hadn't refreshed her as it usually did. How could it when she'd only had to look in the bathroom mirror to see the slightly bruised look to her lips and the wildness of her hair from where Jake's fingers had become entangled in its long length as they'd made love—several times!—the night before?

As for the satisfying ache in her body—she didn't even want to *think* about that.

Caro's hand was trembling so badly that she had to place her cup quickly back in the saucer before she spilt coffee all over her.

'What did Gavin have to say about Christmas?' She changed the subject abruptly as she kept her gaze determinedly on the table in front of her.

'Merry...?' Jake taunted.

Caro looked up with a frown. 'That was it?' she muttered disgustedly. 'That was my irresponsible brother's sole contribution to the mess he's landed me in?'

'You know Gavin.' Jake shrugged.

'Only too well!'

Jake's mouth compressed. 'Caro, this is only a *mess*, as you call it, if you allow it to be,' he pointed out patiently.

'No, Jake,' she breathed wearily. 'However you choose to look at this situation, it *is* a mess.'

Jake sat back in his chair to look at her through lowered lids. Caro was still spoiling for that argument she had tried to have with him earlier. An argument Jake had no intention of taking part in. Not now. Not in the future, either.

He gave another shrug. 'Now that we've decorated the tree—'

'*You've* decorated the tree,' she corrected pettishly, making it plain to Jake that she wanted him to realise she had taken no part in the Christmas activity.

'Magdalena and I have decorated the tree,' he stated firmly. 'That done,' he continued, when Caro didn't react, 'I thought we could all go outside this morning and look for some holly to decorate the inside of the house.'

'Holly?' Caro stared at him incredulously. 'I'm sure

it hasn't escaped your notice that there's a foot of snow outside!'

Jake nodded. 'Admittedly some of us might be somewhat vertically challenged by the depth of the snow.' He gave Caro's lack of height a pointed look. 'But it could still be fun, don't you think?'

She shook her head. 'No, I *don't* think!'

He raised mocking brows. 'Ever heard of making the best of a bad situation, Caro?'

'This isn't bad, Jake—it's catastrophic!' she assured him with feeling, her expression of disgust turning to a chagrined frown as Jake began to laugh softly. 'Would you care to tell me what you find so amusing?'

'You,' he acknowledged indulgently.

Her mouth fell open. *'Me?'*

'You.' Jake sat forward to reach out and put his hand over the top of hers where it rested on the table-top, his fingers curling tightly about hers as she would have snatched that hand away. 'Caro...' His voice gentled as he looked up into the stiff rigidity of her face. 'Can't we just forget about the past? It would make all of this so much easier if you could.'

'This?' Caro echoed warily.

He waved an expansive hand. 'Us.'

'There is no *us*,' she told him exasperatedly, finally managing to wrench her hand from beneath his—probably bruising her fingers in the process. 'Last night was—'

'Do *not* say last night was a mistake!' he grated between clenched teeth.

'We both know that it was an unnecessary complication,' she groaned.

Jake's mouth thinned. 'I've said I'm willing to forget about the past.'

'*You* might be willing to forget about it, maybe. But *I* certainly can't,' she said.

'Caro, I will not continue this argument in front of Magdalena,' he told her firmly. 'I heard more than enough arguments between my parents during my own childhood to want to put Magdalena through the same torment. As did you,' he added.

Caro had no idea when she had first become aware of her parents' unhappiness together, but it certainly hadn't been as a baby of Magdalena's age. Although she *did* accept that their young daughter was capable of picking up on the tension around her...

Caro gave an abrupt nod. 'We'll continue this conversation when Magdalena takes her morning nap.'

Jake relaxed slightly. 'And in the meantime can we all go outside to look for holly?'

'I don't remember you as being this much into Christmas,' Caro said, giving him a perplexed frown.

Jake smiled. 'There's a child in the house now.'

Maybe that was what all this talk of 'forgetting the past' was about? Caro accepted heavily. Jake had made it more than obvious that he wanted Magdalena. And he must know that at this point in time Magdalena and Caro came as a package deal...

'ADMIT IT, CARO—it was fun!' Jake teased later, as Magdalena slept upstairs in her cot and the two of them sat beside the lit fire in the drawing room, drinking hot chocolate in order to thaw out from their venture into the snow looking for holly.

Of which there had been an abundance at the bottom of the huge garden. And an old rope swing hanging from the huge oak tree there. Along with a tree-house nestling in its branches.

This house—and the garden especially—had been built for a family, for children to live and play in...

It was hardly the sort of house a man would buy for his mistress to live in.

The thought came unbidden. And unwelcome. Because Caro could think of no other reason why Jake would have bought this house a year ago.

Jake saw the look of determination on Caro's face as she stood up to move over to the huge bay window, the weak December sun turning her hair to the same spun gold as the angel that now resided at the top of the decorated Christmas tree, with its dozens of brightly coloured lights twinkling so merrily.

This really was the most perfect Christmas Jake had ever known—but he had a feeling that what Caro was about to say was going to change all of that!

She kept her back towards him. 'As I attempted to point out to you earlier this morning, what happened last night changes nothing.'

'As neither of us used contraception last night, might I point out that it could change *everything*?'

Caro turned swiftly, her eyes widening, the colour coming into her face and then as quickly fading as Jake's gaze moved pointedly down to the slender slope of her belly. Where his child, Magdalena, had once nestled so safely. Where, after their lovemaking last night, another baby might already be taking up residence...

'*No!*' Caro's gasp was agonised as that same realisation hit her, and her knees began to buckle beneath her.

Jake dashed across the room and gathered Caro up into his arms before she made contact with the carpeted floor, holding her tightly against him as he carried her back to the chair and sat down with her still in his arms. It was a testament to how shaken Caro was even by the *possibility* of another pregnancy that she made no attempt to escape those restraining arms. Instead her head dropped down weakly against his shoulder.

Jake looked down at her in concern, relieved to see that some of the colour was returning to the paleness of her cheeks. 'Would that really be such a bad thing, Caro?' he asked gently.

'You're asking *me* that?' she groaned softly.

'You don't want more children?' Jake moved so that he could look directly into Caro's face. She was still a little paler than he would have wished, and her eyes had taken on a haunted dullness.

'Of course I would like more children! Just—'

'Just not with me, hmm?' Jake realised, suddenly experiencing an icy feeling in his heart.

Caro gave a pained frown, wondering how on earth the subject had jumped so quickly from their lovemaking last night to the possibility that she might be pregnant. Let alone how she came to be cradled in Jake's arms, so aware of the hard warmth of his chest and the lean strength of his thighs!

She shook her head even as she pulled out of Jake's arms to stand up and move away from him. Away from the temptation those arms represented. 'I'm sure that I won't become pregnant from just our one night together,' she said firmly.

Jake scowled. 'And if you do? Would you tell me this time, Caro? Or would you decide you have the right to keep the existence of another of my children from me?'

She gave a shaky gasp at the raw pain she could hear beneath his accusation. 'I never wanted it to be like this, Jake.' She put a hand briefly over her eyes, before taking it away and looking at him. 'It could all have been so different!' Her voice broke emotionally. 'I was so excited when the doctor confirmed my pregnancy. Couldn't wait to get to New York and tell you about it. It was to be my first wedding anniversary gift to you—'

'Just a minute, Caro,' Jake interrupted slowly, suddenly tense as he sat forward in his chair to look up at her intently. 'Are you telling me that you changed your mind about the trip to New York? That you were coming to join me after all?'

She nodded. 'I told my editor I was going, had my flight booked, when—when I received the telephone call that changed everything.'

Jake looked stunned now. 'What telephone call? I deliberately didn't call you from New York.'

'I'm well aware of that!' Caro exclaimed painfully.

'I had been looking forward to sharing pre-Christmas New York with you,' Jake explained. 'I thought we could go ice-skating together, walk around all the lighted shops. I was so damned angry with you for not going with me that I deliberately didn't call you. Extremely childish of me—I realise that now—but at the time I hadn't expected to be delayed for that extra day, and in doing so miss spending our first wedding anniversary altogether.'

'Did you even *care*?' Caro scorned.

'Of course I damn well—!' Jake stopped and drew in a controlling breath. 'You were already packed and ready to leave me when I did get back.' He suddenly looked agonised. 'I didn't even have the chance to tell you about—' He broke off abruptly.

'To tell me what?' Caro prompted when he didn't go on.

'It doesn't matter now,' Jake dismissed with a shrug.

'No. You're right. It doesn't matter,' she acknowledged wearily. 'We were all wrong for each other from the start, Jake. We wanted different things from life,' she said sadly. 'You were perfectly happy with our life in London—your business, the penthouse apartment, the meaningless round of parties. Whereas I...' She gave a rueful shake of her head. 'I was tired of all those things, Jake. Oh, I enjoyed my career still—but the other things...?' She grimaced. 'I wanted a home and a family. A *real* home and a *real* family with you.'

'Do you think I didn't know you well enough to realise that?' Jake stood up abruptly, a scowl still darkening his brow as he stood only feet away from her. 'Why else do you think I bought this house a year ago?'

'I know *exactly* why you bought this house, Jake!' Caro said angrily.

'Then—'

'How could you?' she accused, her eyes dark with pain as tears sparkled on the darkness of her lashes. 'How could you bring Magdalena and I to a house you initially bought for your mistress?'

'*What?*' Jake barked. 'What the *hell* are you talking about, Caro?' His hands were clenched at his sides as he stared at her disbelievingly. 'I bought this house for *you*, damn it. It was meant to be a surprise. A first wedding anniversary gift.'

Caro stared at him.

Jake had bought this house for *her*...? As a wedding anniversary gift...?

Oh, dear God...

CHAPTER TEN

'YOU EITHER *ARE* PREGNANT, Caro, or this fainting is becoming a habit!' Jake attempted to tease her as he felt her beginning to stir in his arms.

Once again he had managed to catch her before she actually fell, gathering her up in his arms to carry her back to the armchair. Caro had been completely out of it this time, and the longer she'd remained unconscious the more worried Jake had become.

She had regained her senses several minutes ago but had remained silent, unwilling for a moment to give up the luxury, the sheer joy, of being held in Jake's arms. She would surely have to once he learnt of the assumption, the complete mistake she had made a year ago. Of the way she had denied him knowledge of his daughter because of that mistake...

It was too late to tell herself that she shouldn't have just left Jake that day. That she should have stayed and listened to what he had to say. That she should never have just disappeared in that way, let alone kept Magdalena's birth a secret from him. It was far too late for that because she had already done all of those things.

All those unforgivable things...

Her throat moved convulsively as she tried to hold back scalding tears that refused to be denied as they fell hotly down her cheeks. She turned to bury her face against the warm strength of Jake's shoulder as those sobs racked her body.

'Hey.' Jake shifted so that he could see her face. Her eyes were still closed, but the cascade of tears down her cheeks told him this was a deception—that she was fully conscious now. And hurting. 'Don't cry, Caro,' he pleaded, even as his arms tightened about her. 'I can't bear it!'

'*You* can't bear it?' She sat up, her eyes deep blue wells of pain as she looked at him. 'Jake, I thought—you must know what I thought! You see, the estate agent telephoned the apartment to let me know that the sale of this house had been completed.'

'The idiot!' Jake growled. 'I gave him implicit instructions *not* to do that—I told him the house was a surprise for my wife. What the—'

'Don't you see, Jake? That isn't the point!' Caro wailed her distress. 'From that single telephone call I made an assumption— Well, not that single telephone call,' she recalled with a wince. 'I also telephoned your hotel suite in New York, to let you know about the estate agent's call. When a woman answered—a woman with a sexily husky voice—and told me that you couldn't take the call because you were in the shower—'

'Caro, could we go back a couple of steps?' Jake cut in grimly. 'Exactly *what* assumption did you make when that stupid estate agent told you about the house?'

Caro swallowed hard before standing up to move away from him. 'There was the woman in your hotel suite, too...'

He nodded. 'Who I can only assume was Mrs Williams...'

'Your PA?' Caro shook her head in denial. 'It didn't sound like Mrs Williams at all.'

'She had a cold,' Jake explained. 'A single day in the

below-zero temperature of New York and she caught what she assured me was the worst cold of her life. It was because I finally had to send her off to her bed, making it impossible for her to assist me with the paperwork on the deal I was making, that I was delayed in New York for that extra day.'

This just got worse and worse! Caro realised achingly.

The woman who had answered the telephone in Jake's hotel suite in New York *could* have been Mrs Williams with a cold.

No—it was no good trying to make excuses, Caro reproved herself; it *had* been Mrs Williams with a cold. As Jake had said it was. Just as he had bought this house for *her* as a wedding anniversary gift. As he said he had.

'Caro,' Jake spoke slowly, carefully, as if he wanted there to be absolutely no more misunderstandings between them, 'are you telling me that you left me a year ago because you thought, you *assumed* from those two telephone calls, that I was involved in an affair with another woman?'

Caro's heart seemed to stop and she could no longer breathe; that was *exactly* what she had thought. What she had assumed!

Jake would never forgive her. How could he when she had left him, denied him knowledge of his own daughter, because of a mistake? She didn't deserve to be forgiven.

'Caro, can you ever forgive me?'

She blinked across at him dazedly. 'Can *I* forgive *you*…?' she whispered. 'You mean it's true after all?'

'No, of course it isn't true, damn it!' Jake stood up suddenly to cross the room in two long strides, standing only inches away from Caro as he reached out to take both of her hands in his. 'Caro, do you have *any* idea how much I love you?' He looked down at her searchingly.

Her lips moved, but she uttered no sound. Instead she could only stare up at him with wide, disbelieving eyes.

'No, of course you don't,' Jake muttered in self-disgust. 'I've never told you that, have I? Never once in all the time we were together.'

The pink tip of her tongue moistened her lips before she spoke. 'I— No, you haven't.'

'No,' Jake acknowledged grimly. 'Caro, I've been so busy protecting myself from the same heartache my parents suffered, because they really *did* love each other, but just couldn't live together, that by not telling you I had fallen in love with you the moment I first saw you I actually created the situation that led to the two of us parting.'

'But I left you,' she gasped. 'I kept Magdalena's existence from you.' She shook her head. 'In the circumstances, that was completely unforgivable!'

'Caro, I think you should let *me* decide what is or isn't forgivable,' he chided huskily. 'Yes, I regret that I wasn't at your side during your pregnancy, during Magdalena's birth and the months since, but…'

'*You* regret it?' Caro echoed, still in shock. 'Jake, I was *wrong*. About *everything*. Because of that I—'

'Stop beating yourself up, Caro.' Jake gave her hands a gentle squeeze. 'Do you still love me?'

She swallowed hard. 'I— You—'

'No, you probably don't,' he accepted heavily. 'But will you give me a chance to try again, Caro? Not because of Magdalena, but because I love you more than life itself. This past year without you has been absolute hell,' he admitted, lowering all his barriers and making himself completely vulnerable to her for the first time.

'You could live here with Magdalena. I could come down and visit both of you. Perhaps spend weekends here. We could get to know each other all over again. At least think about it before saying no, Caro,' he pleaded when she didn't answer him.

Caro couldn't have spoken at that moment if her life had depended upon it. Jake loved her. He had always loved her. From the first moment he saw her.

'I can't—' She stopped, not even knowing where to begin telling Jake how much she loved him.

He gave a pained wince as he released her hands and stepped back. 'You can't love me again?' he guessed sadly. 'Perhaps I deserve that.' He ran an agitated hand through the dark thickness of his hair as he turned away. 'I should have told you how I felt when I asked you to marry me. Should have taken the risk and stopped protecting my own damn heart.'

'No, Jake. I mean—yes, Jake. You should have told me how you felt when you asked me to marry you,' she corrected as she saw the way his face had paled. 'But you weren't the only one to blame for the misunderstandings between the two of us. As you said, we—we're both a product of our upbringing. Your parents spent holidays together because they sincerely believed it was the right thing to do for you. As you know, my own parents stayed married to each other because of Gavin and I.'

'Neither is exactly good PR for the perfect family,' Jake acknowledged ruefully.

'No.' Caro gave a humourless smile. 'Jake, I— Did I ever tell you that my father had affairs? Oh, they were discreet enough. But nevertheless as Gavin and I got older we always knew whenever he'd become involved with someone new. He and my mother would get along better, and he would take Gavin and I out to the cinema and shows. All in an effort to salve his conscience because he was sleeping with another woman.' She bit her bottom lip. 'It isn't an excuse for the way I've behaved, but I think—believe—that in my heart of hearts I always felt the same thing might happen to me. That if I ever married my husband would eventually grow tired of me and turn to other women. But when I met you, fell so deeply in love with you, I forgot all about those fears. I was so sure that we would have a good marriage. A happy marriage.'

'And instead I never told you that I loved you, allowing those fears to resurface,' Jake realised, clenching his fists in agony. 'To the point that my buying this house and the presence of a woman in my hotel suite that day all pointed to my behaving in the same way your father had.'

'Yes…' she whispered.

Jake groaned and shook his head. 'Caro, I haven't so much as *looked* at another woman from the very first moment I set eyes on you! Damn it, I can tell you that until the end of time,' he rasped. 'It isn't going to matter at all when you no longer love me!'

'But *of course* I love you, Jake,' Caro protested emotionally. 'I've always loved you,' she told him. 'And I always *will* love you,' she vowed. Then, because she could no longer bear to be apart from him, she launched herself into his arms. 'I love you so much, Jake, that this past year apart from you has been absolute hell for me, too!'

Jake kissed her long and deeply, trembling slightly minutes later as he drew back to rest his forehead against hers. 'I really thought you would come back that day, you know. Believed you were just upset that I hadn't managed to get back for our wedding anniversary.' He smiled shakily. 'After two days I went to see Gavin—was convinced you would be staying with him.' He breathed raggedly. 'Gavin didn't even know you had left me, let alone where you were.'

Caro winced. 'I thought at first that if you did bother to talk to Gavin after I left, it would be easier for him to deny all knowledge if he really didn't have any idea where I was.'

'*If* I bothered?' Jake repeated incredulously. 'Once I realised you weren't coming back I was frantic! I spoke to all your friends. Your work colleagues. I checked with Gavin several times a day to see if he had heard from you. But no one had any idea where you were.' His face was haggard with the memory of those days and weeks of searching for her. 'Then Gavin said something to me that forced me to stop making a damned nuisance of myself...'

'*Gavin* did?' Caro frowned.

Jake nodded. 'He pointed out, quite bluntly, that if you had wanted me to find you then I would have done so.' He gave a shuddering sigh. 'I realised that he was right. That as far as you were concerned our marriage really was over.'

'Oh, Jake!' Her arms tightened about his waist and she clung to him. 'How can you ever forgive me?' she choked.

'Quite easily, when I love you so much,' he assured her firmly. 'And by knowing that there's two ways we can do this. I can lose my temper because you distrusted me,' he explained as she looked up at him questioningly, 'and we can waste another year—or two—until either you've forgiven me or I've forgiven you. Or we can both just accept, hard as this last year apart might have been for both of us, that without it we might never have got to *this* point.'

Tears glistened in Caro's eyes. 'I don't understand...?'

'Don't you see, Caro, that without that telephone call from the estate agent, without the mistake you made about Mrs Williams, you would have flown to New York that day and surprised me, told me about your pregnancy, given birth to Magdalena? And all without my ever feeling any need to tell you how much I love and cherish you.'

'Well...yes. But—'

'Just think about it for a moment, Caro,' he encouraged huskily. 'I'm more than willing to forget the pain of this last year for what we have here and now—how about you?'

Could they do that? Could they really start again and forget all the past heartache?

If he could do that, then so could she!

'Oh, yes, Jake,' she said brokenly. 'Let's do that. Let's start again,' she pleaded as she clung to him. 'Let's live in this house together from now on. Fill it with love and children and—'

'God, I love you, Caro!' Jake groaned as his arms tightened about her like steel bands. 'In future I intend telling you that a dozen times a day. A hundred times!' he vowed fiercely. 'I never, ever want you to doubt my love for you again—let alone even think of leaving me!'

Caro gave a shaky laugh as she looked up at him, with her own love for him shining brightly, clearly in her eyes. 'Now that I know you love me I won't ever doubt you again, Jake. Or leave you,' she promised. 'From now on we'll make every day as happy as this Christmas now promises to be.'

Jake reached up to cradle each side of her face as he looked down intently into her eyes. 'I'll love you until the day I die, Caro Montgomery. Longer! You're the air that I breathe. The sun, moon and stars to me.'

'As you are to me, Jake Montgomery,' she whispered emotionally.

It was more than enough.

Much, much more than enough…

* * * * *

TWINS FOR CHRISTMAS

Alison Roberts

Dear Reader,

Christmas… Merry Christmas. Happy Christmas. Christmas blessings. The word invokes emotion, doesn't it? A sense of caring. Being able to show that you care for the people you love and for others who might be in trouble.

An emergency department is not where anyone wants to be on Christmas Eve. This particular emergency department on the outskirts of London is certainly not where my hero, Rory, wants to be because…well…Kate's there, isn't she? And she's pregnant, and clearly *he* isn't the father.

It's not where a busload of orphans want to be either, but there's magic in the air.

Christmas magic. I hope some rubs off on you.

Happy reading!

Love,

Alison

CHAPTER ONE

'GOOD GRIEF! IT CAN'T BE—'

Kate Simpson glanced up from the computer screen in time to see the back of a tall man who must have climbed out from the back of the ambulance in the bay to give the crew space to unload their patient.

'Of course it isn't,' she told Judy.

Her colleague's eyebrows rose at her tone. 'Looked like him for a sec, though, didn't it?'

Kate shrugged, pretending interest in the screensaver that had just kicked in on the screen in front of her. Santa's sleigh, being pulled by ridiculously happy-looking reindeer, emerged from one side of the screen and then took a circuitous route to the other side amidst snowflakes and the soft jingle of bells. A clock in the bottom right corner of the screen ticked off the countdown until Christmas Day. Five hours and fifty-nine minutes to go.

Of course it wasn't *him*.

How many times, she reminded herself, had she caught a glimpse of a masculine figure with some feature familiar enough to make her heart miss a beat? Broad shoulders, perhaps, or dark hair. Even a hand with elegantly long fingers or a way of moving with quiet confidence.

How many times had she taken a second glance and felt the weight of disappointment? An echo of the loss she'd never really had the right to feel in the first place.

'You OK, Kate?'

'I'm fine. Why?'

'I dunno. You look kind of…sad.'

'Bored, more like. I'm not cut out to be a receptionist, and it's so qu—'

'Don't!' Judy held up her hand in a stop signal and the quick movement of her head made her festive bell earrings jingle. 'Don't you dare say the Q word! I'm off duty in an hour and I've still got Christmas shopping to finish.'

Kate smiled. 'OK. So far I've logged in one broken ankle, a kid with tonsillitis and a septic finger. It's…shall we say…restful?'

'Restful is exactly what you need. You should be at home with your feet up.'

'I'd rather be doing the job I'm trained for, thanks.'

'You can't get close enough to a bed to take a pulse unless you turn sideways. Anyone would think you were carrying triplets instead of just twins.' Judy turned to look out through the double doors ringed with bright red and green tinsel that led to the ambulance bay. 'They're taking their time.'

'Probably finishing their patient report form or something. Can't be urgent.' Kate had been resisting taking that second glance. The one that was such an ingrained habit after so many months. Her soft sigh was an admission of defeat. It was too compelling to resist.

What *was* it about the man still standing out there as the paramedics finally lifted a stretcher from the back of the vehicle? The sense of him *listening*, for want of a better word, she decided. Standing so patiently when it had to be freezing, with the sleet that now appeared to be thickening into real snow falling heavily just beyond the overhang. He gave the impression of waiting but still being active. Absorbing everything happening around him. Ready to act on information instantly if necessary. A sense of control. That was what it was. He might be wearing civvies, but you'd pick him as the person in charge.

No. Kate gave herself a mental shake. It couldn't be him. She didn't want it to be. Not now. Not when she finally felt in control of her life enough to be looking forward to the future. She transferred her gaze to the patient propped up on the stretcher as the double doors slid open to admit the new arrivals to the emergency department of St Bethel's Hospital—a choice made easy by the fact that the paramedics were now blocking the figure of the man accompanying the frail-looking, elderly female patient.

Judy moved to the other side of the reception desk to do her assigned task of triage, which meant that she would greet the patient, listen to the hand-over and decide where the patient should be taken first.

Kate's job was to collect the copy of the patient report form that had the patient details, input them into the computer program, then order sticky labels and request notes from previous admissions if appropriate.

Except that the small entourage had moved enough to reveal the man again, and she couldn't stop staring because it *was* him.

Rory.

He was staring back at her, his expression unreadable. He couldn't be as shocked as she was because he'd had the advantage of being prepared for the possibility of this encounter, hadn't he? No surprises there. He'd always had the advantage over her.

He looked…as gorgeous as ever. A little thinner, perhaps. Different. But that could be because he was wearing clothes he would never have come to work in. Black jeans. A leather jacket over a black fisherman's jersey. His hair was longer than she remembered, and there were beads of moisture caught in the dark waves. Melting snowflakes? No wonder they were melting. Had something gone wrong with the heating in here?

The voice of the paramedic telling Judy about the patient was a background blur of sound, only partially comprehensible.

'…seventy-two-year-old woman…. Parkside Rest Home… Advanced Alzheimer's…'

Kate hadn't set eyes on this man for six months. No one had. Rory McCulloch had simply vanished. One minute he'd been the senior consultant of this very department and the next he had been…gone.

The day after she'd… After they'd…

'Query urinary tract infection,' the paramedic was telling Judy now. 'She's tachycardic with a heart rate of one twenty. Pyrexic—temperature's thirty-nine.'

The woman being discussed made an alarmed cry, and Rory looked away from Kate. He stepped forward to touch the woman. A gentle touch on her forehead, smoothing long strands of nearly white hair from her face. It was an action that spoke of familiarity and deep affection.

'She's more confused than usual,' he said to Judy. 'And she's had quite severe abdominal pain. She had five milligrams of morphine, but I'm not convinced it's reduced the pain scale significantly.'

Judy's jaw had dropped as she turned her gaze to the speaker.

'Dr McCulloch! It *is* you! Oh…my goodness. You're back!'

'Briefly,' he conceded. 'This is my mother—Marcella.'

'Oh…' Judy was looking around the department now, as though searching for a suitably senior staff member to take charge of this case. 'Let's put Mrs McCulloch in

Resus 2,' she told the paramedics. 'We're quiet enough for the moment.'

The triage nurse was so flustered she didn't even notice she'd uttered the banned Q word. The stretcher lurched into movement, but then stopped as the woman cried out again in fright.

'Jamie! Where are you?' Then her tone changed to one of terror. The language also changed and became a frantic babble. What was she speaking? Was Rory's mother Italian?

That might explain why Rory had never looked as Scottish as his name and the slight lilt of his voice suggested. Why his hair was so dark and his skin so olive and his eyes that amazing chocolate-brown.

Rory took a stride to catch up with the stretcher, his face set in lines so grim it took Kate straight back to that night. The night before he'd disappeared. Her heart gave the same kind of squeeze it had then. A kind of pain. Wanting to know what was so wrong.

Wanting to make it better.

He took his mother's hand, saying something soothing in the same language, but she clung to him, tears coursing down a face so lined it made her look much older than she apparently was.

'Jamie,' she sobbed. *'Dio mio...* Don't leave me!'

'I won't,' he said. 'Shh, now, Mamma. It's all right.'

Judy frowned. 'Why—?'

A quick glance from Rory coupled with a tiny shake of his head was enough to stop the obvious question. The triage nurse regrouped.

'Kate, have you got all the information you need?'

Kate finally looked at the copy of the paperwork the ambulance crew had left on the desk in front of her. She scanned the details.

'Is the Parkside Rest Home her permanent address?'

'Yes.' The word was clipped and gave nothing away about whether Rory was happy with where his mother resided.

'Has she had any recent admissions to hospital?'

'Not that I've been informed about. I've been out of the country for six months.'

'Yes.' Kate's mouth felt dry. 'So you have.'

She couldn't help looking up to catch his gaze, and then she couldn't look away. Was there a message there? Remorse? An apology?

No. But there was something. An intensity that made her feel as flustered as poor Judy had been when she'd tempted fate by uttering the Q word.

'I'll come and talk to you if I find I need anything else,' she said, dropping her gaze.

Rory gave a curt nod at the dismissal and followed the stretcher into one of the well-equipped resuscitation bays.

Hopefully she wouldn't need anything else. If she had to get up from this chair and move beyond the screen of the counter he would realise why she wasn't on active duty tonight. The bagginess of the tunic top of her uniform was no longer enough to disguise her impressive bump.

Her heart was racing as she considered the implications. This was no way to learn of impending fatherhood. What would he say? Would he be angry that she hadn't told him earlier? A lot, lot earlier?

But how could she have when he'd simply vanished? Resigned from his job and walked away without leaving even a forwarding address. People had talked about it for weeks. Made jokes about interplanetary abductions. Asked, far more seriously, where Dr Rory McCulloch could possibly have needed to go in such a hurry. And *why*?

Maybe some of those questions would be answered tonight. Word was spreading fast. Kate saw the man who was now in charge of the department, Braden Foster, shaking Rory's hand and greeting him like a long-lost friend. Nurses were flocking to the bay, vying for the privilege of caring for his mother. Some things certainly hadn't changed. Even Judy had gravitated in that direction, leaving Kate alone at the desk.

The prettiest nurses had always made themselves available to Rory McCulloch in the two years Kate had worked in St Bethel's. She had always been in the background. A bit short and round and plain. Just like her name. Nondescript. Invisible.

Until that amazing night...

The radio behind the desk crackled into life and Kate reached for the microphone.

'St Bethel's—emergency department,' she responded. 'Receiving you loud and clear.'

'How are you placed for multiple casualties?'

Kate didn't need to look around to know how 'restful' the department was. 'How many?' she queried briskly. 'And what status?'

'We've got a mini-bus from the Castle that's gone down a bank.'

'Oh, my God!' Kate couldn't help the unprofessional response. The Castle was actually an old stone house just a few miles from St Bethel's on the outskirts of London. Its owner, Mary Ballantyne, had been well-known in the district for many years, welcoming all the orphans and foster children she could manage into her home. It had been one of 'her' children, so impressed with his new accommodation, who had announced he was now living in a castle, and the name had stuck. The house—and Mary—were a local legend.

'Ten children on board,' the voice of the person from the emergency services continued. 'And Mary was driving. Maybe half of them are injured, and a couple look serious, but we haven't extricated everybody yet. It would be preferable if we could bring them all to the same hospital, and St Bethel's is closest.'

'Of course.' Kate took a deep breath. 'Bring them here. We'll be ready.'

They would be—but Kate's first task was to alert the trauma team, who would clear the resuscitation bays, gather equipment and put the other staff on standby.

To do that she had to tell Braden Foster what was happening, and the department's head consultant was still talking to Rory about his mother.

There was no time to consider the implications. Kate stood up and moved from behind the shelter of her desk. She walked into Resus 2.

'Dr Foster? There's a multiple casualty incident in progress on the motorway and we're the closest casualty department.'

Both men in front of her were staring. Braden Foster was looking at her face.

'How many?'

'Possibly eleven. The mini-bus from the Castle has gone over a bank.'

Judy's voice carried to the now silent staff around them, and it was an echo of Kate's reaction to the news.

'Oh, my God! On Christmas Eve? That's awful!'

'Put Mrs McCulloch in one of the cubicles,' Dr Foster ordered. 'Let's get her bloods off and a urine specimen before we get too busy. Put out a call for everyone in the trauma team, would you, please, Kate?'

Kate nodded and turned—but not before she glanced at Rory. She was too aware that he was still staring at her. He seemed to sense her gaze and lifted his own. He might not have been shocked at seeing her on his arrival, but he certainly was now.

Kate held his gaze for just a heartbeat as she watched his mental calculations. Remembering dates. Counting weeks.

Yes, she told him silently. I'm just over six months pregnant.

And you're the father.

CHAPTER TWO

SHE WAS *PREGNANT*.

No wonder she had looked different when he'd seen her sitting at the desk. Rounder. Softer. The soft waves of her hair that almost touched her shoulders had been catching the light and shining like a golden halo. If it was true that pregnancy gave all women a special glow, then Kate had turned it up a notch. She shone as brightly as the light at the end of a very long tunnel.

The way he had remembered her being anyway—but she was *pregnant*.

Enormously pregnant. Way more than six months along, so she must have already been pregnant that night.

And that hurt, dammit, because the memory of that night had been the single bright note in those first dark weeks.

Rory had to help hold his mother's arm still while blood was drawn for the necessary tests. And the insertion of a catheter was the only way they'd be able to obtain a urine specimen from a patient who couldn't co-operate because she had no understanding of where she was. Or why. It was a miserable but mercifully short period of time.

'It's all right, Mamma. It'll be over soon. You're being brave.'

He managed to keep up a stream of soothing words, in both English and his mother's native Italian, even as he reeled from the shock of seeing Kate's condition—as unexpected as it had been to be bringing his only living relative here tonight.

He hadn't questioned the destination. He'd already made the demand for extra medical attention for his mother and, given that he no longer carried any authority within this medical hierarchy, it had seemed prudent to put up with what might be a difficult time revisiting St Bethel's. If he was honest, part of him really wanted the opportunity to see Kate Simpson again, but he'd been wary. He knew quite well he might have made her into something she wasn't.

A life-saver.

Some kind of saint. An angel, even.

He'd known he'd have to face the probability that she wasn't all that he had built her up to be in his head—and his heart. But not like this. Not this slap in the face that told him she'd been already pregnant by another man that night. That her words and her touch and the…*love* he'd felt had not been genuine.

As if it wasn't bad enough to have his mother's illness tipping her to a place where she was convinced that her prayers had been answered and she had her precious Jamie with her again. Now Rory also had to deal with the most precious thing *he'd* had in his life for the last six months being exposed as a fraud. As a dream that had no basis in reality.

The tiny Christmas tree on the central desk, beside a donation box for some worthy cause, caught Rory's eye as he slumped farther into the chair beside his mother's bed when the blood test had been completed. He closed his eyes for a moment as he put a hand to his forehead and pressed on both temples—his thumb on one side of his head, his middle finger on the other side.

Merry Christmas, he told himself bitterly.

Merry bloody Christmas!

HE LOOKED AS THOUGH he was wishing himself a million miles away from this place.

Why? Because he had to face the prospect of fatherhood? Of *her* being the mother of his children?

Well, tough! Kate's face tightened as she moved swiftly past the cubicle the McCullochs were in, making her way to join Judy as she spotted the arrival of the first ambulance from the scene of the accident involving the minibus full of children. Two stretchers and some ambulatory patients were being ushered into the department by paramedics and police officers.

It was probably all for the best that she had no choice but to ignore Rory and his distress right now. He needed time. She'd had more than enough to get her head around the new direction her life was going in, and she'd come to terms with it. More than accepted it. She already loved these babies. Passionately.

That love was comforting to remember. Empowering. And for the first time Kate realised *she* actually had the advantage. In a neat twist of fate, she wasn't going to be in the background, watching other women claim Rory's attention. Eventually he was going to have to seek her out so that they could talk about this. Or she would find him. It didn't matter, because she was in control.

It was something that might have thrown her completely six months ago, but Lord knows she'd had more than enough practice in discriminating between fantasy and reality. She was an expert. There was no danger of having that control undermined by any hope that her situation would magically change.

Hope got crushed.

It was only when you removed the fuel from unrequited love that it had any chance of burning out.

And the easiest way to remove it was to focus on something else entirely.

Like the teenaged girl on one of the stretchers. Her lower leg was splinted and propped up on a pillow. One arm was also splinted and in a sling. She was sobbing hysterically.

'This is Helen,' a paramedic informed them. 'She's sixteen years old and has a fractured right tib and fib and a Colles' fracture of her right wrist.'

'Vital signs?'

'All within normal limits.'

'Resus 3,' Judy directed.

'Noooo,' the girl sobbed. 'Don't take me away from Danni.'

Judy was already moving to the second stretcher as she did her job of triage.

'Who's Danni?' Kate queried.

'This is. Danielle.' An older woman was standing beside a policewoman. She had a pale face and a blood-stained bandage on her head. She was holding a wailing toddler. 'She's Helen's baby.'

'Is she injured?'

'They didn't think so at the scene,' the policewoman responded. 'And Florence insisted she was OK to come with her.'

Kate eyed the older woman. 'You know these children?'

'Yes. I'm the housekeeper up at the Castle.'

'Great. You'll be able to help me with the information I'll need.' Kate was all too aware of the need to start gathering that information and filling in paperwork before it got out of hand with this influx of new arrivals.

Another paramedic was handing a new case to Judy, just behind her.

'Wally's twelve and he was KO'ed. Unconscious for possibly ten minutes. Responsive, but his GCS is down to thirteen. Repetitive speech pattern and some nausea.'

'Wally?' Judy crouched beside the boy, who lay flat on his back with a hard collar protecting his neck. 'Do you know where you are, love?'

'We've been at a party.' A white grin appeared in a very dark small face. 'Christmas. Da-da-da... Da-da-da...'

It was a tuneless rendition of what sounded like 'Jingle Bells'. Judy caught Kate's glance and they smiled.

'Resus 4,' Judy directed, with another glance at Kate, who nodded. Resus 1 needed to be kept free in case more seriously injured victims arrived.

Helen was still sobbing, and the ambulance crew were unsure of whether to increase her distress by separating her from her child.

Kate crouched down, which was no easy task these days. She had to catch the bar on the side of the stretcher to keep her balance.

'The doctors need to take care of you,' she told the girl. 'And we're going to take very good care of Danni for you.'

'Is she all right?' Helen grabbed Kate with her uninjured hand. 'Oh...*God*! I couldn't hold onto her, and I tried... I really tried...'

'I know, sweetheart,' Kate said. 'We'll check her out thoroughly. Try not to worry. You need to trust us.' She squeezed Helen's hand. 'Can you do that, do you think?'

There was anguish in the girl's eyes, but she nodded. What choice did she have? The poor girl was hardly more than a child herself, but the bond she had with her baby was palpable. It wasn't helping either of them to be hearing the other sobbing so miserably.

'Good girl.' Kate smiled. 'Now, take a deep breath for me. And another one.'

Helen complied, controlling her sobs with difficulty. 'I—I'm sorry.'

'You don't have anything to be sorry for.' Kate gave her hand another squeeze before heaving herself upright again. 'Let the doctors take care of you, and we'll have you back together with your little girl just as soon as we can, OK?'

Helen nodded again, her lips clamped shut on another sob as she was wheeled away. Wally was still singing as he was taken to the team waiting to assess and treat him.

'Could you put Florence and Danni into a cubicle, please, Kate?' Judy was writing furiously on the big whiteboard, putting the names of the patients into boxes that would track where they were and what treatment was underway. 'I'll find a doctor to come and see them. Oh, and could you check on Mrs McCulloch? Do her vitals if you get a chance. I think her nurse is caught up in resus now. I'll try and get someone in to cover the paperwork.'

An empty stretcher was on its way back to the desk. 'You can expect the next ambulance in about ten minutes,' a paramedic said. 'Possibly longer. The driver and another child were still trapped when we left. The fire service is working on getting them out.'

IT WASN'T SO MUCH of a shock being close to Rory this time. Her skin still prickled, and there was that odd feeling deep inside her belly that had nothing to do with any movement from all those tiny limbs in there, but Kate could cope.

She had to.

She fitted a clean earpiece to the tympanic thermometer. 'So, your mother's Italian?'

'Yes.'

'I never knew that.'

'Why would you?'

Why indeed? But the curt response was unnecessary. Unkind. Kate concentrated on her task and inserted the earpiece as gently as she could, but Marcella stirred and moaned.

Rory said something to his mother in Italian. Something so soothing that Kate could feel the words rumbling into her bones. No wonder his mother's eyes drifted shut again.

'Temperature's thirty-eight point four.' Kate reached for the chart on the end of the bed. 'It's coming down.'

'Good.'

Kate carefully wrapped a blood pressure cuff around the elderly woman's arm, trying not to wake her. She felt for a pulse, keeping her eyes firmly on what she was doing, because she really didn't want eye contact with Rory. He was giving the impression that he considered this to be *her* fault.

Fair enough—to a point—but, unlike many, she had never chased this man. Never let him know even by a glance how she felt about him. She'd certainly never, ever expected to share her bed with him. And, yes, it was her fault as much as his that they hadn't used any protection, but the possibility of pregnancy had seemed as unreal as everything else about that night.

Kate pumped up the cuff and let it down slowly, listening for a pulse to reappear. She took her time, because she would have to look up when she'd finished and she could feel Rory staring at her.

Sounds from the adjacent cubicle were muffled, but still audible. A junior doctor was talking to Florence.

'How old is she?'

'Nearly two.'

'And she lives at the Castle?'

'Yes. Her mum, Helen, came when she was fourteen and pregnant. She's still living there. She helps with the other kids and gives me a hand with the cleaning and so forth.'

Kate unhooked the stethoscope and wrote down the blood pressure. Then she put her fingers back on Marcella's wrist to time her heart rate.

'How many children at the home at present?' the doctor was asking Florence.

'Nine—if you count Danni, here. Ten if you count Helen—and she's still a child, really, poor lamb.'

'And you were at a Christmas party?'

'Yes. Big charity do where they give us sacks of gifts for the children. They're still in the back of the bus. Oh, no! You don't think someone will steal them, do you?'

'I'm sure the police will take care of that. Danni seems fine. Let's have a look at that head of yours.'

Kate could hear the noise level in the department increasing, presumably due to a new wave of arrivals, but that wasn't what made her brow furrow in concern.

'Is your mother's pulse normally irregular?'

'Yes. She has chronic atrial fibrillation.'

'I might see if I can find a twelve-lead ECG machine that's free. I'll check to see if any results are back on those tests as well.'

'You might be needed more urgently elsewhere.'

'Help!' someone was shouting. '*Help* me…'

'It *hurts*!' a child's voice cried. 'It really, *really* hurts!'

It was a cry that would have torn anybody's heart. Kate looked up deliberately to catch Rory's gaze.

'You could help,' she heard herself suggesting. 'While your mum's asleep.'

'No.' The word was a harsh dismissal. 'I'm no longer a doctor, Kate. It's out of the question.'

She stared at him. This wasn't the man she knew. Or thought she knew. The brilliant doctor who'd never missed a beat, no matter how much pressure he was under. The leader who had thrived on coping and still being fanatically careful with his treatment of every patient. The physician whose diagnostic abilities were a legend and his skills with highly invasive procedures even more so. The man colleagues had admired and respected. That patients had adored. That women had fallen in love with.

Like Kate had.

And to ignore a child like the one who had just cried out! She'd seen him with children in the past. He'd always gone to whatever lengths were necessary to help a child.

Who was this man? The lines on his face were as uncompromising as his tone had been. The topic was clearly not open for discussion, but surely Kate had the right to know?

'You left medicine? Just walked away?'

'That's exactly what I did.'

'What have you been doing?'

'Not that it's any of your business,' Rory said coldly, 'but I've been building roads. New mining development in the south of Australia.'

No wonder he looked so tanned and lean. Toughened by a harsh climate and physically demanding work.

'But...*why*?' The word came out as a whisper. It just didn't make sense.

Marcella stirred, probably disturbed by the now chaotic noise level in the department.

'Jamie?'

The change in Rory was subtle, but Kate didn't miss any of it. She'd had too much practice watching this man in the past. She saw what amounted to physical pain at hearing the wrong name. She could see the instant tension in his body, the shadow in his eyes, and it reminded her so strongly of the trouble he'd been in that night.

She was no closer to understanding what it was all about, but—stupidly—she still wanted to help. She almost reached out to touch him. To convey that desire. What stopped her was seeing the fierce determination in his face. Confidence. So something *had* changed in the months he'd been gone. Whatever it was, and however hard it might be, Rory could deal with this by himself this time. He didn't need her comfort.

'Leave it, Kate,' he said wearily. 'It really is none of your business.'

'Oh?' The tension had been contagious, and Kate didn't have access to whatever inner strength Rory had just tapped into.

And, yes, the fantasy of seeing the dawning joy in his face on learning he was soon to be the father of twins was over-the-top, to say the least, but to reject her like this was unfair.

Unacceptable, really.

Maybe it *wasn't* any of her business, but Kate could at least live up to her responsibilities. She could do what should have been done a long time ago.

'It might be helpful if you could leave some kind of forwarding address the next time you decide to vanish,' she said.

'Why?'

Kate's smile was wry. 'So that I can let you know when your children are born.'

CHAPTER THREE

'*CHILDREN?*'

The colour in Rory's face was draining, but Kate's gaze didn't falter.

'Twins,' she confirmed.

'Kate?'

Judy's voice was coming from behind the curtain screening the cubicle, but something had clicked for Kate. Something important.

'It's in your family, isn't it?' She didn't give Rory time to respond. 'You have a twin. That's why your mother keeps calling you Jamie.'

'Kate?' The curtain was twitching now, but Kate was still watching Rory. Seeing the pain that darkened his eyes to an impenetrable black.

'*Had.*' His voice was so low and raw the words were almost inaudible. 'He died. A long time ago.'

'Kate? We need help in Resus 1. I know you're supposed to be on light duties, but are you up for it?'

'Of course.'

Judy's glance turned to Rory. 'Dr Foster asked me to bring you, too, if possible, Dr McCulloch. It's a Code Red.'

Meaning that this was a crisis. They had more serious cases than they could safely handle with the staff they had available.

Rory shook his head.

'We can find someone to sit with your mother. Now that she's started antibiotics there's not much more we can do for the moment.'

'No,' Rory said aloud. 'I can't help you. I'm sorry.'

Judy stared with the same incredulity Kate had experienced only a minute ago. She flicked Kate a 'what on earth is going on?' kind of look, but couldn't linger.

Neither could Kate. But neither could she let Rory get away with dismissing his moral responsibilities like this. He'd taken an oath when he became a doctor. One that Kate considered if not sacred at least equal to the kind of obligation and responsibilities that came with becoming a parent. If he could ignore that oath and the patients that needed him in a situation like this, what sort of father was he going to make to her children?

It simply wasn't good enough.

'There are children out there,' she breathed. 'Frightened, injured children who thought they were going back to the only home they know to put their Christmas presents under their tree. They need help. *Your* help.'

It was more than pain in his eyes now. More like agony.

'You don't know what you're asking, Kate.'

'Yes, I do.' Kate was already moving. She took a quick glance over her shoulder. 'And if you can't do it, you're not the man I thought you were. And you're certainly not a father I thought my children could be proud of.'

The sharp stab of discomfort in her chest as Kate walked out of the cubicle felt remarkably like a piece breaking off from her heart.

Or the death of a dream she'd never quite been able to relinquish.

IT TOOK LESS THAN thirty seconds to get from the cubicle Mrs McCulloch was occupying to the resus bay where she was needed. Ahead of Kate was the job she was trained to do. A job she loved. The complicated and often challenging task of assessing and stabilising the condition of injured or sick people. Trying to reduce suffering. Saving lives.

The pull towards that duty and the desire to perform to the very best of her ability was a powerful force.

But Kate could feel a pull from behind her as well.

A link to the man she was walking away from in disgust.

A voice as compelling as the cry of the injured children was inside her own head. Telling her she was wrong.

Reminding her...

Strange how thirty seconds was long enough for a series of impressions to flash through her mind with such clarity. Or maybe not so strange. So much editing had been done to those memories they were now condensed into a single image that was far more than a picture. It could touch her senses and capture her emotions even when she was wide awake.

Every step Kate took seemed to trigger a new image. Another sense. Following one from another. But the first was an image printed on her heart that never failed to stir something painfully poignant.

The way he had been sitting that night. Alone. On that bench in the little park that was halfway between St Bethel's and her small apartment.

The sight of a lone man late at night should have frightened Kate. It had—but she hadn't been afraid for her own safety. She had been alarmed because she'd recognised Rory, and for him to be sitting there like that, so alone, was so completely out of character she'd known something was wrong. Terribly wrong.

Rory McCulloch was never alone. He was a man who

played as hard as he worked. A man who could make anybody laugh and feel good about themselves. At least smile if a day or a job had been particularly distressing.

His philosophy on life was so well-known someone had printed a card and put it on the noticeboard outside the staffroom. It had Rory's photograph on it and below was the caption: *Life is short. Eat dessert first.*

Time away from work was all about life's 'dessert' for Dr McCulloch. It was time to recharge one's batteries by having fun.

He wasn't having fun right now. Kate could see that by his solitude and by the body language in shoulders slumped enough to suggest the weight of the world was too much. By the look in his eyes when she got close enough, having veered from her path without hesitation.

A look of…defeat?

Asking if he was all right was such an obviously redundant question that Kate said nothing at all. She sat down beside him and took his hand, and just sat there. Listening to the ragged edge to his breathing. Hearing the oddly thick note in his voice when he finally spoke.

'You should go home, Katie. It's very late.'

Nobody else ever called her Katie. It didn't suit the person she was at work. The efficient, competent nurse she was proud of being. She had thought he might have seen something nobody else had seen about her. Something attractive. A quiet little dream that had been a pleasure all on its own.

He needed someone tonight, though. She could see it and hear it, and she was the one who was there and, dear Lord, she wanted to be the one to help.

'Come with me,' she said simply.

'Why?'

'Because you need a friend.'

Amazingly, when she'd tightened her grip on his hand and stood up to move he'd come with her. They hadn't talked, and that had made Kate all the more aware of other sounds. Their shoes on the pavement. The creak of the steep stairs that led to her bedsit. The scratch of her key in the lock. The click of the lamp beside her bed as she switched it on so that she could see Rory's face to help her try and find words to ask what was wrong so that she could offer comfort.

'Don't ask,' he'd said softly. 'Please, Katie. Don't ask.'

It was actually easy to give comfort without knowing what it was for, because it was an expression of love. Unconditional.

The images that flowed from that point were ones Kate could easily suppress if she wasn't alone. They were too private and too precious.

The taste of that first kiss.

The smell of Rory's skin.

The touch of his hands and lips.

Her breath escaped in a soft sigh of submission. The pull was too strong.

Kate was almost there, on the other side of the department. Ready to focus completely on the people who needed her now. In the present. She just couldn't stop herself taking one last peek into the past.

To where Rory was, once again, sitting alone.

Except he wasn't.

He was right there, a step behind her, and he still had that look of grim determination on his face. He walked right past her into Resus 1, where there were two new patients crowding the area.

Braden Foster was bent over a small boy who was on one of the beds.

He nodded at Rory, who stepped towards the other bed onto which ambulance staff were transferring a grey-haired woman who had to be Mary Ballantyne.

'Tell me about this patient,' he instructed a paramedic.

'Kate?' Braden Foster caught her glance. 'Could you give me some cricoid pressure here, please? We need to intubate this lad.'

Her focus was narrowed to just one of the patients occupying this area set aside for major trauma, but Kate was aware of Rory in the same room. Aware that he'd stepped through some kind of personal barrier to be here.

For her? For his children? Because of what she'd said?

It didn't matter. He was here, and her heart had been right not to let her believe the worst about him.

He was still the man she thought he was.

The man she loved.

CHAPTER FOUR

THIS WAS A NIGHTMARE.

Not quite his worst, but only because he was tasked with treating the older female patient tucked into the corner of the area and not the little boy who was the primary focus of concern.

He could still hear the alarms going off on the monitoring equipment, however. Hear the tension in the voices of the staff dealing with the emergency.

'Oxygen saturation dropping.'

'Blood pressure's dropping.'

'Heart rate's irregular. Ectopics increasing.'

'I need some suction, here. Can't see a damn thing.'

Focus, Rory told himself. Shut it out. You don't have to take responsibility for that patient. Look after the one you've got.

On first glance it didn't look good. Strapped to a spinal board, the woman was wearing a neck collar, and her face was largely obscured by blood and an oxygen mask.

'Facial injuries,' the paramedic had informed Rory. 'This is Mary Ballantyne and she's seventy-two years old. She was driving the mini-bus and thinks her face hit the steering wheel as they went over the bank.'

'Are you having any trouble breathing, Mary?'

'By dose is blocked.'

'Keep breathing through your mouth for the moment.' Rory turned back to the paramedic. 'Was she knocked out?'

'I don't think so.' The paramedic had a hint of a smile. 'GCS was fifteen on arrival. Mary was trapped, but still trying to organise everybody else—including the emergency services.'

'I'b fine,' came a surprisingly strong voice from the bed. 'Get be out of this ridiculous contraption. I need to look after by children.'

Rory smiled at the feisty tone. He leaned closer. 'I'm Rory McCulloch, Mrs Ballantyne. I'm the doctor who's going to be looking after you.'

'Get on with it, then, young ban,' his patient directed. 'And call be Bary. Everyone else does.'

Mary's nose was still bleeding. Rory pulled on gloves as the paramedic lingered to pass on all the information they had gathered so far.

'All she's complained of is a sore nose and nausea, which is probably due to the amount of blood she'd swallowed by the time we got her out. She denied any cervical tenderness but, given the mechanism of injury, it seemed prudent to immobilise her spine.'

'Let's get that nose packed,' Rory directed. 'I don't want her losing any more blood. I'll get a line in and we'll hang some fluids. What's the blood pressure now?'

'One-fifteen on sixty,' a nurse relayed.

Not too bad, considering. 'Do you have any medical history I should know about, Mary?'

'No.'

'No problems with your heart or blood pressure or breathing?'

'I get a bit of angina. Nothing buch.'

'Any chest pain at the moment?'

'No.'

'I'm going to loosen this collar and check your head and neck, but I don't want you moving just yet, OK?' Rory was surprised to see just the flash of a twinkle in the pale blue eyes watching him. Was Mary actually weighing up whether she would co-operate or not?

'OK,' she agreed.

Rory smiled. He could see beneath that twinkle. He could see the fear that her condition might prevent her doing what she desperately needed to do, which was to look after all the children she had chosen to take into her care. The trust being put in him was one he would do his utmost to honour. He admired what this woman was doing with her life, and how she was coping with a potentially disastrous situation.

He would do whatever he could to help her, and it was a privilege to be in a position to do so. He'd missed this part of medicine more than he had allowed himself to admit.

'We need X-rays,' he ordered moments later, having checked for obvious injuries to Mary's head and neck and found nothing. 'C-spine, chest and pelvis. The sooner we can clear Mary, the sooner we can untie her.' They couldn't use the overhead X-ray facilities in this trauma area because they were over the bed the boy was occupying. 'Is X-ray free?'

'Yes,' a nurse responded. 'Helen's just gone through to the plaster room.'

'Let's move Mary, then.'

There was huge relief in being able to issue the instruction. He could move away from what was happening in here. An intubation attempt to secure the airway of a child that had clearly failed.

'Bag him,' Braden Foster was ordering. 'I need a guide wire, Kate. We'll have one more try.'

Rory almost managed to escape. The bed Mary was on was being wheeled through the door and he was following. Relieved to be moving. Confident that a broken nose was the worst of Mary's injuries and that she was in no immediate danger.

It was Braden's voice that caught him.

'Rory?' The tone was quiet—a warning all by itself. 'I need you.'

He had to turn. To face the concern he knew he would see in his colleague's face. The fear that he was losing his young patient.

God, he knew that fear. He had lived with it every day he had been a practising doctor. Statistically, it was a ticking bomb. You couldn't be a specialist in emergency medicine without losing the battle to save a paediatric patient at some point.

It hadn't happened to Rory, but the fear had finally crippled him. Would have destroyed him if it hadn't been for Kate. And he could feel even before his gaze moved the way Kate was looking at him.

There was a plea in her eyes. She knew how much he didn't want to do this. Maybe she knew he was convinced he *couldn't* do it, because there was also encouragement in that steady gaze. A belief in him.

You can do this, her gaze told him.

For just a heartbeat he could feel it again. The memory of her touch. The feeling that he *was* worth the space he took up on the planet because this woman felt that way. The seed of strength he had taken with him to the most distant corner of the planet he'd been able to find.

He couldn't let her down.

Facing that fear again *was* his worst nightmare, but he had to step into it. He had to *try*. He owed Kate that much, at least.

IF ANYONE COULD save this child, it was this man. Rory McCulloch.

And Kate was there. Right beside him.

There were lots of other people as well, of course. Other doctors and nurses, technicians and a surgeon with his registrar, but it was Rory who took over trying to make sure this boy could breathe—because if he couldn't he was going to die, very, very quickly.

Rory had fresh gloves on by the time he reached the head of the bed. So did Kate. She unrolled a kit onto the top of a trolley, containing what she knew Rory would need.

'Fold a towel and slip it under his shoulders,' Rory directed another nurse. 'Kate, can you prep the skin, please?'

Wordlessly, Kate picked up a swab in some forceps and dipped it into the antiseptic solution someone was tipping into a kidney dish for her. She swabbed the front of the boy's neck, swallowing hard herself as she thought of what had to be done.

She watched Rory feel for the anatomical landmarks and then stabilise the small Adam's apple with one hand. His other hand reached out to Kate and she placed a scalpel into it.

Their hands touched for only an instant in time, but Kate could feel Rory's tension. She held her breath. Everyone else seemed to do the same and movement stilled, the atmosphere so tense it felt as if the world might shatter at any moment.

Rory didn't hesitate. His movements were smooth and sure, despite the grim necessity of actually cutting into the little boy's throat. The tube was slipped into place and suction used to clear it. Then the bag mask unit was attached.

And finally the small chest rose as air entered the lungs. Everybody breathed out in a collective sigh of relief in time with the boy's outward breath, but Rory wasn't finished. He was watching the respiratory efforts intently.

Braden handed Rory his own stethoscope and Kate allowed herself to watch his face, because he was too intent on his patient to notice her scrutiny. It was ridiculous to feel so proud of him, but there it was. Kate had to blink the threat of tears away.

Rory turned his attention to the monitors next, and then to his colleagues. A theatre was on standby, but they had to make sure that their patient was stable enough to transfer and find out the extent of the trauma they would need to deal with. Kate left the room for a minute or two while a series of X-rays was being taken. She returned as the images were coming through on the computer, but she still stood back.

This felt so right. As if Rory had never been away. If it wasn't for the huge bump of her belly it would have been easy to dismiss the gap in time. He was here again, *now*, doing the job he did so brilliantly, and another life had just been saved.

How could he have walked away from doing this? From being able to make such a difference?

The little boy, Michael, was now breathing well on a ventilator, and his vital signs were stable and within acceptable limits. His care was passed to the paediatric surgeon who led the team transferring him to Theatre. Braden was going to accompany the entourage.

'I'll be back directly,' he said as they left the resuscitation area. 'We've dealt with the worst here, but there are still a lot of patients that need attention. Rory, I hate to ask, but—'

Rory's smile was lopsided. 'I'm here,' he said. 'I'll help if I can.'

'You already have,' Braden told him quietly. 'Thanks, mate.'

RORY WAS STRIPPING off his gloves as Kate reached his side. Other staff had dispersed to urgent tasks. Only a nurse aide was left, and she was busy cleaning up. Kate couldn't help her wide smile.

'I knew you could do it.'

He didn't return the smile. 'You knew more than I did, then.'

Kate held his gaze. Maybe he wasn't relaxed enough to smile, but that unbearable level of tension was gone. And there was something else in both his look and those words. Something that recognised the link between them. An acknowledgement that Kate knew more than anyone else because she'd been there that night. She had seen him in a space no one else here would dream he could ever be in.

He'd let her share that space then. Would he let her in again?

'What I don't know,' Kate said cautiously, 'is why you stopped doing this. Why you had to leave.' She swallowed hard. 'Was it because of me?'

That shocked him. He was holding his gloves over the rubbish bin, but he forgot to let them go. 'Good God, Katie! Why on earth would you think that?'

He'd called her Katie again. It was a struggle to keep her tone light. To give a shrug that belied her history of painful agonising over this.

'Oh, I don't know,' she said quietly. 'You'd never taken

any notice of me. Not in—um—*that* way. And then we had that amazing night. But you creep out of my room hoping that I'm still asleep and—'

The flush of colour would have been welcome on his pale face if it hadn't been due to embarrassment. '*Weren't* you?'

'No. I pretended to be, because it was obvious you didn't want to talk to me.'

'I—'

'And then,' Kate rushed on, 'I get to work to find you've gone. Resigned. Vanished. Can you blame a girl for thinking that you'd gone to rather extraordinary lengths so that you didn't have to see her again?'

The quiet sound he made was almost a groan. Rory dropped the gloves into the bin and caught Kate's shoulders.

'Don't ever think that,' he said softly. 'You have no idea how important it was. How often I thought about that night.'

'As often as *I* thought about it?' Kate's voice caught. 'I don't think so, Rory.'

There was a moment's silence as they stared at each other. There were too many questions hanging in the air between them. So much that was a mystery. But one thing was clearer now.

He hadn't been avoiding *her*. Kate knew with a certainty that gave her a new sense of peace that she had had nothing to do with his decision to leave. That the decision had been made well before she'd met Rory that night.

And he remembered their time together.

It had been important.

A glimmer of something like joy flickered within Kate, but then Rory's gaze dropped. To her belly.

'I'm sorry,' he said.

'I'm not,' Kate responded steadily.

His gaze flicked up. 'Really?'

She drew in a deep breath. How could she tell him she already loved these babies because of the way they had been conceived? Because she'd known for a very long time that she would never love another man the way she loved their father?

She couldn't tell him. Not when he was 'sorry'. Sorry that he'd made a mistake in allowing it to happen.

The faint glow of joy was snuffed out. Perfect timing for someone to come close enough for them both to be distracted.

'Could I ask you both to help mop up in the cubicles?' Judy asked. 'There's a woman next door to your mother, Dr McCulloch, who needs a head wound sutured. There's nobody available from Plastics, and if anyone could do a job that won't leave too much of a scar it would be you.'

Rory didn't seem to notice the compliment. 'Is my mother still asleep?'

'Yes. Quite peacefully, and her temperature's still dropping.' Judy's smile was openly admiring as she turned to hurry away again. 'Fabulous job there with Michael. Just like the old days.'

Rory said nothing, but Kate kept pace with him as he headed in Judy's wake.

'She's right, you know.'

'Is she?'

'You stepped back just the way you left. In a blaze of glory.'

Rory stopped just in front of the double doors that led from the resuscitation area back to the main department. The halt was so sudden Kate almost bumped into him. Her belly brushed his hand.

'What on earth are you talking about?'

'The last case that day. Don't you remember? The toddler with meningitis?'

'I remember.'

'He'd been discharged,' Kate continued, speaking fast because she knew they were needed elsewhere, but this was somehow important. 'The houseman had filled him up with paracetamol to get his fever down and decided his rash was due to fleabites. You ran after them. Stopped them driving out of the car park. Made the parents bring him back.'

'I remember,' Rory repeated, grimly enough to let Kate know she wasn't wrong in assuming the importance she was assigning to this part of their history. 'It was why I had to leave.' He was moving again, his hand on the doors. He didn't want to talk about this.

'But you *saved* him.'

Her words were quiet. A thought that was spoken aloud unintentionally. But Rory turned his head.

'It wasn't enough,' he growled. 'Not that day. Come on, Katie.' He pushed open the swing door. 'We've got work to do. There'll be plenty of time to talk later.'

CHAPTER FIVE

THE CASUALTY DEPARTMENT of St Bethel's Hospital had gone from being 'restful' to completely chaotic.

A nurse was walking up and down in front of the central desk, holding the toddler who'd come in with the first wave of patients. Danni was still crying.

'Someone needs to check that child again,' Rory said.

Other patients had come in while they'd been involved in the resuscitation area drama. Cubicles were full and staff were flat out. An ECG machine was being wheeled to one bedside. Someone was having a seizure in Cubicle 6 and a very inebriated person in a Santa costume was yelling for attention in Cubicle 5.

And there seemed to be children everywhere they looked. Cubicle 1, beside the woman they were assigned to see, had a thin, worried-looking girl peering out.

'Rhys?' she called nervously. 'Alex? Come back here!'

A small girl, maybe four or five years old, was tugging on an older child's arm.

'Lucy? Why is Father Christmas shouting? I want to go *home*!'

'Are you all right?' Kate asked as they got closer.

The girl nodded. Then shook her head. 'I can't see the boys and I'm supposed to be looking after them.'

'What's your name, sweetheart?'

'Lucy.'

'And how old are you?'

'I'm eleven.' Lucy was looking past Kate now. 'Are you a doctor?' she asked Rory.

'Yes, I am.'

'Did you…? Is…?' Lucy's inward breath was a gulp. 'We saw Michael being taken away and…'

Her face crumpled. The face of the smaller girl, who had been staring upwards, was like a mirror. Both girls burst into tears simultaneously.

Kate's gaze flicked automatically to Rory. Would she see the man she'd fallen in love with so long ago?

Yes. Her breath escaped in a sigh of what felt like relief as she saw the softening in his face. The compassion that had always made him go the extra mile for any young patient.

He bent down and scooped up the smaller girl. He put his free arm around Lucy.

'Come with me,' he directed, drawing them back into the cubicle. He sat on the bed and patted the space beside him, and without hesitation Lucy climbed up to sit beside him.

'Michael got hurt in the crash,' he said quietly. 'And he was very sick for a while.'

Lucy nodded, tears streaming down her face. 'I know. He…he couldn't breathe properly. I saw them with the football thing.'

'That's called a bag mask,' Rory said in the same calm tone. 'It's scary, but it's very useful. All it does is collect air inside the football bit, and when you squeeze it, it helps people to breathe when they can't manage very well on their own.'

'Did it help Michael?' Lucy had inched closer, her gaze glued on Rory's face.

'Yes, it did. But then we had to do some more to help him. He needed a little tube inside his throat to make sure the air could get where it was supposed to be.'

A glance towards Kate included her in this interchange. Gave them that link again of knowing things no one around them could know. Kate could feel her own gaze softening this time. Acknowledging the simplification of what had been a major intervention. That tiny gap between life and death and the battle that had been fought. And won.

Lucy accepted the explanation. It was almost all she needed. 'Why?' she asked quietly.

'Sometimes when things get bumped they can break or bleed, and if that's happening in the spaces where air is supposed to be, it makes people very sick.'

'Where is he now?'

'He's gone to have an operation. To fix any broken bits and to make sure nothing's bleeding inside.'

'Will he be all right?'

Rory was as focussed on Lucy as the girl was on him. His arms were still around the smaller girl, who had put her thumb into her mouth and was leaning back, looking up, as though she was also listening and finding reassurance in his words.

Kate was watching, too. So captured by this scene she hadn't even thought of moving. It was no surprise when she found a small boy by her side. And then another on the other side. Rory had always drawn people towards him. Especially children. Her hands seemed to find their hands without any conscious effort and they stood in a little row. Hand in hand.

Watching. Listening. Holding their breath as they waited for the verdict on Michael to be delivered.

The children on either side of her wouldn't be seeing what Kate saw. A man who respected children enough to be as honest as their level of understanding allowed. Someone so sincere they instinctively trusted him. Did he know he won that trust so easily? Was that why he'd always been so honest with them?

This was the man Kate had come to love so much. Not the brilliant physician or the fun-loving party animal. Not even the gorgeous poster boy with the perfect look for a model young doctor. He could have been short and dumpy and bald and she would still have loved him for the way he cared so much.

'Michael's still very sick,' he told his small audience gravely. 'But there are lots of people who are working very hard to try and make him better. Our job is to be brave while we wait and to look after each other. Can you do that?'

Lucy nodded slowly. 'But what about Aunty Mary?'

'I'll go and find out for you.'

'She had a sore nose,' one of the boys beside Kate piped up. 'I saw *lots* of blood.'

'I saw more than you did, Alex,' the other boy said. 'I got some on my shirt—see?'

The small girl pulled her thumb from her mouth. 'I want to go home,' she informed Rory.

'What's your name, poppet?'

'Nicola.'

'And you don't have anything that's sore?'

A small blonde head shook vigorously. 'We have to go home,' she said with considerable urgency. 'Josie's having her baby.'

Rory's eyebrows rose and his tone evinced surprise. '*Is* she?'

Lucy scrubbed at her face. 'She *might* be having her baby,' she said, with all the authority of being the eldest. She gave Rory a look that put them on an equal footing in the authority stakes. 'She's late,' she explained. 'Aunty Mary says she can't for the life of her understand why she hasn't had her baby already, but maybe it's because it's Christmas and she wants it to be a present for us all.'

Rory nodded, but the glance he sent Kate held a distinct edge of concern. 'And Josie's at home? All by herself?'

'In the stable,' the boy called Alex confirmed.

'That's where she lives,' the other boy added.

Kate could see Rory relax. She saw the beginnings of a smile that made her grip the small hands within hers a little more tightly.

'And Josie is...?'

'Our *donkey*,' the children chorused.

'Her real name's Josephine,' Lucy said. 'Because of—you know—donkeys and Christmas and stuff. Mary was riding a donkey because—'

'Not *Aunty* Mary,' Alex interrupted. 'The Mary in the story.'

'Shut up, Alex,' the other boy said.

'No, *you* shut up, Rhys.'

Lucy glared at them. 'Mary was riding a donkey because she was too fat to walk to the stable.'

'She was having a *baby*!' Rhys crowed triumphantly.

Alex leaned forward. He stared at Kate's stomach and then up at her face.

'You're fat,' he told her. 'Are *you* having a baby?'

Kate smiled. 'Yes, I am.'

'Why?'

'Ah...' Kate caught Rory's gaze, still smiling. How huge was *that* question?

She was having a baby because of one amazing night. A night when she'd been needed by the man she loved as much as she had ever wanted to be needed. It had been her gift and it could never be something she would regret.

Especially now, knowing that he'd remembered it. That it had been important.

To her amazement, Rory smiled back at her. A real smile. The kind she remembered, but hadn't seen for so, so long. And something inside Kate melted.

Alex bounced up and down, trying to catch Rory's attention. 'Why?' he demanded again.

Rory cleared his throat. He didn't take his eyes off Kate. 'Sometimes it just happens, mate,' he said cautiously. 'And it's a surprise. A really big surprise.'

'I like surprises,' Alex nodded. ''Specially at Christmas.'

'Are you having a baby because it's Christmas?' Rhys asked. 'Like Josie?'

Nicola's eyes were wide. 'Is it a present?'

Kate's smile wobbled. 'Kind of,' she said. She was holding Rory's gaze, talking to him, her voice quiet and sure. 'It's certainly a gift as far as I'm concerned. Something very special.'

'We've got presents,' Alex told her.

'Not any more,' Rhys said sadly. 'They're in the bus, remember? They'll be all mushed up.'

'I want to go home,' Nicola said in a small voice. 'And I want to see the presents under our tree.'

'We could ask that Santa.' Alex was leaning around Kate so he could talk to Rhys. 'Did you see him?'

'I didn't like him,' Rhys said worriedly. 'He sounds cross.'

Their anxiety level was increasing. Rory eased himself from the bed, gently disentangling the small arms that wound themselves around his neck.

'He's not the real Santa,' he told the children. 'He's just dressing up like one. Kate and I are going to find out what's happened to those presents,' he promised. 'And about Aunty Mary and everybody else. And then I'm going to find a nurse who can get you all something to eat. Who likes ice cream?'

'*Meee!*' The combination of several enthusiastic voices made the word into a verbal bomb.

Judy appeared as if by magic. 'What's going on in here?'

'We need ice cream,' Rory told her seriously. 'It's an emergency.'

Judy grinned. 'I'll see what I can find in the freezer. Are you going to see Florence?'

'We're almost there.' Kate lifted the edge of the neighbouring curtain and was horrified to see the woman with the bandaged head sobbing silently.

'What's happened?' she gasped, rushing to the head of the bed. 'What's wrong?'

'I was listening…' Florence caught her breath and gave an enormous sniff. Then a tremulous smile. 'What a lovely man that doctor is.'

'Yes.' Kate knew perfectly well that Rory had left his following with Judy and was now standing right behind her. 'I think so, too.'

Rory left Kate to infiltrate the impressive laceration on Florence's forehead with local anaesthetic and then clean the wound thoroughly.

'I want to check on my mother,' he'd said.

'We're fine,' Kate assured him. 'I'll let you know when we're ready for suturing.'

He'd only been telling half the truth. Of course he wanted to check on his mother, but he also needed the comparatively private space of her cubicle.

Amazingly, given the noise level, with only the curtain for a screen, Marcella was fast asleep. Her face had lost some of the redness that had been due to her high fever and her skin felt much cooler and drier. Her pulse, while still erratic, felt stronger beneath his fingertips.

Rory's fingers trailed up from his mother's wrist to touch the heavily bandaged splint that was protecting her IV line. She needed fluids to correct the dehydration her fever had brought, and antibiotics to fight the cause, but how sad was it that she had to be treated like a baby who might pull the line free at any time?

Would she still be so distressingly agitated when she woke? Hopefully she would be back to her normal level of confusion, where she recognised nobody—including himself. Not that calling him by his twin's name was due to recognition. How could it be, when Jamie had died at the age of seven?

Michael's age.

The cry for her lost child was coming from her heart. It was a cry that had always been there, but it had been silent for twenty years. Until the anchor his father had provided had been lost with his death and his mother had simply allowed oblivion to take his place.

She was—most of the time—in a peaceful state, and Rory prayed that she would be again when this illness was dealt with.

Could he find such a state for himself?

He thought he had. In a far corner of the world where no one knew him, where physical strength and sheer determination and guts were the only things a man was judged on.

He hadn't bargained on revisiting the past like this.

It was tempting to stay by Marcella's side for longer than the time needed to check her condition. This was his first chance to get his head around what was happening tonight. Too many things to know where to start, in fact.

His conviction that he would never again put himself in a position where a child's life was dependent on him had just been blown out of the water. And it had happened in the wake of being pulled back to the origin of his fear, thanks to both his mother's presence and her confusion. But he'd done it. He'd coped. And part of him knew that he would have coped even if the outcome had not been a success—because Kate had been there.

His touchstone.

His angel.

Who would have thought that the idea of her being pregnant by another man could have been so intensely painful? Had he really thought that she was some kind of saint? That she hadn't had—or wouldn't have—a relationship with another man? It wasn't as if she'd had anything like a relationship with *him* anyway. It had been a one-off. Because she'd felt sorry for him.

But she was carrying *his* baby.

Babies, he corrected himself.

And there was another conviction he'd had no intention of overturning. He'd never wanted to be a father. Why would he, when he'd lived through the dark side of what parental love could do? He'd always taken great care to ensure an accident would never happen, but he hadn't taken care that night, had he? He'd been offered something he'd needed so badly he hadn't stopped to think at all.

Comfort.

Kate hadn't even known what she was comforting him for, which was a testament to his lifelong ability to disguise his demons no matter how much influence they might have in every choice he'd made. But Kate had found him at a point when he'd been as vulnerable and afraid as he'd been when he was seven years old.

When he'd had to watch his brother die and know that it had been *his* fault.

Rory drew in a breath that felt as if it was inflating his lungs for the first time. Painfully. He touched his mother's forehead with a gentle finger and then turned away.

Kate hadn't known, but it hadn't mattered because of who she was. She had given him the only thing that could have made a difference—her touch. The feeling of being loved. An affirmation of life. And she had done so with a sweetness and generosity that made his heart ache every time he remembered it.

She deserved better than what he'd given her in return. A shameful exit from her life. He hadn't even said goodbye because he hadn't been able to begin to explain where he was going. Or why.

She should hate him, but clearly she didn't. She had agreed with Florence, who thought he was 'a lovely man'.

And she thought her pregnancy was a gift.

And it was twins. Why hadn't that thought occurred to him when he was judging the duration of her pregnancy by her size?

Because it was just too ironic?

Fate had brought him in a very neat circle, here. Back to a place where he had to face his past *and* his future.

And right in the middle was Kate.

CHAPTER SIX

'IT WASN'T HER FAULT, you know.'

'What wasn't, Florence?' Kate lifted the dressing she had put over the wound on Florence's head until Rory came back.

'The accident. We came round a bend and there was this car stuck in the road. It had skidded into a truck coming the other way. Nobody was hurt, and they'd got out and were all walking around. Some children had started a snowball fight. Mary had to swerve or she would have hit one of those children.'

'When did you last have a tetanus booster, Florence?' Rory didn't seem to be listening.

'Oh, heavens—I can't remember.'

'We'll need to give you another one, then. Kate?'

'I've got one here.'

His smile was brief but approving. The nod that followed was thoughtful. 'Of course you have. You always were the best.'

Kate tried to suppress the glow his words gave her. She had to remind herself that he'd always treated everybody like that. Made them feel special. Brought out the best in their performance. It didn't mean anything. Or rather it didn't mean what she'd like it to mean.

'We weren't even going fast.' Florence was apparently distracting herself from the way Rory was probing at her wound. 'Mary had been worried about the weather before we even left the Castle. She wouldn't have gone out at all if it hadn't been for the Christmas party, and she made us leave early. She knew she could handle the road if we took it slowly, and she drives that bus like a professional. Well, she would, wouldn't she, when she's been doing it for nearly forty years?'

'What made her start?' Kate was happy to let Florence cope by talking. 'Looking after children, I mean?'

'She lost her own.' Florence clicked her tongue and sighed sympathetically. 'Her whole family. Husband and two little girls. He'd taken them up for a ride in his new plane. He ran into trouble and then got tangled up in power lines when he tried to make an emergency landing.'

'Mary must have been devastated.'

'Oh, yes. Nearly destroyed her, I think. Though she never says much about it. I know it took years for her to want to face the world again, and she decided she would never marry or have any more children of her own. She says it was because there were too many out there already who needed help, but I reckon she just needed to fill a dreadful gap in her heart.'

'She must be a very strong woman.'

Something in Rory's tone made Kate look up from where he was pushing a curved needle through one side of Florence's impressive cut. She had always loved watching him when he was focussed like this, with that furrow in his forehead, the way his dark hair flopped down on one side—a perfect match for the tangle of unfairly luxuriant eyelashes. He'd often had that shadowing of stubble late at night, too.

This was the first time she'd noticed it with the knowledge of how it felt against the smoothness of her own skin, however. Just as well her hands were occupied holding

Florence's head still, because the urge to reach out and touch that roughened skin was almost irresistible.

Was it the movement of one of her babies that sent such a delicious tingle right down to her toes? Kate sucked in a breath and dragged her gaze away from Rory's chin. Back to that furrow in his brow which made her recall the note in his voice that had caught her attention in the first place.

His mother had lost a child, as Mary had. Had she not been strong? Had she never been able to face the world with positive determination again? It was possible that such a tragedy could have caused a depression severe enough to contribute to the deterioration of her mental function.

How old had Rory been?

He'd said they would talk later. Kate was going to have a raft of questions by then. Was she way off beam thinking that he might be of Mary's ilk—had devoted his life to medicine in order to help people who were at risk of suffering the same kind of loss he had?

Except it didn't quite fit.

It was lucky that Rory was concentrating on his task of trying to bring the edges of the cut together neatly enough to leave Florence with very little scarring. He wouldn't notice how intently Kate was staring at him as she supported the older woman's head to keep it perfectly still, unaware of the deep furrow on her own forehead.

Surely such a tragedy in his past would have left a mark? The Rory she remembered had always been so upbeat. Not so much 'eat dessert first' as 'why bother with vegetables at all?'

And life's 'vegetables' had been things like commitment. Marriage and mortgages.

And babies.

Maybe she wasn't so far off beam. His tragedy might have affected him in a similar way as Mary's had affected her. It wasn't beyond the realms of possibility that he had also made a conscious decision not to have children of his own.

If that was the case, Kate was not only presenting him with the certainty of unwanted parenthood, she was unwittingly twisting the knife because it was twins.

The heaviness pulling at her spirits was sympathy for Rory.

Or was it? Maybe Kate was feeling sorry for herself.

How could she have forgotten the way Rory had neatly sidestepped any hint of a long-term relationship?

'You'll be feeling a bit of tugging,' Rory was telling Florence as he tied off a stitch. 'Not painful at all, is it?'

'No, lad. You keep going. I need to get out of here and help with the children. Lucy's probably got her hands full with those little scamps.'

'I think most of them are in the staffroom at the moment,' Kate reassured her. 'Probably being stuffed full of toasted sandwiches and ice cream.'

'And they're all right?'

'Mostly. There's a few bumps and bruises. Michael got the worst of it.'

'He wouldn't stay sitting down. He fell down the aisle as the bus tipped and there was nothing to break his fall. And the seat at the front broke. He was still trapped beneath it when I got out. How's he doing now—do you know?'

'We haven't had a progress report from Theatre,' Rory said. 'I'll go and check when we've got your head sorted. You don't have a headache, do you?'

'Not much.'

'On a scale of zero to ten, with zero being no pain and ten being unbearable, what score would you give it?'

'Oh, a three, I guess.'

'I'll get Kate to give you some paracetamol in a minute.'

The mention of that medication took Kate back again to the last time she had worked with Rory. With its action of reducing inflammation and fever, paracetamol had masked the early symptoms of meningitis. And those bright red spots on the lower legs *could* have been flea bites. Kate had been there when Rory had quizzed the younger doctor on his management of the case. She had seen the dawning alarm on his face and been as astonished as everyone else when Rory had actually run from the department to try and catch the family. It had been a desperate struggle to save that child, but they'd succeeded. Not that Rory would know how he'd been discharged a week or so later, with remarkably few lingering effects from the deadly disease, because he hadn't hung around to find out.

Not that day, he'd said. As though something much worse had happened. What could have been bad enough to have negated his triumph at saving that child?

They hadn't dealt with anything out of the ordinary. Broken bones and cuts that needed suturing. Abdominal pains and chest pains and difficulty breathing from one cause or another. Headaches. A man with a fish-hook in his finger. Someone who'd been kicked by a pony. A heart attack. There *had* been a DOA, but Rory had been in the middle of cutting out that fish-hook at the time, and Kate had been assisting. The patient hadn't even made it inside the department, and it had been Braden who'd gone out to the bay to do the paperwork required before the ambulance could move on to the morgue.

Kate could remember pretty much the entire day, because she'd been over and over it in her head so many times. It had been business as usual, and that had meant Rory knowing everything that was happening in his department. Taking charge of anything serious. Smoothing over any bumps.

Always interested. Always smiling. Always flirting a little because it came as naturally as breathing. It was his way of making women feel special. From an elderly female patient to a nervous new nurse aide.

'Nearly there, Florence,' Rory was saying now. 'We'll get a dressing on this, then I reckon it's going to heal and you'll be just as gorgeous as ever.'

'Get away with you!' Florence scoffed, but Kate could feel the cheek muscles under her fingers bunching as the older woman smiled broadly.

Kate wasn't smiling. He hadn't changed at all, and right now, the Rory McCulloch they all knew and loved was about as far as she could get from the image of a family man.

It had been a stupid fantasy, pulling fragments of time out for closer inspection. A smile, perhaps, or a compliment—like *you always were the best*—and making it into something it could never be.

Kate had honestly believed she was finally over doing that. She had been dealing with this pregnancy and planning her future on the basis of being alone. Rory had walked into her life tonight and here she was, doing it again. Watching his interaction with Lucy and the other children and thinking that he could be that way with his own children.

That he could be the perfect father if he chose to stay in London.

But how hard would that be? Having to see him every

second weekend as she handed over her babies? Knowing they would be together but she would be excluded? Knowing that he would love his children but she would only ever be their mother? Having to hear about a series of 'special friends' of Daddy's? The ever-changing parade of woman that Rory would no doubt include in his life because he always had.

What on earth had ever made her think that *she* could offer him enough to make him want to change?

Fantasy evaporated, and the reality of what she might have to face was daunting. Kate wasn't some kind of saint. And she wasn't going to be a martyr. She deserved better than this, dammit!

It was her job to put the dressing over Florence's beautifully stitched wound.

'You'll need to keep this clean and dry,' she advised automatically. 'If it gets red or painful or has a discharge you'll need to come back in or see your own doctor.'

'When will the stitches have to come out?'

'In five to seven days. I'll check with Dr McCulloch.'

'He's gone to see Mary, hasn't he?'

'Yes. I think he'll be checking up on the children, too. Try not to worry.'

'I don't have to,' Florence said with a smile. 'Not if *he's* in charge.'

'SO YOU'LL MAKE SURE everything in the bus is kept safe? Particularly those Christmas presents?'

'I'm onto it,' the young policeman assured Rory. He unclipped the radio from the shoulder strap of his protective vest. 'You just leave it with me.'

Knowing that the gifts intended for the children would eventually reach their destination was satisfying.

So was discovering that he'd been right about the extent

of Mary Ballantyne's injuries and that it wouldn't be long before she could be discharged.

Braden Foster, who was treating Mary now, had also been able to give a report on Michael's surgery, and the news was good.

'He'll make it,' Braden had said. 'Thanks to you.'

'It was a team effort,' Rory had responded.

Like the way the staff were currently dealing with the overcrowded department. Efficiently and cheerfully. Judy was still here—and hadn't someone said she was supposed to go off duty some time ago? If he was still head of department here he would be proud of them all.

Even the orderly, who was wearing a pair of red felt reindeer horns on his head as he came past with an empty wheelchair.

'Could I borrow that?'

'Sure. Merry Christmas, Doc.'

'You, too.' Rory pushed the wheelchair towards the cubicles. He had one more request to honour, and then he was going to do something for himself.

Or rather for Kate.

For both of them, perhaps.

Things were starting to clear in his head. He was being given an opportunity here to repay Kate for what she had given him—albeit unwittingly. He could make life easier for her. Support her.

He wouldn't have chosen to become a father, but it was happening—and, dammit, if he was going to be a father he was going to be the best he could possibly be.

Pulling back the curtain, he found Kate helping Florence to sit up.

'Just take things easy,' she warned her patient. 'You've had a bump on the head and you've been lying down for quite a while. You might well find you're a bit dizzy if you try and get on your feet too quickly.'

'Mary's fine,' Rory informed Florence. 'She's about to have a small blood vessel in her nose cauterised, and when the bleeding's definitely stopped the fracture will need strapping. She'd like to talk to you.' He smiled as he deftly manoeuvred the wheelchair into the cubicle. 'Your chariot, ma'am.'

'I don't need that.' Florence slid her not inconsiderable weight onto her feet. Seconds later she paled and clutched Kate's arm.

Kate helped lower her into the wheelchair. 'Better?'

Florence still looked pale. And not very happy. 'How am I going to help Mary with the children if I come over all peculiar when I stand up?'

'Give it some time,' Rory advised as he turned the chair and started wheeling Florence to where Mary was being treated. 'Nobody's going anywhere for a while yet, and I prescribe a nice hot cup of tea.'

There was another prescription he was going to make as soon as he could. One for Kate.

KATE TIDIED UP, putting the suture needle and the syringes from the local anaesthetic and the tetanus booster into the sharps bin, and all the disposable material and anything contaminated with blood into the hazardous waste bag.

A glance at her watch showed that it was now two hours since the first victims of the mini-bus accident had arrived. No wonder her feet and her back were aching and she was feeling so tired. Helping to deal with a Code Red would have been enough all on its own. To have to factor in all the confusing and still overpowering feelings she had for Rory had made it a marathon.

Maybe she could put her feet up back at the desk, and take over what must be a vast amount of paperwork.

Or maybe not.

She was smoothing a clean sheet onto the bed when someone came into the cubicle behind her.

It was a surprise to hear the curtain being whisked shut, and even more of a surprise to turn and find Rory standing there.

He was smiling at her. As though he was genuinely pleased to see her. It was impossible not to respond. Not to feel that incredible *warmth*. Kate smiled back and forgot all about her sore feet.

'When are you due?' Rory asked quietly. Not that there was any chance of anyone overhearing above the noise in the department.

'My obstetrician seems to think they'll come early, but we're hoping for at least another eight weeks. Any time from Valentine's Day, probably.'

'And have you told people?'

'That I'm pregnant?' Kate couldn't help her lips twitch. 'It's been a bit hard to hide lately.'

Rory's gaze was intense. Serious now. Kate bit her lip. 'I haven't told anyone who the father is.'

He blinked. 'Why not?'

'Because I hadn't told you. It wouldn't have been fair. I...thought you might come back.'

His gaze wavered for a heartbeat. Had he guessed what she had almost confessed? That she had hoped he would come back? Dreamt of it too many times to count? Maybe not.

'Where will you live?' he asked.

Kate could cope with meeting his gaze now. 'I've started looking for somewhere.'

'So you're still in that bedsit? Up all those stairs?'

'Yes.'

'How will you manage? Financially, I mean?'

He was going to offer to help, Kate thought in dismay. This was how it would all start. Financial support. Legal documents. Custody arrangements.

'I'll manage,' she said quietly.

'You don't have to,' Rory said. The curl of his lips might have gone, but the smile had returned to his eyes. 'Not by yourself. Marry me, Katie.'

It was fascinating how Kate could mentally rewrite her future in the blink of an eye.

She wasn't hearing the children tell her about Daddy's new 'friend'. Or sitting alone. She was in the same house as the twins.

With their father. Her *husband*.

Always knowing that he had offered marriage only for the sake of the children and not because he wanted her as a partner for life. Watching resentment build because he was trapped.

It was equally instantaneous to realise which of the scenarios would be the worst.

There was humiliation to be unearthed from this in the not too distant future, Kate realised.

And grief. Dreams that simply had to be given the burial they deserved.

Tears were dangerously close, but she wasn't going to cry in front of Rory. She had some pride. *Somewhere.*

'You're proposing to me?'

'Yes.'

'That's very generous of you.'

'No...' Rory gave his head a tiny shake. 'I *want* to marry you.'

'Why?'

His expression went blank. He didn't understand. Why

would he? It was obvious why he was asking. She was pregnant and he was the father. He was going to fix the terrible mistake he'd made. Put things right.

She stared back. It wasn't a mistake, and she didn't need gestures that came from someone feeling sorry for her. She was proud of who she was and the decisions she had made, and she could manage. By herself. She was independent. And strong.

At least she would be when she'd had a bit of time to herself to get her head back together. There were only precious seconds of control left right now, however. Kate lifted her chin.

'The answer's no, Rory,' she said softly. 'I'm not going to marry you.'

CHAPTER SEVEN

SPLASHING COLD WATER on her face did little more than disguise her tears.

Rory had proposed to her.

The stuff of fantasy—except that there was no romance in the proposal. Worse, there was no way she could have done anything other than refuse. Kate felt as if she'd been offered a gift she wanted more than anything in life, but when she'd unwrapped it the pretty box had been empty.

A sham.

And that was what their marriage would have been if she'd accepted.

Six months ago she might have thought differently. She might have even convinced herself that it could work. That love could grow from a commitment that had been made for other reasons.

Just as she'd convinced herself that one night with the man she loved was worth it, even though he had been with her simply because he'd needed *someone* and she'd happened to be there.

Kate was older and wiser now. She knew the repercussions of such self-deception. Pain that even a river of tears would never completely wash away.

'Get a grip,' she ordered her tear-stained reflection. 'You're a strong, independent woman—remember? You have to be. You're going to have two little lives dependent on you in the very near future.'

Her hands smoothed the roundness of her belly. Felt the delicious ripple of movement. And finally the tears ceased and Kate smiled. A secret smile. Nobody else could share this joy. This wonder of new life within her. She was going to protect and nurture these babies with everything she had.

She might be alone, but she was never going to be lonely.

'You can do this,' she said to the mirror.

And, with a nod, Kate turned away to dry her face with a paper towel.

She *could* do this.

Rory was probably relieved that she'd refused his impetuous proposal. He'd done the right thing in offering, she'd refused, and that was that. They could move on.

There was even relief to be found in the end of fantasy. Peace. The cloak of serenity that Kate pulled around herself as she left the female locker room behind her might be transparently thin, but it was far too busy in here tonight for anybody to be looking hard enough to see through it.

Even Judy, who was preoccupied by finally being able to head home.

'I'll be buying my final gifts at the all-night grocer's,' she lamented. 'But everybody likes chocolate, don't they?'

'Of course they do.' Kate hugged her friend. 'Have a wonderful day tomorrow. Merry Christmas.'

'You're coming for dinner, don't forget. Oh, help! I hope they've still got stuffing in the shop.'

'I won't forget.'

'You should be going home now, too. Melanie's here from Medical Records. She's doing the paperwork.'

Except poor Melanie wasn't coping. She was virtually in tears when Kate went to find her.

'It's a mess,' she confessed. 'I'm missing details on more than half the people in here, and I don't know where to start trying to catch up.'

'You go home,' Kate told her. 'I'll fix it. Go home and get some sleep, and have a really happy Christmas Day tomorrow.'

'Are you sure? Oh, thank you! You're an angel!'

Kate would have laughed except that she'd spotted Rory approaching, and he was already close enough to have overheard Melanie's effusive gratitude. She tried to smile and found it easier than she had anticipated. Maybe that was the way to move forward. Keeping things light.

'Apparently I'm an angel,' she quipped.

'I've thought that myself,' he said. 'More than once.'

Good grief, he sounded as though he wasn't joking! Kate dragged her gaze downwards. To the sea of half-completed forms that lay in a messy heap beside the computer. The screensaver was back on. Bells still jingled and the clock still ticked over. Two hours and eighteen minutes to go now.

Kate sighed as she began to pick up papers. 'I've got my work cut out for me here.'

'Kate.' Rory was close enough to lower his voice. 'We need to talk.'

He never called her Kate. It sounded wrong. Formal. As though he was about to start discussing legalities. His parental rights. She couldn't do that right now.

'There'll be plenty of time for that later.' She hoped she didn't sound as desperate as she felt. 'You said so yourself.'

'I know.' His hair was decidedly ruffled, and she could

see why when he raked his fingers through it again. 'Just think about what I suggested in the meantime. Please?'

Her headshake was unconscious. Protective. She wasn't going to let herself think about it any more.

'I didn't mean it to sound quite like it did.' Rory's low voice was compelling. 'As though it was just because of the babies. Look, Kate...I never thought I'd be even thinking of marriage, but—'

Kate's headshake was deliberate this time. 'You don't have to now, Rory. There's no obligation.' She glanced up from the sheaf of papers in her hand. 'This is a new century, you know. There's no horrible stigma attached to being a single mother. Some women actually choose to have a family that way.'

'Is that what you're doing?'

'In a manner of speaking, I suppose it is.'

Surely it wasn't disappointment she could see in his eyes? No. More likely to be anger as he gave headroom to the notion that she might have actually *planned* this situation. She couldn't leave him thinking along those lines.

'There was a choice to be made early on,' she said carefully. 'And I made it. You had by popular vote been abducted by aliens, so I knew I was making that choice on my own. That whatever the future held I would be dealing with it. On my own.'

His face was expressionless now. 'And is that how you *want* it to be?'

Oh...God! Want had nothing to do with the way it had to be. For everyone's sake.

She was spared the agony of having to deny what she really wanted aloud. Lucy was beside the desk, a younger girl clinging to her hand.

'Excuse me,' she said, 'but Eve's knee is bleeding again. I think she might need a new plaster.'

'Does she now?' Rory dropped to a crouch so that he was at eye level with the girl, who had a pixie face and long dark braids. 'Hello, Eve.'

'She doesn't talk,' Lucy said. 'Well, not to people she doesn't know. Do you, Eve?'

The braids wobbled as Eve shook her head.

'But you hurt your knee?' Rory spoke directly to Eve, and sounded as though it was no big deal that he wasn't going to be answered.

'She fell over when we were climbing out of the bus. The nurse said it was just a graze.'

'*Just* a graze?' Rory eyed the bloodstained dressing on a small knee. 'It's sore, isn't it, Eve?'

He was rewarded with a tentative nod.

'You know what I think?' Rory lowered his voice, making his opinion a secret. 'I think it needs a *real* bandage. One that's guaranteed to make it feel better. Shall I find one for you?' He held his hand out.

Kate saw Lucy's expression of astonishment when Eve's hand crept into Rory's. He stood up and led her to the end of the counter. Then he scooped her up and sat her on the top.

'Bird's-eye view,' he said. 'You get to be in charge while I find a bandage. Keep your eye out for anybody that's being naughty. Especially that Santa over there. See?' Rory jerked his head towards the cubicle where 'Santa' was sleeping off the effects of festive overindulgence.

A loud snore sounded faintly through the busy noise and Rory raised an eyebrow. 'Strike one,' he said sternly. 'Snoring.'

Eve's lips twitched, and then she giggled.

Lucy looked at Kate, who could only shake her head and smile. She couldn't explain how Rory did things like that. He had the ability to win hearts effortlessly. He was more relaxed now, she realised. More like the way he used to be. She saw a nurse go past with a bedpan discreetly covered with a towel. Her face had been set, indicating her desire to complete a less than pleasant task as quickly as possible, but then she noticed Rory and Eve and her lips curved in a smile.

He was good at that, too. Changing the atmosphere of the whole department by his presence. Making it feel happier. More alive. The same kind of effect he had on her.

Kate tried to concentrate on sorting the paperwork as best she could as Eve sat on the counter and swung her legs, her gaze firmly on the misbehaving Santa. Twelve of the forms were from the mini-bus passengers, and many had only first names recorded.

'How old is Eve?' she asked Lucy.

'Seven.'

'And Rhys?'

'Four. Nearly five, I think.'

'Do you know his last name?'

Lucy shook her head. 'Aunty Mary knows.'

'I'll go and talk to her. You all right for a minute?'

Lucy nodded. She was watching Rory returning, pushing a dressing trolley in front of him. Kate saw a young police officer catch his attention, and Rory indicated the resus area she was heading for herself. When she got there she found Florence beside Mary's bed, and they were both looking appalled.

'How *could* they?' Florence was saying. 'On Christmas Eve!'

'Problem?' Kate queried.

'Someone's stolen all the gifts that were in the mini-bus,' the police officer told her. 'Someone said they'd been sent, but Mrs Ballantyne says she didn't arrange anything.'

'No, I most certainly didn't!'

'The poor children.' Florence looked close to tears. 'As if they haven't had enough to deal with tonight.'

'The guys from the tow truck reckon they got a plate number. We've got road patrols keeping an eye out, but I wouldn't bank on getting them back immediately.' The police officer was sympathetic. 'I'm really sorry.'

Mary's nose was swollen, she had black circles under her eyes, and when she spoke it sounded as if she had a very bad cold—but, amazingly, she was smiling. She patted her housekeeper's hand.

'We're lucky, Flo. Our wee Michael is going to be all right. What does it matter if the gifts have gone when we've all still got each other? Let's get organised. They're going to let us take Wally home and look after him there, and Helen will be ready to go when her plasters have dried a bit more. We'll arrange some taxis for you, and I'll stay here with Michael.'

'Is he out of Theatre?' Kate hadn't had a chance to catch up on the most seriously injured child.

'Just a few minutes ago.' Florence wiped her eyes. 'He's going to be fine, but he'll be in hospital for a while.' She sniffed and turned to Mary. 'And *I'll* stay with him. The children need you to take them home.'

'Let's get on with it, then.'

'I need just a couple of minutes,' Kate said apologetically. 'I've got a lot of gaps in these forms I need to fill in. Surnames and dates of birth and things for some of your children.'

'You go,' Mary directed Florence. 'Be with Michael for when he wakes up in Recovery. You'll have to be quick,' she warned Kate. 'I need to go to… Where are the children, Flo?'

'The relatives' room. We've made beds on the couches and most of them are asleep.'

'I'll show you,' Kate promised. 'This will only take a minute or two.'

RORY WAS PUTTING the finishing touches on a magnificent bandage, but he knew that Kate was returning to the desk. He could feel her approach with a curious mix of pleasure and tension.

He'd added to that tension considerably. Of course she didn't want to marry him. And she was quite right. There was nothing unusual about women raising families on their own. Where had that idiotic suggestion of marriage come from, anyway? He'd only gone in there with the intention of taking the first step towards involvement. To offer assistance and support.

He ripped off a length of tape to hold the end of the bandage in place.

They barely knew each other. One night together. Hardly enough time to warrant even thinking of the possibility of being a couple. Except that they'd worked together for a long time. Long enough to know each other very well on a professional basis. He liked Kate. He respected her.

He was very grateful to her. And, thanks to that gratitude, she had been in his head frequently for months, and it felt curiously as though he knew everything he needed to know about Kate Simpson.

One more strip of tape should do the trick. Rory pressed gently as he attached it to Eve's knee.

He should have expected that fierce streak of independence in Kate. She'd been left to cope alone, and that was exactly what she'd done. What he would have expected her to do. There had always been an aura of... What was it about Kate? *Peace* was the best word he could come up with. She was quiet and competent, and a bit of a loner in some ways. Happy with her own company. She had rarely joined in the social events that Rory's life had revolved around.

They had been complete opposites.

But Rory had changed. He had faced solitude for the first time in his life, and there was nothing quite like Outback Australia to give you that experience. He'd been wrong in thinking he had to face his past tonight. He'd done that, hadn't he? He was in a very different place than he had been six months ago.

Different enough to think that his future could change? That he could marry and have a family dependent on him?

No. If he stopped to think about it he knew the prospect would be terrifying.

'I don't *think* you need a wheelchair, but let's see, shall we?' Rory put Eve carefully back on the floor. 'Testing...' he said solemnly. 'Weight-bearing? Check. Walking? Check.' He tugged one of Eve's braids gently. 'Better?'

Eve nodded and grinned.

'Can you say thank you?' Lucy prompted.

Eve shook her head, but as Lucy was leading her back to the relatives' room, she turned to smile at Rory.

'Thank you,' she whispered.

Rory smiled back, but he could feel a painful lump in his throat. God, he'd missed this. That touch on his heart when he'd been able to make a difference. To take away someone's pain. To make life a little bit better. Especially for a child.

But he couldn't go back. He'd moved on now. It was

time, in fact, to make sure his mother was in the best of care and then go home. They were just waiting for a consult from the cardiology registrar and for a bed to come available on the ward now. The Code Red was over and there was nothing else Rory needed to do. Apart from making sure he left an opening for further communication with Kate, that was. He couldn't leave with things the way they were. He leaned over the counter.

'Why did you tell me?' he asked quietly. 'If you didn't want me to be involved?'

'You had a right to know.'

'Do I have a right to be involved, as well?'

'Of course.' Kate seemed to be taking a steadying breath, but she didn't look up. 'If you're not somewhere down a mine in Outback Australia.'

'I won't be,' Rory said, knowing it was true. 'I'm not going back, Kate. I'm staying right here.' For his mother. And now more for Kate.

Braden Foster was dumping some patient notes on the end of the counter where Eve had been sitting. His head turned sharply sideways.

'You're coming back?' He moved to grip Rory's shoulder. 'That's the best Christmas present I could get. I've only been filling in, you know. We were all waiting for you to reappear.'

No. He'd moved on. Yet why did Braden's words give him a curious thrill that felt oddly like excitement? He didn't want to come back to this. Or maybe he did want to. But he couldn't. Yes, he'd won with Michael tonight, but that statistical bomb was still ticking and it was that much closer to detonating.

Maybe he'd felt that he might have coped because Kate

was there, but she wouldn't be around to help him pick up the pieces if he did come back, would she?

She'd be away from work. Raising his children.

Without him.

CHAPTER EIGHT

THERE WAS ONE HOUR and twenty-nine minutes left until the start of Christmas Day.

Twenty-nine minutes until Kate's shift was due to finish.

'You OK, Kate?'

'I'm fine, thanks, Braden.'

'Still busy?'

'Not really. I'm up to date with the paperwork, and I've just spent some time with Mary Ballantyne going over the head injury watch-list. She's a bit worried about taking Wally home.'

'I'll talk to her. His CT scan was absolutely fine. It's only a mild concussion.'

Kate nodded. 'He was lucky. How's Michael doing?'

'Very well. But they'll keep him in ICU until they're sure the airway isn't compromised by any swelling.' Braden Foster moved to one side to allow an orderly to approach the desk.

'I'm here for a Mrs McCulloch?' the orderly said to Kate. 'To go to the cardiology ward.'

'Cubicle 3,' Kate told him. 'Her son is with her. Dr McCulloch.'

The reminder that they were dealing with the relative of someone who had been a senior staff member here was not lost on Braden.

'We need someone to accompany them.' He glanced

at his watch. 'Hand-over's due to start any minute, and I need to talk to Mary.'

They both looked around the department. The registrars and other doctors were all busy. So were the nurses, now thin on the ground as many were heading to the office for the shift hand-over. Kate could see an ambulance pulling into the bay outside. Her gaze shifted, and she saw the orderly kick off the brakes on the bed he was about to move.

'Kate? Would you mind doing the honours?'

She hesitated for just a moment. It was a long walk to the cardiology ward. Not that weariness was the reason for her hesitation. It was more the thought of the return journey without Rory's mother and the orderly.

It would just be her and Rory. And long, quiet, empty corridors.

But they needed to talk, didn't they? Maybe it would be better to get it over with now than to spend her Christmas Day agonising over what the future held for herself and her babies.

'Kate?'

Marcella's bed was moving. Nearly level with the desk. Kate gave a single nod and got to her feet. She picked up the patient notes from the end of the counter and fell into step beside Rory.

The orderly was pushing the bottom end of the bed. A big paper bag labelled 'Patient Property' was on the pale blue cover between the end and the lump that was Marcella's feet. Rory had one hand on the side of the bed beside his mother's pillow, helping to steer. His other hand steadied the bag of IV fluids that was swinging with the movement.

Nobody said anything. Marcella's eyes were open, but she stared at the ceiling moving overhead and seemed unaware of what was happening. They left the hum of noise in the casualty department behind them as the double doors swung closed. To one side Kate caught a glimpse of the relatives' room, and the shapes of children fast asleep on the couches. Mary Ballantyne sat in an armchair, a toddler asleep in her arms.

The corridor leading to the empty outpatient waiting area was silent, but then they turned a corner into the corridor that would take them to the lift they required to reach the third floor of St Bethel's. On the far side of the lifts was the hospital chapel, and a midnight carol service was clearly in progress. The sweet sound of 'Silent Night' filled the dimly lit corridor and brought the sting of tears to Kate's eyes.

What was it about Christmas songs that created such a sense of nostalgia? The yearning for the kind of uncomplicated joy that childhood allowed for?

The orderly pushed the button to summon a service lift that was large enough to accommodate a bed. The overhead panel indicated its current position to be on the fifth floor, and Kate closed her eyes for a moment, pulling the comfort of the music around her.

It was easy to remember the best that this time of year was capable of bestowing. The celebration of family. Her mind was only too happy to escape the tense silence of the people around her by putting on a rapid fantasy slideshow that was a mix of memories and hope for the future.

A beautifully decorated tree.

A glass of milk and cookies waiting for Father Christmas.

A cold foray into a dark garden to put out a bucket of water and a handful of hay for the reindeer.

The smell of cinnamon and special treats.

Waiting until the children were asleep before taking

brightly wrapped parcels from their hiding places and arranging them under the tree.

Firelight and fairylights and mistletoe.

And…and…*Rory.*

The yearning was so intense it was physically painful. Kate's eyes snapped open as the discordant 'ping' announced the arrival of the lift just as the carol was ending in the background.

Rory had moved to the other side of the bed. Opposite Kate. He was holding his mother's hand, but it was Kate he was looking at—and his face was so sombre she had the impression he had guessed her thoughts.

Was he thinking about Christmases to come? The fractured family they would represent? The inconvenience and amount of compromise that might be necessary?

It was hard to think of anything else *but* Christmas celebrations once they reached the ward. The staff up here had gone all out to make the surroundings festive for people unfortunate enough to be confined to a hospital bed at this time of year.

Garlands of tinsel were strung across the central corridor. Snowflake patterns had been sprayed onto the windows of the rooms. An enormous Christmas tree with coloured lights was positioned by the ward office, and it had an impressive pile of gifts beneath it.

'We've got a private room for your mother,' the charge nurse told Rory. 'It's a full on day here tomorrow, with the chaplain visiting everyone and carol singers and Christmas dinner. You're most welcome to come and join in the fun.'

Rory smiled, but Kate had the impression he might be gritting his teeth.

'I'll be in to visit, of course,' he said. 'But I think the

festivities might be a bit much for my mother. She's not aware of the season and she needs to rest.'

They settled Marcella into her room, and the electrodes for the cardiac monitor were put in place and attached to a monitor. Marcella was still staring at the ceiling, taking no notice of what was happening around her. A nurse raised the sides of the bed.

'I'll have a nurse sitting with her as much of the time as possible. Is she likely to try wandering?'

'I doubt she's up to climbing over these rails.' Rory leaned over and smoothed his mother's hair. '*A domani*, Mamma,' he murmured. '*Buon Natale*.'

'*Buon Natale,*' Marcella echoed. She didn't look at Rory, but she smiled sweetly. '*Buon Natale,*' she said again as Kate followed Rory from the room. '*Buon Natale…*'

'That means Happy Christmas?'

'Yeah.' It had touched something deep within Rory, hearing the seasonal greeting in his mother's native Italian. Something very poignant.

'She sounded happy.'

Rory sighed as he stepped into the lift. 'I don't think "happy" is a word I've associated with my mother for thirty years.' But he could hear her voice again as the lift descended. See that smile. 'You're right,' he said as the doors opened again. 'She seemed…content.'

'You sound surprised.'

He tilted his head to acknowledge the correct assumption. 'Christmas was always the hardest time of year for my family. After Jamie died.'

Kate was walking beside him. The top of her head barely reached his shoulder. He could look down and see the gleam of gold in the honey-blonde waves of her hair. She was so small. Why was there such a large amount of comfort to be found in her presence?

'What happened?' she asked. 'To Jamie?'

This wasn't comforting. It wasn't something Rory talked about to anyone. Ever. But Kate wasn't like anyone else, was she?

She had seen him…*saved* him…when he was at his lowest. She was carrying his babies. She had the right to know the story of their father. With his mother left content upstairs, it seemed an appropriate time to take away the barrier he'd always kept between his past and his future.

'We were walking to school,' he said quietly. 'A car came around the corner too fast, mounted the kerb and hit Jamie. He died instantly.'

'Oh, *God*!' Kate whispered in horror. 'And you were right beside him? How old were you?'

'Seven.'

'Michael's age.' The words were so quiet Rory barely heard them, yet he could hear her comprehension of exactly what he'd been through tonight.

They walked in silence for a minute. Along a totally deserted, dimly lit corridor.

And then Kate spoke. 'That must have been so lonely for you.'

Rory found his steps slowing unconsciously. How had she done that? Touched on the single emotion that had coloured his world for ever after that day?

'Why do you say that?' His words sounded harsh. He stopped. He had to watch Kate. To listen to what she had to say. He didn't want even the distraction of walking. 'I was the lucky one. I was walking on the inside of the footpath. I didn't even get a scratch.'

Kate's eyes looked over-bright as she looked up at him. 'Your parents had each other,' she said slowly. 'And they still had you. You lost your *twin*.'

Rory swallowed hard. 'Yeah.'

'Do you have any other brothers or sisters?'

'No.'

'And your mother never got over losing Jamie.' It was a statement, not a question, but Rory answered anyway.

'I don't think she could. Dad tried to help. So did the doctors. I did my best, but the only comfort she found was to shut herself away. She gave up on living. Slowly. Inexorably. By the time Dad died there was nothing left. Except me. And I'd always been a reminder of what she'd lost.'

'That's awful,' Kate said fiercely. 'It wasn't *your* fault.'

'No.'

'But it felt like it, didn't it?' Kate held his gaze and Rory saw a tear escape and roll down her face. 'Dear God, Rory, you were only *seven*.'

He caught the tear with his fingers, but he couldn't quite swallow the lump in his throat.

'You didn't deserve that,' Kate said with a catch in her voice. 'Nobody does. I'm so sorry, Rory.'

He opened his mouth, intent on saying that he didn't need anybody to feel sorry for him, but no words emerged.

'I'm sorry you had to carry a burden like that,' Kate continued softly. 'And I'm sorry your parents couldn't find a way through their grief and realise how blessed they still were.' She gave a sniff and let her breath out in a sigh. 'But things shape our lives, and maybe it was because of Jamie that you ended up becoming a doctor. If your mother could understand how many lives you save, and how many people you help when *they* have terrible things happen to them, she would be *so* proud of you.'

She caught her breath. '*Why* wasn't it enough?' she asked. '*That* day? When you saved that little boy?'

She could see how hard it was for him. He closed his

eyes and swallowed noticeably. Then he opened his eyes and looked directly into hers.

'Do you remember what happened earlier on in that shift?'

Kate nodded. 'I remember it all. A compound tib and fib. Big MI. Appendicitis. The fish-hook. You did a wonderful job stitching that man's hand. I'll bet he didn't even end up with a scar.'

'Do you remember what happened when I was doing that job? The ambulance that arrived when I was halfway through the incision to get the hook out?'

'The DOA?' Kate nodded again, but her frown was a little puzzled. Of course it affected everybody when that happened. A sombre ripple would go through the whole department even when the details had not been discussed. And they hadn't been that day. Braden had said nothing, so why did it have extra significance for Rory? 'But it was Braden who dealt with that,' she said slowly.

'And it was me that Braden came to talk to. To tell me it had been a kid. A boy on his way to school who should have been safe because he was using the zebra crossing to get over the road.'

'Oh, no!' Kate breathed. The pull back in time would have been *so* hard, and nobody knew about Rory's history so there would have been no one for *him* to talk to.

'Braden was almost in tears,' Rory continued. 'Said he could only imagine how devastating it was going to be for the kid's family.'

'But you didn't have to imagine, did you?' Kate asked softly. 'You knew.'

Rory gave a slow, single nod. 'I couldn't think of anything else for the rest of that day. I was distracted, and it could have meant the death of that little boy with meningitis. I'd lost the ability to focus and the risk was terrifying. I had to get out. And stay out. For everyone's sake. But I knew I was leaving what I'd wanted to do for the rest of my life and it was tearing me into pieces.'

Kate was touching him. Her hand on his arm. But it was her eyes that held him. They were like a mirror. He could see his own pain. Not just at that particular time of his life, but for its entirety.

'It was never your fault,' she said. 'What happened to Jamie. You don't have to try and make the world a perfect place to make up for it.'

The power of speech deserted Rory. How did Kate know him so intimately when they'd only ever had that one night together?

She knew things he'd barely formed as thoughts himself. She understood how it had been to lose his brother. How lonely he'd been. He knew how he'd tried to make it up to his mother by being the best he could be in everything he did. How afraid he was to deal with the death of a child professionally. And why.

And she'd known long before he'd told her anything. Because her touch—all those months ago—had done the same as her words were doing now.

Absolving him.

Making him feel special. Worthwhile.

Rory cleared his throat. He found the hint of a smile as he bent his head and kissed Kate, very softly, on her lips.

'You…' He had to clear his throat again because his voice sounded strangely hoarse. 'Are going to make the most amazing mother.' He touched her belly, and it was firm and warm beneath his fingers. 'These two are the luckiest babies.'

'Yes.' Kate's voice sounded a bit strangled as well. 'They are.' She brushed at her cheeks with her fingers and her smile wobbled. 'They have you for their father.'

What did she mean by that? Rory had to start walking again, as though movement might jog the puzzle into place. Did she want him to be involved in their upbringing?

To the point where she was reconsidering his impetuous proposal?

He hoped so.

And not just for the sake of his unborn children. Rory wanted to be with Kate for himself. To be with someone who instinctively understood him and was prepared to accept him for who he was. With all his scars.

To be proud of him, even.

It was as much as anyone could hope for, wasn't it? A partnership that was based on acceptance and respect? And maybe love could grow from that. Maybe Rory could learn to open the part of his heart that he'd locked away. And maybe Kate would grow to love him the way he knew she would love their children.

The carol service was winding up as they passed the chapel. 'Away in a Manger' was being sung softly, and Rory found he had to increase his pace a little to overcome the sudden urge to pull Kate into his arms and hold her.

Never let her go.

Rounding the corner, they saw Mary Ballantyne talking to a police officer. It was a relief to have something else to focus on before he did something that might shock Kate even more than his proposal had.

'Everything all right?' he queried briskly.

The police officer was smiling. 'We've caught the gang who stole the kids' Christmas presents. They're all being loaded into a patrol car as we speak, and will be here in no time.'

'I'm going to order some taxis,' Mary added. 'Just as

soon as I've popped upstairs to see Michael and Flo. We can load the presents into them.'

'I've got a better idea.'

They all turned to look at Kate.

'Let *me* take the presents,' she said eagerly. Her smile was strong and sure this time, and it lit up her face. 'I'll get there first and put them under the tree... It'll be as if Father Christmas remembered while they were all in here, and it'll be...' Her smile widened. 'A bit of Christmas magic after all the bad stuff they've had to deal with tonight.'

'It's snowing,' the police officer said cautiously. 'Driving conditions are appalling.'

'Braden Foster's got a big four-wheel drive. He'll let me borrow it.'

'I don't know, dear.' Mary was frowning, which seemed to make her swollen nose and black eyes look all the more serious. 'It's a lovely idea, but in your condition...'

'I want to do it,' Kate said. 'Please?'

Rory's heart twisted as he saw the plea in Kate's eyes and heard it in her voice. She wanted this so much. To help others. To make their Christmas special.

She was...amazing.

They were all looking at him now, as though he had the authority to give permission or not. And he did. And he took it.

'No,' he said. 'I'm not going to let you do that, Kate.'

CHAPTER NINE

KATE WAS STUNNED.

Rory was going to stop her doing this? Doing something that she desperately wanted to do because it would bring joy to a bunch of kids who'd been through possibly the scariest Christmas Eve of their lives?

His face was so stern. Implacable. The decision had been made and that was that.

Well, she'd see about that! Kate sucked in her breath and lifted her chin, ready to do battle. It was only then that she realised Rory was still talking. She had to pull words almost spoken back into her head.

'Not without me. I'll drive. And I'll carry anything remotely heavy.'

'We could send a patrol car,' the police officer suggested.

'No.' Rory's lips curved into a smile. One that held an invitation. 'We want to do this ourselves—don't we, Katie?'

She could only nod, and hope that the action wouldn't dislodge the moisture accumulating rapidly in her eyes.

Mary didn't bother trying to stem her own tears. She looked from Kate to Rory and back again. She smiled and sniffed loudly.

'Bless you,' she said. 'And while you're there do you think you could have a quick peek at Josephine? She's our donkey, and she's out in the stables behind the main house. Across the courtyard. She's well overdue to deliver a foal and I'm a bit worried about her.'

'We heard.' Rory nodded. 'But a vet might be more appropriate than a doctor and a nurse.'

Mary looked at them both again. 'I doubt it,' she said sagely. 'I have the feeling that the two of you could manage anything.'

KATE FELT LIKE THAT, too, when they pulled out of the ambulance bay in Braden's car only a short time later.

'It was nice of Braden to let us borrow this.'

'It was.' Rory was fiddling with the controls—turning the heater up, because it was freezing outside, and speeding up the wipers to cope with the thick sleet they were heading into.

'And those police officers were so helpful—shifting all the gifts.'

Kate looked over her shoulder. The back seats of the large four-wheel drive vehicle had been folded down to create a space the size of a small storeroom. A space that was crammed full of wonderful-looking parcels. The two tricycles weren't wrapped in colourful paper, but they had tinsel wrapped around their handlebars and a huge red bow attached to the seats.

The main roads around the hospital were clear and the traffic light, thanks to both the bad weather and the time of night. Most people would be tucked up safely in their own homes by now, Kate thought. Drinking eggnog, maybe, and admiring the twinkling lights on their Christmas trees. Or stuffing small gifts into the stockings they would hang on the ends of their children's beds, or over the handle of bedroom doors. There were probably a few stressed mothers out there, fretting about the logistics of catering for a large family gathering, knowing how tired they would be because of being woken up at some ungodly hour by over-excited small people.

It would be magic, wouldn't it?

Rory was concentrating on his driving as the houses became more sparse and the snow on the road deeper. Kate didn't want to distract him by talking, so she closed her eyes and allowed herself just a moment or two of fantasy.

Of imagining herself and Rory in a huge old bed with a soft feather quilt and lots of pillows. They were sound asleep. Then being woken by small bodies leaping onto the bed. Two little faces peering at them. Girls? Boys? Not that it mattered, but this was fantasy so Kate made them boys. With dark curly hair and big brown eyes like their father. It was so easy to imagine the glow on those faces.

'Father *Christmas* has been!' they'd shriek. 'Come and *see*!'

Or maybe she and Rory would get up after they'd been woken by suspicious crackly noises, and they'd creep hand-in-hand, through the dark house to find two naughty children with half the gifts under the tree already unwrapped.

And they'd look at each other…and smile.

'THIS IS GETTING WORSE.'

'Is it?' Kate yanked herself back to reality and peered through the windscreen. Visibility was reduced to only a few feet. 'We're not going to get stuck, are we?'

The thought was disturbing. Not that she wouldn't want to spend time alone with Rory, but it might be very hard, and she might end up telling him something he really wouldn't want to hear.

'I don't think so. The actual road surface isn't too bad

yet. As long as we take it slowly we should be fine. I'm not sure about the advisability of a fleet of taxis full of children trying it, though. Not at night, anyway.'

'They could stay in the department overnight. Or maybe the police could help.'

'Mmm.' Rory was driving very slowly.

'Turn left.' The seductive female voice with a strong deep southern USA accent coming from Braden's satellite navigation system was startling. 'In two hundred metres, turn right.'

Kate laughed. 'I know Braden's keen on working in the States, but this is just sad!'

'He wants to leave London?'

'He's ready for an adventure. Like you were.'

'I didn't go for adventure, Katie.'

'I know that,' she said softly. He'd gone because he was broken. He'd fled to try and heal himself. 'Did you find what you needed?'

'I think so...yes.' Rory took the right-hand turn with care. Tiny flakes of snow amongst the drizzle shone in the glare of the headlights. It felt as if they were having an adventure of their own. Driving into the unknown. A dangerous but compelling journey.

'That's good.' Kate's mouth felt suddenly dry. 'I'm... glad you came back. And that you're going to stay.'

He took his gaze off the road for just a heartbeat. Long enough to touch hers. 'Me, too.'

'Do you know what you want to do?'

'No. I haven't thought that far ahead. I only know I can't go back to what I did.'

Kate couldn't think past the need to try and make Rory reconsider such a huge decision.

'Why not?'

'You know damn well why not.'

She could see the way his hands tightened on the steering wheel. She could hear the anger in his words. She had to summon a lot of courage to carry on.

'Not really,' she said cautiously. 'What I do know is that you're absolutely brilliant at what you do. Or used to do. You proved that again tonight. And, yes, I know that you would find it a lot harder than anyone else to deal with losing a child, but I know that you could if you had to. I think you know that, too.'

The headshake was terse. 'I proved I couldn't. I ran away. I'm not strong enough.'

'I think you're incredibly strong. The strongest man I've ever met.'

'What?' The car was inching along a road that had thick snow piled on the tops of hedges on either side. The American voice told Rory to take the second exit on the roundabout they had just encountered. Rory complied, and then looked across at Kate. 'Why did you say that?' he demanded.

'You care,' she said simply. 'You always have. That's what makes you so good at your job. I saw it again tonight, in the way you talked to Lucy and the other children. In the way you treat your mother. And in the way you're dealing with the shock of finding you're going to become a father. You *care,* Rory, and that takes strength.'

He made no response. The only sound was the flick of the windscreen wipers, the background hum of the heating system and that unique, sucking sound that tyres made in snow. Was he listening? Kate hoped so.

'The problem is that you've been trying to carry the whole world on your shoulders since you were seven years old,' she continued gently. 'Giving and giving and not letting anyone give back.'

Still no response. Kate bit her lip hard enough to hurt.

'Nobody can do that for ever. You have to fill the well, and there's only one place you can get new strength that really lasts. And it's not the Australian Outback, Rory.'

'Oh? Where is it, then?'

'In here.' Kate touched her heart. 'It's love, Rory.' She took a very deep breath. 'When we love someone we nurture them and we give them strength. Any amount. It never runs out.'

'It ran out for my mother,' Rory said harshly. 'Do you think she wasn't loved? My father loved her. *I* love her.'

'But she shut herself away, didn't she? If you can't let someone love you because you're afraid, then you can't love them back. It has to go both ways. You should know that better than anyone. Or maybe you don't—because you've never really had it, have you?' Kate had to struggle not to cry. '*You* were the strong one. For your parents and then your patients and your colleagues. You've just never let anyone close enough to love you, and that's why you ran out of the strength you need. If you love someone and you're lucky enough to be loved back then there's always new strength to be found. For ever and ever. It never stops and…and you can face anything.'

'I…can't.'

'What? Let someone close enough to love you?'

'I don't think I'm capable of it.'

'Why not?' Kate's heart was breaking. 'Do you think you don't deserve it? Do you think you have to spend your whole life proving there's a reason why Jamie died and you didn't?'

There was an awful silence that went on and on. Kate had gone too far, hadn't she? Ripped open an old, excruciating wound.

'You have reached your destination.' The voice from the satellite navigation device was jarring.

Still the silence hung over them. Rory drove slowly through the open iron gates of Mary Ballantyne's property. Up a drive lined with vast, ancient oak trees. Up to the steps leading to the front door of a beautiful, old two-storeyed stone house. He turned off the engine, but then he just sat there, gripping the steering wheel with both hands, staring ahead sightlessly.

'Yes,' he finally bit out. 'That's exactly what I've always thought.'

'Well, you're wrong,' Kate informed him. 'And it's too late, anyway.'

'What?'

'You've kept people away, and you don't want them to love you, but it's happened, Rory.' Kate's inward breath caught and she made a sound like a sob. '*I* love you. I have all along.'

Oh...God! She'd done exactly what she had been so sure she wouldn't do. Confessed what should have remained a secret. Now she'd have to hear Rory say that he could never return that love because he wasn't capable of it, and that he was sorry, but he would still be there to help with the children.

And it wasn't enough. It wasn't nearly enough. Kate tried to fight her tears but couldn't. She fumbled with the door latch instead.

'You unload the presents,' she choked out. 'I'm going to go and find that donkey.'

HE HAD TO GO AFTER HER. Unloading the presents would have to wait.

She shouldn't be running through the snow. She could trip, slip and hurt herself, or the babies. Except she wasn't running. Kate might be moving with speed and purpose, but she was being careful. As capable as always.

By the time Rory was out of the car and taking in that first, painfully cold blast of fresh air, Kate had vanished around the side of the house.

He set off to follow, but he was moving more slowly than Kate had. Not that he realised it. His brain was so preoccupied that what his feet and legs were doing had a low priority.

What Kate had said. About strength and love.

It made perfect sense.

He hadn't consciously recognised what she'd given him that night, but he'd taken it with him and had known it was precious. He'd taken it out again and again with his mind, held it and watched it grow. And he'd known how precious it was because it had given him hope. Belief in himself.

Strength.

Kate had given him love. She *loved* him. The revelation was so overwhelming he had to pause for a moment when he reached the corner of the house. Centre his balance before he walked on to where he was confident he would find the courtyard and the stables. Of course he would.

Kate was there.

Had he really believed that what he felt for her was simply gratitude? The need to repay a debt to which he'd added admiration for how good a mother she was going to be?

It was so easy to think back to the first day he'd seen her, when she'd come to work at St Bethel's and he'd noticed her sweet, rather shy smile. To remember his growing respect for the way she did her job. The way her quiet presence had always made his work smoother and more satisfying.

She'd been giving him strength all along.

Even easier was to remember the awakening of sexual

interest. He would never forget their night together. The way she'd kissed him and touched him. The way passion had flamed and—at least temporarily—burnt away the pain of ultimate failure. Of course he would never forget. He'd been savouring fantasies centred on that night ever since.

The kind of fantasies he'd never allowed himself before. A fantasy that had a face. A name. A real person. Wanting more had always been his signal to pull the plug on any new relationship. To escape before he crossed the line into territory that led to marriage and children and the kind of misery he'd finally escaped. But it had been safe to play with thoughts of Kate when he was tucked away in a part of the world where no one would ever find him. Safe to remember every little thing he'd ever noticed about her. To dream about touching her again.

Rory had reached the courtyard. A low building made of the same stone as the house marked the opposite side of the square. A rank of heavy wooden doors were divided into halves, and one set had an upper half that was open. A light was glowing inside.

Was it possible to fall in love retrospectively?

No.

He'd been in love with Kate all along, hadn't he? That was why he'd instinctively kept his distance. Why he'd gone all out to make sure every waking moment was filled with either work or lots of other people. He'd generated a force field he'd probably never have noticed if she hadn't smashed her way through it that night.

Being in love… Having someone love him like that… He might not have articulated the prospect, but he'd sensed the added intensity of his need to escape. To run. Like the coward he'd been for far too long. Even now his heart rate was picking up and his mouth was dry. Fear was part of the icy drizzle settling on his head and his skin, seeping under his collar. Enveloping him. Threatening to paralyse him.

But this was *Kate*, and she said she loved him, and the truth of that was blinding because he knew that was where his new strength had come from.

From knowing he was loved.

His final steps crunched through the layer of snow on cobbles and Rory reached for the ancient iron latch on the stable door with a sensation of…relief.

Of reaching home.

He didn't need to run any more.

What he needed was…Kate.

CHAPTER TEN

THE ONLY THING Rory could see in the limited light from a single bulb high on the stable wall was the profile of Josephine the donkey, standing on a thick carpet of clean straw. She swung her head to see who was entering her space.

Rory stopped, carefully pulling the door closed behind him and slipping the latch into place. He stayed still, not wanting to frighten the creature, but when he turned back he saw long ears pricked forward and got the impression that he was more an object of interest than alarm.

He'd never been this close to a donkey. She was shaggy and grey, with liquid, dark brown eyes and a tuft of brown hair on the tips of those extraordinary ears. She was quite small and she was very round. Very pregnant-looking.

Rory put out his hand, and Josephine stretched out her pale muzzle to sniff his fingers. Then she looked up at him again, and Rory took a step closer.

'Hello, Josie,' he murmured, moving his hand to stroke her neck. 'Are you all right? You *look* all right. That's good, isn't it?'

The donkey's coat felt softer than he had expected. It was mousy grey except for the amazing dark stripe across her shoulders and down her spine. And now that he was this close he could see over the top of the round little donkey to where Kate was kneeling in the straw.

In front of her stood a baby donkey. Dark brown and

fluffy, and very, very small. It looked like a soft toy, except that it wobbled a bit as it stood there on long, knobbly legs, and it was nuzzling the fingers of Kate's outstretched hand.

Kate looked up at Rory. Her face was tear-streaked, but she was smiling.

'Isn't it the most beautiful thing you've ever seen?'

Rory couldn't look away from the joy in Kate's eyes. 'It certainly is,' he said softly.

'Come and see,' Kate invited. 'I don't think Josie minds at all.'

'She doesn't seem to.' Rory's movements were still cautious, however, as he moved to her other side. A glance behind showed him the upper half of the stable door, ajar enough to see that snow was falling thickly now, the white flakes catching the light from the stable. It looked like a curtain, shutting them off from the outside world. This stable was a private place right now. Warm and musty and full of the joy of new life.

'I thought Josie was still pregnant,' he confessed. 'Shows how much I know about donkeys.'

'She's probably always fat.' Kate smiled. 'The baby's completely dry, so he must have been born a while ago. Probably just after everybody left to go to the Christmas party. Touch his coat, Rory. You won't believe how soft it is.'

Rory dropped to a crouch and gently touched the tiny creature. 'He's a very different colour from his mother.'

'He's gorgeous.'

'Josie's pretty, too. Aren't you?' Rory looked sideways to find Josephine watching him carefully. 'You have an amazing stripe,' he told her.

'The cross.' Kate nodded. 'Lucy told me Josie's called a Jerusalem donkey. They were given the mark of the cross in honour of having carried Mary to the stable on Christmas Day. What…?' She was staring at Rory. 'Why are you smiling like that?'

'It just occurred to me.' Rory's smile widened. 'I'm in a stable. On Christmas Eve. With a pregnant woman.'

'But I intend to stay pregnant,' Kate said hurriedly. 'For as long as possible.'

'Good thinking.'

She seemed to shrink inwards at his approval. Shutting herself away from him?

'Katie—'

'You don't have to say anything else, Rory,' Kate interrupted. 'In fact, I'd rather you didn't. It's perfectly understandable that you're not keen on these babies arriving.'

'I was only referring to this particular date. It's too early, isn't it? We want them as healthy as possible before they arrive in the world, and being inside you is the best place by far.'

Kate was silent. It felt as if she was holding her breath.

'Besides…' Rory wanted to smile, but this felt too big. Too important. 'How awful would it be to have their birthdays on Christmas Day? It's bad enough being a twin and having to share your party with someone else. Imagine if you had to share it with half of mankind?'

'You didn't like sharing your parties?'

Rory took in a slow breath. 'I didn't mind at all,' he said softly. 'I would have given anything to be still sharing parties. But I've never even had one since Jamie died.' He was silent for a breath. 'After Dad died there was no one to even remember the date except me. And no gifts. Until this year.'

The baby donkey tried to move and fell over. Josephine

nudged it back to its feet and closer to her body. It lifted a fluffy head and searched for sustenance.

'Do you think it needs help?' Kate sounded anxious.

'Just wait.' Rory felt for Kate's hand in the straw and grasped it. 'He knows what he needs. I think he can find it.'

Sure enough, the tiny muzzle soon gave up on the outside of his mother's flank and edged behind her leg, then up to the underside of that round belly. A moment later and the blob of fluff that was the baby's tail gave a triumphant flick. They could see matchstick legs bracing, and in the utter silence of the night they could hear determined sucking noises. Josephine gave a sigh and lowered her head. Her eyes drifted half-shut.

The baby donkey wasn't the only one to know what he needed. Rory's hold on Kate's hand tightened a little.

'This year I got the most amazing gift anyone could have ever given me,' he told her. 'I knew it was very special, but until tonight I didn't realise exactly what it was and why I needed it so much. Why I will always need it.'

Kate's eyes looked huge. And puzzled. 'What was it?'

'You.'

Her lips parted in astonishment and Rory swallowed. Hard. He needed a moment before he could say anything else. And then all he could say was, 'Do you have any idea how beautiful you are?'

'I'm not—'

Rory pressed a finger to her lips to stem the denial. He smoothed damp tendrils of hair from her cheeks and then he touched her lips again. Softly. Totally blown away by how touching her was making him feel. So powerful. Capable of protecting this woman from anything. Nurturing her. Spending as long as it took to convince her of just how beautiful she was.

Kate closed her eyes, and he felt movement on his fingers as she tilted her head forward to press her lips on his hand in a kiss.

Something inside him simply melted away.

'I thought you were giving me comfort,' he told her. 'Because you felt sorry for me. I didn't want that. But I knew you were giving me strength, and I *did* want that. I kept it the whole time I was away. Something pure and warm and *good*, and I needed it *so* much.'

He lifted her chin gently and waited for Kate's eyes to open.

'What I didn't understand was that you were giving me love. I didn't know it was there, and I hadn't asked for it, but you gave it to me anyway.'

'I had to,' Kate whispered. 'Because I do love you.'

There was still no way Rory could find a smile. 'I've thought about it so much,' he continued. 'It was like you were some kind of a guardian angel while I was gone. You were a whole world and another lifetime away, but you were still there with me. Every day.'

'And you were here with me. With *us*.' Kate's hand went to her belly and Rory covered her hand with his.

'You said these babies are a gift, and you were right. Not just because of the new life they represent, but because they're bringing us together. Making us a family.'

He felt Kate flinch. 'I don't want you to marry me because I'm pregnant,' she said. 'Or because you're… I don't know…grateful, or something, that I love you.'

'I'm not saying this right.' Rory's hand was still on her belly, but his eyes were on her face. Seeking her gaze and then holding it with an intensity he could feel so deeply within him that it had to be touching his soul.

'I love *you*, Katie. I need you. You saved my life. But it's more than that. You *are* my life. I can't believe I couldn't see this a long, long time ago. This has nothing to do with the babies. They're a gift. A bonus. A…' This was so important—but how could he make her understand?

'A two-for-one Christmas special?'

Finally he could smile. He could see the joy blooming in Kate's eyes and knew that he didn't need to say anything more. She believed him. She trusted him.

'I love you.' His voice was stronger now. Sure and confident. 'I always will. I suspect I always did, but you were right about that, too. Not letting anyone close was so ingrained I didn't even see it. You're a wise woman, Katie Simpson.'

She was smiling now. 'Just as well there aren't three of me, or this would be getting spooky.'

Her humour just added another layer to his joy. 'I had no idea I could feel this…this happy. That *love* could feel like this. I want to love you and protect you, Katie. I want to give you the kind of strength you've given me. For ever and—'

The flow of his words stopped so abruptly that Rory's mouth was still open. Kate's hand was moving beneath his in a curious wave-like motion, and then he felt a vibration. The aftershock from the kick of a miniature foot.

A baby's foot.

One of *his* babies.

The reality of it all hit him. The love. The knowledge that they were making a whole family, here.

It was huge. Wonderful. Poignant. Way too much to take in, let alone confine with any words that could be inadequate.

KATE HAD BEEN SO WRONG.

She'd thought she was the only being who could appreciate the wonder of the new life growing inside her, but she could see *exactly* what she was feeling reflected in Rory's face.

And that magic was a kernel inside something even bigger. The new life that was their love for each other.

Rory loved her.

Kate had absolutely no doubt of the truth of it. She could see it so clearly. Something had been peeled away inside Rory, and what she could see in his eyes was new. Vulnerable. He was giving her a power that could hurt him very badly if she misused it—but how could she, when she was giving him exactly the same power?

They would cherish each other.

Keep each other strong.

They would be friends and lovers and parents. Maybe colleagues again, if Rory was drawn back to his old job—and Kate was sure he would be. The fear might always be there, and one day they would have to deal with its realisation, but they would get through it because they would be facing it together.

Not that there was any pressure. They had their whole lives ahead of them. Time enough for anything, so nothing was urgent. Or maybe something was…

How long had they been in here, oblivious to anything in the outside world?

'What's the time?'

Rory drew his hand reluctantly from her belly to check his watch. 'Just after midnight.' He smiled and leaned forward to kiss Kate. 'Happy Christmas, my love.'

He kissed her again. So slowly and tenderly that Kate had to drag herself back to reality when contact broke.

She had to try and remember what had seemed so urgent only minutes ago.

'We need to get those presents under the tree. What if the children arrive home?'

Rory was already standing up. He held out his hands to help Kate to her feet.

'Mission Santa.' He grinned. 'Go, go, *go*!'

They went.

THEY HAD TO STOP holding hands in order to ferry arm-loads of gifts up the stone steps, across the wide hallway of the lovely old house and into what had once been the drawing room, where a beautifully decorated tree stood by the fireplace, twinkling with every colour of the rainbow in its lights.

Again and again they made the trip, stacking the gifts until it looked like every child's Christmas fantasy. And then they stood back to admire their handiwork.

Kate had called Mary Ballantyne on her mobile phone after leaving the stables, both to report the safe arrival of the foal and to check when she and the children were due to arrive.

It would be any minute now. Kate wanted to stay and see the look on the faces of those children before they were bundled into their own beds for what remained of this extraordinary night.

She had never been this happy. But why was Rory looking at her with a frown furrowing his brow?

'What's wrong?'

'It's Christmas Day. I don't have a gift for you.'

Kate laughed. 'Are you kidding?' She stepped closer and stood on tiptoe, threading her arms around Rory's neck, totally confident in her expectation that he would bend his head and kiss her.

'You've given me your heart,' she whispered. 'It's the most amazing gift I could ever receive.'

His head was moving. Slowly. His lips were curled up at the corners. 'Could be a bit messy to wrap,' he murmured.

Kate smiled mistily up at him. 'I like the packaging just the way it is.' She gave a tug to try and close the gap between their lips. 'It's you. It's perfect.'

'So it is.' She could feel the movement of Rory's lips against her own now. 'So are you...'

* * * * *

For Uncle Allan: a box of tomatoes, stiff gins,
mushy cauli and cheese, pavlova and raspberries,
Spanish cream, plum duff,
your brand of chocolate...
I can still have all these things this Christmas.
But without you, my heart aches.

THE MILLIONAIRE'S MISTLETOE MISTRESS

Natalie Anderson

Dear Reader,

I do love Christmas—from the songs I've heard and sung a zillion times, to the crazy race in the supermarket for the last pack of strawberries, to the corny jokes and the silly presents we tease each other with. And, of course, the coming together of family and friends that occasionally brings its own complications!

But sometimes Christmas can be hard—when one is far from home, lonely or has lost someone all too recently. At those moments in the season I try to find the little things to take pleasure in—such as reading a book with a happy ending!

My heroine Imogen is lonely and working in a store surrounded by the trappings of Christmas. Normally she would adore such decoration, but this year she finds it reminding her of what she doesn't have. So I wanted to give her the fairy tale, the finding of home and happiness that many of us long for at Christmas. For me it's a time of tradition, of family, of forgiveness, of looking forward and back, but mostly of being and sharing together.

So I do hope you have a wonderful Christmas and get to spend time, love and laughter with your nearest and dearest.

With very best wishes,

Natalie

CHAPTER ONE

'PLEASE, PLEASE WORK.' Imogen slowly pushed the card in before, just as slowly, pulling it out. Nothing happened. The little green bubble just refused to light up.

She tried again. Pushed it in slowly, then whipped it out fast. Nothing.

Fast in. Fast out. *Nada*.

'Damn.' Getting desperate, she tried fast in, slow out. 'Give me the green light, give me the green light. I do *not* have time for this.'

She didn't have time for anything. A quick glance at her watch showed precisely ten minutes remained until the meeting began. Ten minutes to wash off the mix of mud, blood and sleet and change into the new shirt and skirt she'd bought from the overpriced shop three doors along precisely eight minutes ago.

'Please, please, *please*.' Why did this have to happen now? She wanted to wail. Why…when she'd got all her reports together well ahead of schedule, when she'd found something to wear after her cringe-worthy disaster on the street, when the receptionist had been so sympathetic… why did she have to fall at the final hurdle?

She pulled her wet shirt away from her skin. It was cold and muddy and she felt hideous and sore. She'd gone for such a spin on the icy path—landing awkwardly and sliding flat on her front, ending up in a puddle of nasty water. She cursed the hidden ice that never seemed to melt on these Edinburgh footpaths. She couldn't master walking on them at all. No matter what shoes she wore, she still slipped. And the one time she needed to get somewhere fast, and in one piece, she'd gone for the biggest spill of all.

And still the hotel room door wouldn't open. The smiling receptionist had practically leapt to attention when Imogen had explained why she was there and who she was meeting and what had happened on the way. She'd handed over her wool coat and been assured it would be delivered to the dry cleaners, and had then been given a key card to a room.

'Please use the room to shower and change. No charge.'

The 'no charge' bit was a huge relief, because the emergency outfit she'd had to buy had not been cheap. Nor was it the kind of business clothing she usually wore. Her wardrobe consisted of a neat uniform of black below-the-knee skirts and discreet jackets—nothing attention-seeking at all. Imogen didn't want attention; she just wanted to get on with the job—and do it well. But the nearest clothing boutique had stocked far more stylish and figure-revealing items than her usual mass-produced, form-concealing choices. She'd frantically pulled aside the hangers in a quest for something conservative and simple. And she'd been in too much of a hurry to even try her selection on. Surely the black trousers and green shirt that she now held in the large carrier bag would fit? She was a standard size. Surely—hopefully, please, Lord—it would be fine?

Well, it wouldn't be if she couldn't get into the wretched room to wash and change!

She flicked the hank of hair that had fallen free of its

tie back over her shoulder, breathed in deeply, and tried to control her rising temper with a slow count out.

'One…two…three…fourfivesixseveneightnine*ten*.' She inserted the key card one last time. 'Argh!' she exclaimed in total frustration.

Nine minutes and counting. She was never going to make it. She was going to have to meet the new manager of Mackenzie Forrest wearing a sodden shirt and with dirt on her hands. She banged those hands hard on the door in front of her and swore. 'Open, damn you!'

And then it did. So quickly she stumbled. Regaining her balance with a wince of pain from her knee, she looked up. Then lost all her remaining poise as he spoke—dry and unconcerned.

'Can I help you with something?'

Stunned, she stared, stared and stared some more. He was wearing nothing—*nothing*—but he held a white towel to his…his…lower middle. There was acres of chest…lightly bronzed, so broad, so bare…and he was dripping wet. Imogen couldn't help following the light dusting of hair…down. Couldn't resist following the angles of his muscles…down. Couldn't stop following the drops of water…down, down, down.

Down to where that broad hand was holding the fluffy towel which was catching those slow drips of water. She'd never seen a body so perfect—not even in billboard ads for underwear or aftershave. She'd certainly never seen a torso with such muscle definition. Not body-builder, too-many-steroids, bulging-veins kind of muscles, but strong and smooth and sharp. There was not an ounce of fat for those muscles to hide behind—they were all on show. And she'd never before seen a belly button that her tongue basically begged to touch. In fact, it seemed her whole body had gone brazen—and so had her brain.

She was blatantly watching as his fingers tightened on the towel and his other hand came to support it. Blatantly fascinated as each of his abdominal muscles moved, revealing even greater definition.

'Ma'am?'

Hearing his broad American drawl, she dragged her gaze back up. Looking into his face, she simply stared some more as the brightest of blue eyes captured hers. Peripherally she saw the straight nose, the even brows, the angular jaw, but it was the eyes that held hers, with their unbelievable colour and their focus and their sudden flicker of something that looked a lot like *you wanna dare*?

At that whisper of wickedness she closed her eyes for a second, holding back the wave of sensual feeling that wanted to spread over her, forcing herself to pause the explicit show her imagination wanted to screen and instead get on top of what she was supposed to be doing.

'This isn't your room.' She didn't mean to snap. But she was embarrassed and confused.

'Actually, I think it is.'

Oh, did he *have* to have a voice to match the body? All amused and confident and capable of turning her pause button off again?

'Actually, it isn't.' Pause button back on. She was in control and fighting for her rights. 'The receptionist said I could use it to tidy up and change.'

'Well, that was nice of her. But it's my room.'

'It was a him.'

'Ah.' He nodded, and that dare in his eyes became a very naughty looking challenge. 'I'd have said yes to you, too. Beauty in distress.'

She wasn't distressed, she was flustered, getting hot

and rapidly approaching full-on panic mode. 'I can't get the key card to work.'

'That's because it's *my* room.'

'It's not. It's—'

She broke off as he took half a step closer. 'What's your room number?'

Her pause button slipped and she answered breathlessly, staring at that chest once more. 'Sixty-seven.'

'Ah.'

At that know-it-all sound, she looked up. He was nodding again, and this time accompanying it with a wide smile—perfect white teeth, all too devastating.

'Ah, what?' Her heart couldn't beat any faster. She couldn't feel any hotter. And the wild thing was that she was wishing she could forget the silly meeting with her stuffy new boss and just stand here all day. Staring at him.

'This is my room—number sixty-nine. Yours is just along the corridor a bit.'

She slowly looked behind him and read the number on the door. She could have sworn that nine was a... Oh, hell, could she really be so stupid? 'Sixty-nine?'

'Sixty-nine.'

'And I'm...' Not sixty-nine. Not thinking sixty-nine. Not thinking... *Ohhhhhh*. The sensual feeling rippled. Imagine—those muscles, that size, that heat...and tasting it all.

Her mental X-rated movie started rolling again.

His head angled and he almost whispered, 'You can come in here if you want.'

Unconsciously she mirrored him, angling her head so she could keep watching the same gleam of light in his eyes. Then what he'd said sank in. 'What? No!'

'Oh—okay.' He was out-and-out grinning now. 'I

thought for a second there you looked like you might want to.'

Oh, great. So her lustful moment had been totally transparent. She put her hand to her chest protectively, hoping her nipples weren't prodding through the wet shirt like twin missiles aimed at him. They sure felt as if they were. 'What I want is to find my hotel room.' Frozen speech now. Dignity had to be recovered.

'Well, like I said, it's just along the corridor a little.'

She curled her fingers and pulled the halves of her shirt closer together. This time it was *his* gaze that dropped. His smile widened as he gave her torso a very thorough inspection.

She could feel herself responding even more to his warm appraisal. She couldn't believe she was standing in a hotel corridor being turned on just by looking at a complete stranger—and by him looking at her.

'Okay,' she croaked. She turned—too fast for her recently scraped knee—and couldn't quite stifle her groan of pain.

His glance went lower. 'Hey, you've hurt your leg. It's bleeding.' He stepped after her. 'Can I get you a plaster?'

The change from teasing flirt to concerned gentleman was too fast and too damn sweet. Infatuation threatened to slip over her, to send everything sensible from her head—what little was left.

Embarrassed even more by her ridiculous response to him, she muttered, 'No, I'm fine.' She added, 'Thanks...' way too late as she tried to walk normally, but her leg had really stiffened now.

'Are you sure you're okay?' He followed her into the hall. 'I'm good with first aid.'

Imogen turned back and nodded, unable to stop her

eyes slipping south one last time. She was quite sure he'd be good with everything. Did he have any idea how good he looked right now? His legs were long—really long—and every bit as beautifully muscled as his chest. And the way his hair was wet, sitting as if it had been pushed back with a hand, all added up to a gleaming bronze statue *way* better than Michelangelo's marble *David*—this one was all real *man*. But she didn't answer, and made it to her door instead. The card worked instantly, the little green light flashed, and she heard the lock mechanism sliding. Thank all the gods.

She didn't even try to resist taking one last look. He'd gone back to his room, but had paused in his open doorway—still smiling as if he *knew* everything she was thinking, and still not wearing anything like enough clothing.

Feeling far too hot for this freezing winter's day, she let the door slam behind her and, tiptoeing on her sore leg, taking the weight on her good one, hobbled into the bathroom. Caught a glance in the mirror and froze.

Oh, no.

She blinked. Took another look to be sure.

Oh, yes.

She hadn't realised the extent of the rip in her blouse. The sleeve had all but come away completely from the seam, and there was a tear from her underarm across the front. To make it worse, the way she'd been holding it just now had pulled that gap even wider. Towel Guy had had a first class view of her breast. Her scarlet-bra-cupped breast.

Scarlet and lace bra.

Her mind raced back to her sprint out of the flat early that morning—wanting to get to work and have everything just so for the arrival of her new lord and master.

Usually she wore a black bra, or skin tone—plain, nothing too fancy that would show outlines under the fabric of her simple cotton shirts. But with all the extra study she'd been doing to get her last assignments in ahead of the Christmas madness she was behind on the laundry. Like weeks behind. So she'd grabbed this one from the drawer, figuring no one was going to see it anyway, and besides, wasn't it the kind of day when she needed the extra lift the colour gave her?

She'd bought the set on a whim once in the store's sale, simply because she loved the colour. Just looking at it gave her inner confidence a boost—and today her toenails were painted the same colour, even though they'd spend all day hidden away in her ankle boots. Scarlet underwear; blood-red toenails. Not because she was some sexy vamp, but because that deep, almost burnt red was her favourite, and wearing it gave her a pick-me-up—yes, underneath she was covered in confidence. It was still fake, but it was better than none at all.

Only now she didn't see it as the confident colour of a winner. It was trashy streetwalker in-your-face tarty— and she was crimson with embarrassment.

No wonder the hotel receptionist had been so happy to help and so full of smiles. No wonder Towel Guy had been so bold about inviting her in. She was flashing the world half her scarlet-clad assets.

She glanced at her watch. Less than three minutes. No time to shower—only a quick wash with a flannel and an even quicker fix of her mascara and a swipe of the comb through her hair. She retied it back in a harsh ponytail and got to redressing.

The new shirt was forest-green and silk, and felt deliciously cool on her hot body. She took in a breath and told herself to calm down as she tried to work the buttons through their too small holes. Any last shred of calm dissipated as she pulled on the new trousers—they were way firmer round the hips and thighs than she would usually wear. Definitely too firm round the butt. Her temperature lifted again as she tucked in the shirt and did up the zip and button at the waist. This was the kind of sleek outfit she'd have worn at her old job—emphasising her curves and showing her long legs while still being appropriate office attire. She'd *wanted* to look attractive there. Wanted to be wanted—what a naïve fool of a girl she'd been. She'd learnt more than one painful lesson as a result. One of them being that work and amorous relationships shouldn't ever mix.

So she had no desire to be seen as feminine at Mackenzie Forrest. She simply wanted to be good at her job. But this was only a first meeting, with all the office and admin team. The new boss probably wouldn't even notice her—he'd be too busy giving a speech or something. And at least the trousers covered the ugly graze. She'd fashioned a crude plaster for it out of tissue and sticky tape. That would sponge up the blood and stop her trousers from rubbing against it and being even more uncomfortable. Her elbow was sore, too. And she was thrown by the whole twenty-minute mess.

Imogen tossed her muddy clothes into the shopping bag. One last deep breath and another quick count to ten as she tried to forget the blue eyes that had twinkled at her with that mix of humour and heat and concern.

There had definitely been heat. Oh, yes, there'd been heat.

Awkwardly, she walked out of the room and took another frantic look at her watch—already three minutes late. The door of room number sixty-nine was shut. Good thing too. Turning, she headed for the lifts and—oh, wouldn't it *just* be her luck?

Towel Guy was up ahead, and looking back down the corridor at her. Only he was wearing more now— more as in a tailored suit: it had to be custom-made, the way it hung so smoothly from his tall frame, dark grey, with an ice-white shirt and a blue tie that brought out the sapphiric tint in his eyes. Oh, yes, he was male-modelicious. His hand was on the door to take the stairs, but he paused, watching her hobble towards him. Then he moved away from the door, pressing the button to summon the lift instead. All the while he watched her walk nearer.

Totally self-conscious, she moved towards him, re-fusing to run. He could get this lift and she'd get the next. She didn't want to be red-faced and breathless when meeting the new boss. She was already late, so another minute wasn't going to matter that much. Anyway she couldn't run. Her leg was too stiff.

The lift arrived. He entered. Kept his finger on the door open button long enough for her to get there and get in. For a mad moment she met his eyes, and was nearly fried on the spot.

'Which floor?'

'Two, please.' Imogen looked low to the ground, not really wanting to look into those blues again—they were hotter than hell.

The doors slid shut and she kept her focus hard on the seam in the centre of them.

'The colour really suits you.'

She started, glanced down at the green, felt her embar-rassment increase—but the politeness thing was deeply ingrained. 'Oh…' She took a breath to try and be able to talk. 'Thank—'

'The green is nice.' He cut her off. 'But I was thinking of the red.'

Stunned, she turned, her widened gaze colliding with his—all blue fire. Then the solemnity in his face shattered and he smiled—a full-blown, toe-curling, bone-melting blaze of a smile. It felt as if splotches of crimson heat were being stamped all over her body. So much for not being red-faced when she met her new boss. It was going to take at least half an hour for her to cool down after exiting the lift. But this guy was irresistible, and she smiled back.

Nodding, she stated the only thing in her head that she could share publicly. 'I'm really embarrassed.' She was also really attracted.

'Hey,' he joked, 'I was wearing less.'

'Yes.' Her smile broadened as the lift doors slid open. The comeback bubbled out of her, filled with sassy spark, just as she stepped out. 'That suited you, too.'

She met his eyes with a lift of her brow, beyond trying to hide the attraction now.

'I'd like to…' He glanced at his watch, spread his hands and shrugged. 'But I have to—'

'I'm late for something, too.' Imogen smiled as she closed the conversation. Another time, another place, maybe they'd have talked more, flirted, had some fun?

Imogen hadn't done that in…well, ever. But honestly just the idea of it, the almost-but-not-quite nature of their encounter, was enough to put a little jolt of pleasure in her day. But now real life had to be attended to—she had a meeting to survive and a career to keep on track.

She walked down the corridor, conscious that he was only half a pace behind her. She stopped as she came to a suite of meeting rooms. He stopped right beside her.

For a moment they stood, both reading the sign on the first door.

'We're heading to the same meeting,' he said flatly.

Was the dismay that she was feeling reflected in his face?

He blinked, and in that minuscule moment his whole demeanour changed. He withdrew, and his eyes—those windows to anything personal, to that wild heat—veiled as he became completely professional.

He opened the door. 'After you.' And he ushered her in.

She didn't answer verbally—couldn't as she hobbled as far to the back of the room as she could. Oh, no. He had an American accent. He couldn't possibly be...

'Sorry I'm a little late, everyone. I've been sight-seeing.'

She turned and looked to where he'd walked in and instantly taken command. Sightseeing? Right.

'And it took me a bit longer to get changed than I thought it would.'

A smile flashed—charming, but remote rather than hot. Of course it had taken him longer. One of his new employees had tried to burst into his room when he was taking a shower.

'My name's Ryan Taylor. Please call me Ryan.'

Imogen closed her eyes as he confirmed the worst. Not for the first time in her life she wished the ground would open up and swallow her whole. Opening them, she saw the impossible hadn't happened, and she was stuck in what could only be one of the most embarrassing situations of her existence.

She wished she'd done even a smidge of homework—then she would have known, could have been prepared. But as she'd spent every moment outside of work these last three months studying for the two accountancy papers the company was sponsoring her for, she'd hardly had time to breathe—determined to get as high a grade as she could to prove to them and to herself that she was worth it.

All that she'd known about Ryan Taylor was that he was going to oversee the change in management and steer Mackenzie Forrest into a supposedly bright new future.

And now she knew how magnificent he looked all but naked.

CHAPTER TWO

IMOGEN KEPT HER WEIGHT on one leg as the other suddenly pounded with pain. Silly how just a stupid scrape could hurt so much. She hoped the bandage she'd fashioned would hold. Hoped this would be a sit-down meeting. Hoped she wouldn't have to say anything— because she was still puffing, adrenalin still zinging around her body courtesy of her haste, her accident and her encounter with— Oh, hell—she'd practically had her tongue hanging out as she'd ogled him all over, like some sex-starved spinster. Okay, so she *was* a sex-starved spinster. That didn't mean she wanted her new boss to know all about it!

She caught him looking at her intently, a frown causing the faintest of lines on his brow. She looked away, wishing to be swallowed whole once more, and heard him address the room again.

'Please take a seat everyone. This is an informal get-together. A chance to meet and talk through any issues or questions you may have before I start in my official capacity tomorrow. I'll talk for a bit, and then you can ask some questions, and then we'll have coffee—okay?'

Great.

She moved to a seat near the back. Tried to avoid Shona's concerned look, but clearly failed, as her line manager came and took the seat next to hers. Imogen was never late. She was never flustered. And yet here she was—late and flustered *and* wearing a whole new outfit.

'What happened? You left ages ago,' the older woman said in an undertone as everyone found seats.

Imogen had indeed left in plenty of time, intending to call in at a shop on the way to get a quick sandwich. The humiliating accident on Victoria Street had ended that idea. 'I fell.'

'You okay? You were all red a minute ago, and now you're all pale.'

Imogen nodded. 'Just feel like a dork.'

'Hence the new outfit?' Shona was smiling.

'Complete with grazes.' Imogen held up her palm, just thrilled that someone found it amusing—and Shona only knew half the story.

Her mentor chuckled now. 'The colour suits you.'

Imogen searched out Ryan as Shona echoed his words. Surely he couldn't have heard the comment? But when his gaze intercepted hers the sardonic tinge in his eyes suggested he had.

He was too young. He was far, far too young. Was he even thirty? Even if he was, he was too young to be taking control of Edinburgh's premier department store. Yes, Mr Mackenzie had been ancient, but this guy was too young and too good-looking.

He talked to a couple of her co-workers who were already seated, asked their names. He'd obviously done *his* homework because he could match the name with the job position immediately. He moved around the room, learning faces with names as he went. Frozen, she watched as he came closer—until he was right there, by Shona and her. Saw his lips twitch that little bit as he looked her over—very quickly, so quickly you almost wouldn't have noticed. But she was hypersensitive, and very, *very* focused on him.

He shook hands with Shona, nodding, as they'd already met. All too soon it was her turn. His eyes didn't waver from hers, and there was almost a smile in them.

She took in a deep breath, determined not to reveal wobbly voice syndrome. 'I'm Imogen Hall.'

'Imogen.' He repeated, clearly turning through the personnel files in his head. 'You're the—'

'Accounts administrator—yes, Mr Taylor.' She couldn't call him Ryan. Ryan was too intimate. It made her think of his naked dripping torso and his muscle definition and… Mr Taylor it had to be.

'Accounts,' he drawled, very softly, the veil lifting for a moment and showing her that dry humour again. 'As in *number*-crunching?'

'That's right.' She nodded. She was Shona's second-in-command trainee, and had been given too good an opportunity to lose it now.

'Well…' His teeth flashed as he murmured, only loud enough for her to hear, 'I guess your work should make for interesting reading.'

Her cheeks were on fire, and she went on defence. 'Ordinarily I'm good with numbers. Just not when stressed… I wasn't thinking straight.'

'We'll have to take care not to stress you out, then, won't we?' His eyes lasered through her. *'Imogen.'*

Mortified by the fact that she'd been having fantasies about a stranger who was in reality her new boss, she couldn't return his oh-so-polite smile, couldn't register the slight emphasis on her name, couldn't match his intensity any more. She ducked her head. He didn't seem at all uncomfortable about having met one of his new employees while almost starkers…about having flirted with her so boldly…and having her flirt right back. *Oh, no.* He probably thought she was hopeless at her job. An all boobs, brainless bit of fluff. Wasn't that what George and all his family had thought?

'I always like to sit at the back of a meeting, too.' He stepped away and took the chair two along from Imogen.

The rat. Surely he knew she wanted to get away from him?

Of course he did. Because for one second before he began his well-prepared speech, there was an unholy grin on his face. One she'd seen before—in the hall, as *he'd* glanced down *her* body.

Pen in hand, she stared at the complimentary hotel stationery in front of her as Ryan smoothly talked through his vision for the store. Now she was even more apprehensive about the change. Things had been going well for her at Mackenzie Forrest. She wanted to be able to continue the study course that Mr Mac had agreed to. She could only hope that the staff development programme wouldn't be dropped now that the famous Edinburgh department store had been bought out by the American company owned by the exclusive and reclusive Taylor clan.

Mr Mac had stressed how pleased he was the store was being taken on by a family, rather than a publicly held company. Imogen was cynical about that—family-run didn't always equate with family values or high morals and a decent work ethic. In her experience family-run meant keeping things close, protecting the family at the expense of the company. Blood was thicker than water— even if it was bad blood.

IMOGEN HALL. Ordinarily good with numbers. Ordinarily looking gorgeous. Ryan tried to marshal his thoughts, but all his mind was interested in focusing on was that glimpse of one very scarlet bra and the luscious breast it had contained.

Not ideal. Not when he was meeting the team he was to lead for the first time and she was one of the players. He had to soothe their concerns. Mackenzie Forrest was an Edinburgh institution. Loyal customers, loyal workers. Locally owned since its inception, it had now been taken over by his family—and he knew the idea of foreign ownership hadn't been entirely welcomed.

'Taylors is a family-run business.' He saw the flash of cynicism on her face and it derailed his thoughts again. Why was she so defensive? Surely not the parochial thing? That was no Scottish accent she'd spoken with.

He got back on course, but his blood pumped faster. It was a real shame she was an employee. He could kick himself now for his comment on what colour suited her in the elevator. If he'd known, he'd never have said anything.

It had taken a decade of hard work for Ryan to gain the respect of not just his family but outsiders as well. Being one of the East Coast Taylors had many advantages, but it came with disadvantages, too. Being the 'spare heir', he knew people had preconceptions and misconceptions about him and his ability to actually do the work. Precisely why he'd stayed out of the family business and done his own thing on the continent. But now his brother and his sisters had *asked* for his help—and both they and he knew he had more than the required credentials for the job. They needed his expertise and it was on his terms. But he'd just muffed it with one of his new staff.

He had no intention of getting a reputation for being a Lothario boss. He always kept his flings outside of the office environment. It was easier that way. And he had no problem meeting women. He had more of a problem getting to know them—and with them being able to see through the Taylor mystique to the reality of him beneath. Hence flings. Not relationships. Never a relationship.

So he was just going to have to work hard and jettison this attack of the lusts. Because he had no time for it here. But he couldn't stop his attention sliding, watching as she sat absently clicking and unclicking her pen. Her green eyes accented by the depth of colour in her shirt. Her curves subtly hinted at by the way the soft material sat over them. And all he could see then was her lying back, siren-like in her scarlet underwear, eyes gleaming through heavy lids, a smile on her lips. A smile like that smile she'd given him as they'd stepped out of the elevator—suddenly confident, suddenly sassy, and so enticing.

He looked down at the table and extracted some self-control from deep within. He was going to have to work hard. Very, very hard.

IMOGEN DECIDED TO EXIT as soon as she could. It was sickening. Even Shona, Mr Mac's number one for the best part of thirty years, was smiling. Half an hour in the guy's company and he'd won over the most hardened cynic. Although really, why should she be surprised? It had only taken a split second for her to want to fall at his feet. But there could be no fraternising here—no sycophantic chats with the boss. Not when she'd seen him almost naked. Because that was how she still saw him.

Her face flamed as his image slid into frame again. Frustrated, she focused on those looks. He was way too young for this kind of position. She worked up anger. Most likely nepotism all the way. He'd probably come in and ruin it for all of them. Just as George had ruined it for her back home in New Zealand at Bailey & Co. Sleeping with her boss had been stupid. Trusting a man who'd had everything too easy had been devastating.

Ryan Taylor looked up, saw she was glaring at him. One brow lifted slightly, as if to ask, *What's your beef?*

You are, buddy, she mentally tossed back, with a wide American accent in mind. But he kept his focus on her, and then she got kind of distracted... Goodness, his eyes were blue. Electric. And right now they were honed in on her.

Someone was talking. It seemed he was listening, because she saw his mouth move and heard some kind of noise, but she couldn't have deciphered any sensible conversation. She was lost in the intensity of that look—in the blue skies that were his eyes. It was as if she was in freefall, flying—almost floating—waiting, still waiting, for the parachute to open...

It wasn't in any hurry. She blinked. Maybe she'd just clunk back to earth in a heap.

But she'd been there, done that. And been left bruised and broken. She looked away, realising her grazes were throbbing again. No. One gorgeous heir to an empire was not going to throw her off-course.

CHAPTER THREE

IMOGEN GOT TO WORK early the next day, wanting to be lodged in place behind her desk before anyone else and thus able to avoid comment on her aching limp. Then she couldn't resist doing what she hadn't contemplated or even had time for until now. She opened up the Internet. Typed in his name. Added 'department store' to narrow the search. There were still a zillion hits. She read a few headers.

'The Taylor quartet…' That was a spread in some flash American society mag. Mainly about his elder brother, but he and his sisters had got more than a mention, too. There were photos of them all at some swanky-looking party, with people too beautiful to be real.

'Harvard-educated…grew up in style in New York… holiday homes in Colorado, Italy and the Caribbean…'

She didn't read any more. Didn't need to. She knew the type well and she knew to steer clear. She'd worked hard to build her reputation at Mackenzie Forrest, and she knew how easily it could be ruined. Most of all she knew how fickle guys like Ryan were—guys born with not just a silver spoon in their mouths but with the whole damn canteen of cutlery. Those born into wealth and power grew up with decayed morals. They were always greedy for more. It was not a world Imogen could ever live in. George Bailey-Jones Jr had proved that. His family had added the exclamation mark.

Ryan Taylor's family made the Bailey-Joneses look like nameless nobodies.

Unfortunately he arrived in the office in another made-to-mesmerise suit, his hair still damp from the shower as it had been the day before...

The way her belly squeezed at the sight of him was crazy. Plain crazy. The way her thoughts ran riot if she let them—seeing him naked, seeing her astride his hips with his chest spread before her, bending forward to press her mouth to his bronzed skin, feeling the muscles beneath...

Oh, she was one sick, sick woman. This kind of fever had to be broken. She watched as he coolly greeted everyone by name. He was too relaxed, too confident. And she *knew* he'd be unreliable.

'Good morning, Mr Taylor.' She got in first. Shona had always addressed Mr Mac formally. Imogen had thought it old-fashioned. Now it seemed like a really good idea. Distance—a good way of maintaining the employer-employee boundary. Because she could hardly say to him, *Hey, I don't usually wear a scarlet bra. It's just that I was behind on my washing.*

His eyebrows lifted fractionally. 'Are you able to have the latest financials ready for me by lunchtime, *Ms* Hall?'

'Certainly, Mr Taylor.' She retreated farther behind her computer, hoping to hide the way she blushed as he spoke to her.

'How's your knee? Better?'

No retreat possible. He'd stepped right round her desk.

'All better, thank you.' She didn't look up from her ferocious study of the screen. Determined not to let things get personal. Strictly professionally was how they'd interact.

'That's good to hear.' His soft words went through her insides like a fork stirred through creamy mashed potato.

'Is it just the current month you're after, or last month's as well?' Think work. Think work. Not about being whipped into melting acquiescence by a deep American accent.

'Just this month. I have the other data already.'

Thank heavens he left then—off to the shop floor with the duty manager to meet the front-line staff, before coming back and meeting with Shona for over an hour.

It was well before lunchtime when Imogen knocked on the frame of his open door. He glanced up from his desk. 'Already?'

'Yes.' She didn't look at him, focused on his desk, placing the report on it and walking straight out again.

'Thank you.'

She felt the words like bullets in her back.

Less than an hour later, he stopped by her desk. 'That report was excellent. Not a number out of place.'

Was he teasing her?

'Think I can get you to do me another, with some projections for the next quarter?'

'Of course, Mr Taylor.' She tossed her head as he turned away, determined to reframe his opinion of her and prove her worth. 'There's nothing you can ask of me that I can't do.'

He paused, and it was a miracle she didn't combust as he assessed her with his blue fire eyes. 'Ms Hall, you *do* like to set a challenge, don't you?'

THREE DAYS LATER Ryan congratulated himself on surviving so far—every minute of every day had been arduous.

It shouldn't have been so bad. In fact, he should have been able to say that things were going better than he'd anticipated—the Christmas tills were ringing, the figures were stacking up, and the staff were all accommodating if not bordering on welcoming. All but one. And he wanted her to accommodate him in a way that was thoroughly inappropriate. So much for conquering the lust.

Theoretically, he should be over it. Every day this week she'd been dressed totally differently from that to-die-for green shirt and pants number at that first meeting. If anything she looked downright dowdy in the shapeless shirts and skirts she seemed so fond of. He couldn't understand why she'd want to shroud herself in 1950s-schoolmarm-length skirts, and all he wanted to do was get her out of them. While the rest of the staff were looking festive, she looked funereal. Black, black and black was it. Drab and depressing it should have been. Except that on her the tone emphasised her pale skin, and made her eyes greener than genetically modified grass.

And then there was the fact that it wasn't just her looks he was attracted to. In the open-plan space outside his office, she and Shona were nearest to his door. The door he couldn't bring himself to close—not when he could hear her low-voiced humour. She didn't mix much with the others—just sat quietly next to Shona, passing the time with occasional wry and dry comments that had him hovering ever closer, increasingly interested. Wishing she'd laugh like that with *him*.

And she was damn good at her job—at a junior level, for sure, but with the potential to climb a lot higher. He could see exactly why Mr Mac had agreed to put her through her degree. In early, out late. Always focused, always prepared. Thus far she'd been right—she was able to do everything he'd asked of her. Except he hadn't asked for what he *really* wanted. That was in the 'Not Allowed' category. And she knew it. She wouldn't meet his gaze, wouldn't speak with him unless on a business matter, wouldn't even call him by his first name. So he was tiptoeing around her when in another time, another place, he'd have had her horizontal as fast as possible. And he knew—deep in his bones, he *knew*—that she wanted him, too.

The attraction made him ache. And the impossibility made it worse.

So he spent as much time as he could on the shop floor—away from the temptation of sitting in the admin office. Even so he felt it—the magnetic, compelling instinct to get nearer to her. Much nearer.

Generally Ryan relied on his instincts. He wished this one would go to hell.

LOST IN THOUGHT, Imogen walked as early as ever to work. It was weird walking in the dark. When she walked home it was dark, too. The wintry Edinburgh sun didn't come out to play for long. Despite this, there was one massive light on her horizon. He lit the world brighter than the biggest star in sky—and it wasn't just *her* world. She'd seen the way the women working in the cosmetics department all stood so much straighter when he appeared—and it wasn't an *'uh-oh here comes the boss'* kind of leap to attention, it was definitely a *'suck in your tummy, here comes the sexiest man alive'* pose. Nor was it just the cosmetics hotties, but the kitchenware, nursery, formalwear and lingerie queens, too—both sexes. Wherever he went all heads turned, and on went their *'notice me'* signals. It wasn't just because of his looks. He had an easiness, an open, approachable demeanour, that made people want

to draw closer. And then there was that irrepressible, irresistible glint that suggested he wasn't quite thinking
thoughts as bland as he ought.

Ryan Taylor was blinding everyone with his charm.
Imogen was determined to resist. But, as inevitably as
snow melted in the sun, and for the five millionth time,
she replayed that scene in the hotel hallway, half kidding
herself that it was a good way to combat the chilly wind
on her way to work. She was crossing the bridge, and
had just got to the point when she'd watched his muscles
tighten, felt her own belly tighten in response, when, as
she walked faster to get a grip on herself, she felt her feet
slide...

'Careful!' A strong hand gripped her upper arm, lifting her, just keeping her upright. 'You don't want to graze
your knee again.'

'Oh!' She sucked in a shocked breath. 'Thank you.'
She put a hand out and grasped the railing of the bridge.
Took another shocked breath as she identified her rescuer.
'Thanks.' Her heart thudded faster, but the oxygen didn't
help and she gabbled, 'I'm so useless on this snow.'

Ryan laughed. 'This isn't snow. This is just a bit of
ice.'

'Well, whatever it is, it's too slippery for me.' The
whole world was too slippery. She gripped the rail tighter,
vowing not to move until he'd gone.

He stepped alongside her, so he was no longer in the
way of the other people walking towards their work. He
was breathing faster than normal, too. But that was
because he was wearing navy track pants, had his poly-
propylene-striped arms poking out from the sleeves of a
white tee shirt, and a film of sweat on his forehead.

'You're going in to work early.' He didn't seem to
notice she was impersonating a statue.

'I have some things I want to do. You're...' She looked up at him, lost her train of thought.

'Out for a run—yes.' He smiled.

For the first time in days she stared properly into his eyes—even in the half-light of the late dawn they were vivid blue. She was vaguely aware of her mouth moving into a mirroring smile. Oh, he had it all. One of those American great-all-round types, with his blue eyes and brown hair, his bronzed skin, broad shoulders and... Had she dwelt on his blue eyes already?

'Do you wear contacts?'

'No. Why?' He seemed to be smiling with his whole body.

She couldn't believe she'd asked that question out loud. 'Your eyes are very blue.' Oh, God, she was whispering. *Oh, brain, where art thou?* She jerked back. 'I'm sorry.'

'Why?'

Because that was inappropriate. But she couldn't answer. Looked away to try to clear her head of his almost hypnotic power. 'It's freezing, isn't it?' Hell. Reduced to talking about the weather to distract herself from the fact she'd just made a colossal fool of herself. To try to ignore the way she burnt up in his presence.

'I like the cold. I like the fun of warming up.'

She looked back at him then. Had he moved closer? He had, and now he was taking another step.

'It's easier to warm up than cool down.'

'I don't think so,' she said, just to disagree. 'It can be impossible to warm up.' The brakes on her sensibility were slipping as she stood near him, with him smiling like that. He still had his hand on her arm, and he was edging closer and closer.

'You can *always* warm up.'

Awareness zinged between them.

'No.' She shook her head in the tiniest movement and her last hint of caution melted. 'My lips are so cold they're numb.' The scare from her almost-fall must have addled everything.

'Numb?' He was looking deep into her eyes in a way that obliterated rational brainpower.

She nodded, felt that squeezing inside as his gaze dropped to her lips.

'I don't believe you.' His mouth had that cheeky quirk to it.

'They are,' she insisted. 'I'll have to be careful with my coffee or I might burn them.'

His lashes swooped up and she was pinned in place— just where she wanted to be. 'Well, we can't let that happen.'

Bluer than the brightest summer sky, his eyes gleamed. Spellbound, she watched as he came nearer and nearer.

The kiss was butterfly-light. The faintest brush of his mouth on hers. Not remotely long enough or hard enough or deep enough to satisfy Imogen's burgeoning desire.

'Still numb,' she said, as his mouth lifted and hovered mere millimetres from hers. Her challenge was unmistakable.

His smile widened—and then she got to taste it as his head lowered. Her eyes closed and in her mind she was floating in those skies of blue. His lips were warm, gentle, teasing, before they lifted again, still too soon.

She sighed, resigned. 'I can't seem to feel a thing.'

His brows shot up, but there was a knowing look in his eyes. 'I'll have to try harder.'

This time she met his mouth with her own, wide and hungry. This time he put his hands on her. This time it was longer and harder and deeper.

Imogen moaned. He slid one hand down her back,

pulling her against him while at the same time taking that last step closer. She was sandwiched firmly between the bridge railing and him. Yet still she wanted to be closer. She hadn't lied. It was true she couldn't feel a thing—other than pleasure radiating within her. Emboldened by that madness, she kissed him deeply, searching him out with her tongue, desperate to taste more of him—all of him. Her arms lifted, locking around his neck. Their bodies strained together, arousing, intoxicating, suddenly in an embrace so tight it almost hurt. Until finally he lifted his head and let them both breathe.

But it wasn't sobering oxygen that she inhaled. It was all Ryan. 'Are you sure you don't wear contacts?'

'Imogen.'

She closed her eyes and lifted her chin for more. Almost *heard* his smile. Felt him move impossibly closer, his legs imprisoning her. Feeling them against hers, she was teased by the idea of having all his weight on hers, pressing her down into a big bed, parting her thighs. She ground her hips against his. Heard his groan as he lifted his head a fraction from where his mouth had been sliding kisses along her throat.

'I've wanted to do this since the moment I found you trying to break into my hotel room.'

'Mmm.' She ran her fingers through his hair and held on tight.

'This feels really good.'

Too good.

She moaned when he stood back half an inch. Almost managed to start up her defunct brain. But then he undid the big buttons on her wool coat.

'This is nice, but it's so bulky…'

She trembled as she heard the rough desire threaded in his voice. Underneath was the green silk shirt she'd bought after her spill earlier in the week. She had to admit she liked it—and she knew *he* liked it. Her resistance to his attraction was clearly slipping.

'Such a beautiful colour on you.' He bent and pressed his lips just north of the top button. His hand was between her coat and her shirt now, and still not where she wanted. Bare skin. The idea tormented her. As if he'd heard her mental plea his fingers moved, lifting the shirt, sliding beneath onto the skin of her back.

Gasping, she lifted her chin and he caught her mouth again. All teasing patience gone. Now his tongue demanded—intimately searching, tasting, knowing, as he crushed her to him. His hands moved possessively under her shirt, one running down her back, the other cupping her breast, fingers spreading down on her stomach, firmly sliding further down...pressing hard on her lower belly, right where deep within she was aching and yearning for deeper, more intimate contact. She arched her back against the bridge, thrusting her hips harder into his body.

He tore his mouth from hers. 'If we don't stop soon, I'll be warming you up from the inside out.'

Panting, she opened her eyes. Turned her head and saw the footpath, the people studiously not looking their way. The truth of what he'd said hit her. She was plastered to him, grinding herself against his massively exciting erection, and it was before eight o'clock on a weekday morning in the middle of a busy street.

Oh, no!

His hands loosened. Moved. Not letting go of her, but stopping their intimate invasion. He rested them on her hips—but on the outside of her coat. It was more to stop her toppling over than to turn her on.

'I want you, Imogen,' he said. 'Badly.'

She started shaking her head. He kept talking.

'I know you're not ready for that yet. You tell me when you are. The word I'm looking for is *yes*.'

Not ready? She'd just thrown herself at him. For that she wanted to apologise, wanted to scream her mortification, wanted to rewind time back five minutes and forget.

'But—'

He placed his hand over her mouth.

'There's another word. *But*. Best not to say the rest. If there's a but, that's all there is.'

He didn't want to analyse it. Didn't want it to become any more of a scene than it already was—didn't want complications.

Millions of thoughts were flying in her brain. Was this normal for him? Because it certainly wasn't normal for her. It was terrifying. Since when was she so out-of-control as to be practically having sex with some guy in the *street*?

In the few minutes it took her to get up to Princes Street Imogen wasn't numb any more. She was both frozen with horror and hot with embarrassment. Desire and panic were coming third and fourth. What on earth had she been thinking? This was her boss, her spoilt play-boy boss, and she couldn't ruin the chance she'd worked so hard to get with another cad.

Ryan could feel waves of insecurity and embarrassment almost buffeting into him, so strongly were they radiating from her body. Ordinarily he'd have chuckled about it—made her laugh to lighten the moment. But he was too filled with disappointment and frustration and sheer confusion to be able to laugh himself. He'd kissed her—gloriously, deeply, most satisfyingly, and then even more *unsatisfyingly*. Because he'd wanted more and more and more with every inch he'd explored of her. Instead he'd stopped and breathed. And then he'd stood and watched all the stars in her eyes fade out one by one as reason returned to her head. Each sparkle of desire snuffed out by whatever cynical thought was striking her.

Did he want to know?

He shouldn't. He really shouldn't. He didn't have the time for complicated. He was here short-term to do a job, do it well, and then move on to the next. All his concentration should be on that and nothing else. And just then, in the aftermath of that mind-blowing kiss and then some, she'd looked *very* complicated. Now she looked plain anxious. He liked that less than anything. He had to lighten it up—just for now. So they could have some time to cool off and think this through. Because—oh, boy—*he* needed to think. Since when did he have the hots for someone so bad he'd nearly stripped her in the street first thing in the morning?

'Don't look so worried, Imogen. It was just a kiss.' A bit more abrasive than he'd meant. And who did he think he was kidding—just a kiss?

'And let's face it,' he added. 'It was inevitable.' Hell, yes—it had been. He'd been wanting it—just as he'd said—from the moment he'd found her trying to get into his hotel room. It hadn't been the flash of her bra and the magnificent breast it contained. He'd wanted her before then. One look into her flaming green eyes had jolted him to his core. She was one gorgeous woman.

'Inevitable?'

Frost. No doubt about it. He could see her icing over. What? Because he'd called it like it was?

'Absolutely.' He couldn't resist the temptation to antagonise her more.

She was trying to walk faster. Get away from him. Tough. He could handle icy paths far better than she.

'Well—' her comeback snapped as fast as her heels on the pavement '—now that we've been there and done that, we can move on and forget about it, can't we?'

'You think?' He nearly laughed aloud. There was no forgetting the way she'd just burst into flames, and there was no way in hell he could move on for a while—not when he wanted her with a *want* like this.

'Absolutely.'

At the way she so coolly echoed his word he was seized with the urge to pull her close and kiss her some more, prove her totally wrong. Not a good idea—tempting as it was. His status as her boss was a problem. One he'd give a lot to get rid of—but he couldn't. If anything more were to happen it had to be at *her* instigation. Just as—if she'd take a second to be honest—she'd have to admit that the kiss had been at her instigation. He had to get her to come to him. Outside of business hours, alone, they could work this out.

One thing he knew: she liked his eyes. That was nice, because he really liked hers. He stopped her walking by putting both his hands hard on her shoulders. Stood in front of her and then lifted her chin so that she had to meet him square-on.

She was breathing fast, and he read defiance and the remnants of the desire she was so desperately trying to squash.

He spoke. Slowly, determinedly bringing her back to recognise that this attraction was here and it wasn't going to go away.

'Absolutely *not*.'

CHAPTER FOUR

INEVITABLE. AN HOUR LATER Imogen was fuming in place behind her computer when Ryan walked in. She tried not to watch him as he greeted Shona and the others. Couldn't help but be aware of every move. He walked past her desk.

'Good morning, Imogen.'

For a flash she met his eyes, saw the awareness in them, then looked back to her screen. 'Good morning, Mr Taylor.'

He stopped walking, swivelled, and came right over to her desk, not seeming to care about Shona being well within earshot. 'You're going to "Mr Taylor" me *now*?'

'Yes.' She kept typing. 'Now I have all the more reason to "Mr Taylor" you.'

He'd been right—it had been inevitable. She'd been inevitable. And he'd been so predictable—*just a kiss?* Was that how he thought of it? If so, she was even further out of his league than she'd realised—because no way could she play it like that.

There was a moment longer as he stood beside her desk. She kept typing. Who knew what? But her eyes were glued to the screen and her fingers flew.

'Okay, *Ms Hall*, if that's how you want it.' He stepped closer, crouched down, spoke very quietly. 'But there's one thing I need you to do for me.'

She looked down into his eyes, startled to see their almost pained expression.

'I'm not asking you this as your boss. I'm asking you just to have mercy on a simple man.'

Mystified, she kept staring.

'Would you please never, never, *ever* wear that shirt again?'

Then, for the first time since taking over the management of the store, he walked into his office and closed the door—hard.

Imogen worked through until Shona reminded her there was such a thing as lunch. She wasn't at all hungry. But having her favourite kind of break might provide one way of stopping her mind from lurching between lust-filled fantasies and rank despair. She hadn't had the chance to do it all week, and more than ever she needed to today.

For ten months of the year tasteful classical instrumental music was piped discreetly through the store's speakers. For the other two months it was Christmas favourites. And in the magnificent Christmas store-within-the-store the volume was raised that little extra notch.

Imogen loved the repeat, repeat, repeat of the songs all the day and half the night due to their extended opening hours. She knew the words to all of them and hummed along. Head bent, she stood by the grotto and put the final fold on one of her trademark origami boxes to put a tiny present in.

'Ms Hall.' An American accent, all sarcastically polite, interrupted her. 'May I have a word?'

'One moment, Mr Taylor. I'll just finish up.'

She tucked the boy's gift in the box and quickly wound ribbon around it, curling the ends and fluffing them to sit just so. Reluctantly she handed the present over to the smiling customer. Then she went to where her boss stood, waiting amongst the dazzlingly decorated Christmas trees.

Mr Taylor did not look happy. 'What exactly are you doing?'

'What does it look like I'm doing?' she retorted.

'I think we pay you a little more than we pay the spotty teens who come in to gift-wrap.'

'Are you suggesting it's a waste of my valuable time?'

'Precisely.'

'Well, Mr Taylor, you're wrong. And not one of our teens is spotty—you know that.'

'Actually, Ms Hall, I wasn't looking at anyone but you.'

'*Actually*, Mr Taylor—' she sidestepped the dangerous whisper '—this is my lunch break. I'm free to do as I like. And I like to gift-wrap.'

His glaring blue eyes took on a thoughtful tinge. 'Well, seeing I've eaten into your precious personal time, perhaps you'd better have an extra five minutes.'

'Thank you, Mr Taylor.' She accepted his defeat with extreme graciousness. 'I'll do exactly that.'

She breathed a sigh of relief as he walked away, and focused on wrapping the boxed china tea set that the lovely old lady next in the queue had placed on the table.

Two minutes later Ryan reappeared and stood in her line.

Sadly, the woman after the lovely old lady only had a book to wrap, and it took Imogen less than a minute.

He stepped up to the table. She stared at him.

'I'd like you to wrap this, please.' He met her not so cool gaze with eyes like limpid pools.

She couldn't handle it. Looked down. The matching hat, gloves and scarf set was a deep green, and knitted from the finest merino wool.

'I know someone who needs warming up,' he whispered conspiratorially.

She fumbled with the paper.

'I *had* been thinking about a hot water bottle,' he went on, ignoring her rigid silence. 'But I think she thinks it might be dangerous.'

Imogen picked up the scissors and resolutely decided to play along. 'What about a wheat pack?'

'Not big enough. I was thinking more along the lines of a human hot water bottle. Big and warm—someone that she can snuggle into.'

His eyes weren't quite so limpid now.

Imogen ran the scissor blade along the ribbon. 'She might get too hot.' She might get burned. Imogen already had scars, she didn't need more.

'She wouldn't have to wear pyjamas.'

IMOGEN SPENT THE afternoon in recovery, doing payroll and avoiding Ryan and Shona and everyone. The office team was going for drinks that night—Ryan's first week/ Christmas shout. No way was Imogen going—she never went to staff social occasions, never mixed business with personal. Once bitten, fifty-five times shy. And Ryan's presence was even more of a reason to say no—especially after that 'just a kiss' this morning; especially when he'd flirted with her like that at the gift wrap table.

So she made her usual excuse to Shona and hid out in the Christmas store while the others left. Then she went back up to the office to finish her last sheet of data entry before packing up for the day. She was about to shut the computer down when Ryan walked back in, frowning.

'Aren't you coming for a drink with everyone?'

'I don't drink.'

'Ah.' He rolled his eyes. 'Of course you don't.'

'Mr Taylor?' She was not going to have him poke fun at her.

'Ryan.' He walked to her desk and around it.

'Mr—'

'Ryan.' He pulled her out of her seat.

'No. Mr—'

'Everyone else calls me Ryan. You can, too.' He stood in front of her. Way too close for comfort.

'Don't.'

'Don't what?' He tilted her chin up with his finger.

'I can't…'

'Can't what?' His eyes caressed her, captivated her.

'I can't *think* when you do that.'

'This?' He stroked her hair. 'Or this?' He ran his finger the length of her throat, letting it rest on the hollow at the base.

'Umm…' Her skin burned as she tried to get her head to function.

He smiled. 'Good. Don't think. Just do.'

But her brain flicked back on. 'Like in some sports-wear ad?'

'Sure. I'm thinking athletic. My heart's racing. My body definitely wants a workout.'

She stepped back, broke free of his gaze and his touch. 'I try not to act on impulse.' She'd failed with that this morning—and look at the trouble she was in now.

'Why not try acting on instinct, then? There's a big difference.'

'You think?'

'Impulses can be rash. But trusting your intuition, going with instinct, will never see you wrong.'

'My brain is telling me to run.'

'Precisely my point. You're thinking too much even to

hear your instinct.' He took a step after her. 'Your instinct is that feeling from deep within here.' He put his finger back on the hollow in her throat and then ran it down the length of her sternum, pressed his palm firm against her upper belly. 'Your gut, your bones.'

It wasn't her bones feeling it. 'It's not that easy, Ryan.'

'It is.'

'*I'm* not.'

'Okay.' He smiled then. There was sympathy and understanding in it, but also determination. 'Don't over-complicate things. There's us. There's attraction. Isn't that all that matters?'

Don't over-complicate things? As in search for more? 'No. A lot of other things matter.'

'Tell me.'

'My job. My reputation.'

'Not in doubt. Not relevant to this.'

'How can you say that? You're my boss.'

'Right. But we're on the same team, Imogen, not opposite sides. Besides, my position here is temporary.'

What? So this would only be temporary, too?

'Anything we do outside of business hours is not going to affect your career here.'

Yeah, right.

'No one would know about it if you didn't want them to. I can keep a secret.'

She knew all about secrets. And lies. And she'd rather have someone who *couldn't* keep a secret—that way she wouldn't be set up for any nasty surprises.

'What exactly do you want from me, Ryan?' Was he just up for a quick fling?

'Right now, I just want you. Honestly, I can't think beyond that.' He lifted his hand from her and rubbed his forehead. 'I have a big job to do here, and it's the start of our push into Europe. I need to focus—but that's not to say I can't still have a little fun.' He dropped his hand and shrugged. 'I don't see that as a bad thing. In fact, I'd say it's a great thing.'

He smiled again. She wished he wouldn't, because he smiled with his eyes and his mouth and his whole body, and she couldn't fail to respond. He knew that, didn't he?

'When did you last have some fun, Imogen? You sit here all day, working very hard—and I do appreciate that—then go wrap presents for some nice customers. Then what? Go home?'

'So?' There was nothing wrong with working hard and doing a good job. She was determined to reclaim her work reputation and make something of herself.

'Alone?'

She blushed, and anger surged. 'I've been studying.'

'I know. Good for you.' Did he have to sound so damn genuine? 'But you've finished for now, so why not come out for a drink? It can't hurt, can it?'

With his almost electric-blue eyes he regarded her intensely. Not trying to domineer, but coaxing, tempting—frankly mesmerising.

'It's Christmas,' he said softly.

Her head nodded before she thought better of it. Somehow he had her coat in his hands and was holding it for her to slip her arms into.

'Won't they be wondering where you are?'

'Shona has gone on ahead and opened up a bar tab. The others will be there—just relaxing after work. Having a quiet drink and celebrating the festive season.'

Her arms were in her coat and he'd leant behind her

and switched off her computer. They were walking out the door.

The bar was in a narrow street at the back of the shop. As they walked in she looked around—small, intimate, hip and yet comfortable at the same time. It had been a long time since she'd been in a bar like this.

No nightlife. No social life. She'd avoided it all since arriving over eight months ago.

He was looking at her, that half smile teasing. 'What are you having? Wine? A cocktail?'

'I told you I don't drink.'

'Not ever, Imogen? Not even on Christmas Day?'

He knew somehow, didn't he? That she liked a glass of wine but didn't trust herself—and certainly not tonight.

'A glass of bubbly is lovely on Christmas Day. But we're still a couple of weeks from then.'

'So how about a glass of red?'

It wasn't that she'd fall down drunk. But she didn't want to run any risk of doing or saying anything stupid. He was too much temptation already—look at what she'd done this morning. Just a whiff of alcohol might have her throwing caution to the wind completely.

'I'd prefer a lemon, lime and bitters.'

'Bitters?' he echoed. 'How appropriate.'

With a lethal look she left him and joined the others already sitting around a table. There was only space for one left in the U-shaped booth. Ryan would have to find another chair. But a few minutes later when he walked over, a tray of drinks in hand, he just smiled.

'Bunch up.'

They all bunched up. Imogen's temperature soared as he squeezed against her in the tiny space they'd freed. He was too close. His leg was hard against the length of hers. Their arms were pressed tight together. Then he lifted his and rested it along the top of the seat behind her. Now his body was too close. It would take nothing to lean a little closer and be right in his lap. She had a long sip of her drink and tried to tune in to the conversation.

Christmas plans. They all were sharing them. She had another sip, not wanting to admit to the Christmas Day *she* was headed for.

'What are you doing, Ryan?' Shona asked, and Imogen was all ears.

'Going home.'

She could feel the vibrations in his chest as he spoke.

'It's a big family occasion—my parents, my brother and sisters. A few aunts and uncles, lots of cousins.'

'Do you have masses of decorations and neon lights everywhere? And a giant Santa on the roof like you see on American TV shows?' That clanger was from Angela, one of the marketing team.

Ryan's smile was good-natured. 'We *do* have a tree in the garden that we put lights on. The tree inside only has paper decorations that we make.'

'That you *make*?' Imogen's question was out before she'd even thought it—or thought to stop it.

'Sure. My grandparents originally came from Denmark, and there they call the Christmas season the festival of hearts. We make hearts to hang on the tree. Mum's kept them all over the years. They have our name and the date on the back of them. Now the tree is smothered. It looks pretty good, even for home-made.'

Imogen couldn't believe that his family didn't have one of those trees covered with designer decorations that each cost enough to buy five frozen turkeys. 'Do you still make them?'

'Every year. And on Christmas Eve we put real candles on the tree and my dad lights them. It's a big deal.'

She refused to be touched. 'Isn't that dangerous, with all the paper and wood?'

'Life's no fun without a little danger, don't you think?'

Imogen said nothing, but his thigh pressed a little harder on hers as he glanced away to the rest of the group.

'Then we open presents and eat a lot of food.'

'On Christmas Eve?' Imogen sat ramrod-straight, but was unable to move away from the bone-melting pressure of his leg.

He nodded.

'You open presents on Christmas Eve?'

'Sure.'

'Well, *that's* not right.'

'Isn't it?'

'In New Zealand we open presents on Christmas Day.'

'Oh?' He shrugged. 'Well, we open them on Christmas Eve.'

'But that's just wrong. It's all about the anticipation. About waking up early and getting desperate for all the relatives to arrive so you can get on with it.' She didn't give him a chance to respond—just wanted to score a point. 'Straw poll—show of hands,' she said brightly to the others. 'Do you open presents on Christmas Eve or Christmas Day?'

Christmas Day won by a landslide.

'Different culture,' he murmured.

He was damn right about that. His background was light years from everyone's here—his family hung out with presidents and popstars. She bet they *did* have an overpriced tree with overpriced decorations, and hid the Waltons-esque home-made number in the kitchen.

But as the others chatted about their plans Imogen wondered, and finally gave in to the temptation of asking. 'So what do you do on Christmas Day?'

His face was full of humour. 'Sleep in. Eventually get up and eat. Fish around in our stockings. Eat another big meal all together.'

'You still get a stocking?'

'I'm a very good boy.'

Well, she knew that wasn't the case. 'You mean your mother turns a blind eye?'

'Don't all mothers?'

Every cell inside her chilled. A mother like his would. A mother with money enough to pay off the damage caused by her son's indiscretions. George's mother had done exactly that—refusing to believe the ugly reality of her son's nature, blaming Imogen instead. It was always the woman's fault, right? Especially if she hadn't grown up in the right area and hadn't gone to the right school— then she was definitely the one to blame.

Ryan murmured, way too close to her ear, 'Does Santa bring *you* a stocking, Imogen?'

'Always.'

'That so?'

'I really *am* good.'

'Yes—to my great disappointment.' He smirked into his glass. 'What does Santa put in your stocking?'

'It's been the same every year for some time now.' She tapped her fingers on the table as she itemised the list. 'An orange in the toe, some lipgloss, my own bag of chocolate-covered peppermint creams and...' She turned

her head, met his too-close gaze full-on, and told him
straight. 'Lacy knickers.'

'Really?' His thigh was pressing harder against hers
again. 'How lacy?'

'Pretty lacy.'

'Just the one pair, or several?'

'Several.'

He lifted his drink and took a deep sip. 'I always knew
Santa was a good guy.'

She escaped not long after. Finished her drink and ran
away before she was tempted to flirt back.

SHE AVOIDED MAKING eye contact with him all of the
next morning. But in her lunch break, just as Rudolph
the red-nosed reindeer was being told he'd go down in
history for the fourth time that day, Ryan hit the front of
her wrapping queue again. He had a huge, bulky down
puffer jacket in his arms.

'Could you wrap this for me, please?' There was more
than a hint of devilry in his eyes. Way more.

'Certainly, Mr Taylor.'

He dumped the jacket on the table between them. It
was dark grey. Size triple XL. And it was as if it was
alive. She folded it over and it sprang back. She tried
tucking the arms under. They slipped out. She glanced
up at him. He was smirking.

'It's not a problem for you, is it?'

'Of course not.' She bared her teeth in a savage sort
of smile.

Telling herself he was just like any other customer
who deserved good service, she thought up some polite
small talk. In honesty, she was insatiably curious.

'Is it for a loved one?'

Confusion flickered across his face. 'It's for my cousin,' he suddenly spouted. 'Jodie. She'll like it.'

Imogen pulled on the spool of ribbon in the green and gold colours of Mackenzie Forrest and took in his minor attack of the fidgets. His cousin? Somehow she doubted that.

'She feels the cold, too, you see—needs to warm up.'

Imogen's suspicion hardened as his eyes danced. 'Well, this should certainly do the trick.' She smiled again, docile this time. 'Are you sure you have the right size?'

Dancing eyes narrowed, 'Oh, yes. She likes the layered look. Lots of bulk underneath.'

Good recovery. But she didn't believe a word of it.

Watching her hands, he went on the attack. 'I thought the ribbon was meant to go on the outside of the parcel?'

'Ordinarily. But this will help it look a little neater.'

She'd wound the ribbon round the middle of jacket and pulled the ends tight, fast, knotted it. Then wound another length from top to toe. Another few lengths of ribbon and she had a neat rectangular shape.

She cut some paper to length, now able to wrap it perfectly. She cut yet more ribbon to flourish over the outside this time.

'That looks wonderful.' He didn't seem thrilled to concede.

'I hope she enjoys it,' Imogen said smoothly. 'Even if she is going to open it twelve hours too early.'

He leant over the desk between them. 'Christmas Eve is when the magic happens.'

'Christmas Day is when the world plays.'

He shook his head. 'Are we going to agree to disagree?'

'Never.'

IT BECAME THE ROUTINE. Every lunch break, every day.

'Silent Night'—an oversized toy abacus for his niece Donna, who was still learning her numbers.

'White Christmas'—a giant suitcase on wheels for his cousin Clara, who apparently always had too much baggage.

'Santa Claus is Coming to Town'—a jeroboam of champagne for his Great-Aunt Hilary, who only liked to live it up on Christmas Day, with an oversized twirly straw for her to suck it straight from the bottle.

The presents got more outrageous, more pointed, and more impossible to wrap. And all the while Imogen tried to wrap them Ryan smiled, talked and teased. As hard as she tried not to, she anticipated it—longed for it, lived for it.

Day by day, minute by minute, she was eternally braced for his presence, aching for his appearance, and so on edge she was about to explode. The weekend without work passed slowly and painfully, but the moment of seeing him again first thing on Monday was even more painful with the way her heart raced.

He was wrong. This wasn't instinct—some great inner perception—this was plain old-fashioned lust. It was the instinct to procreate with a fit, healthy male. *Very* fit. Her body wanted his surrounding hers, filling hers.

He wanted her, too—but 'couldn't see beyond that'. She knew why. Once he'd had her, his 'instinct' would be to move on. The marauding male was always driven by an innate need to spread his seed far and wide.

He'd said it didn't need to be complicated. She sure didn't want complicated. But the desire to be with him was complicating everything right now. Maybe it would be better if she gave in to it? Just the once? Then she could forget about it. You always want what you can't have, so if she had him then she wouldn't want him any more—right?

She argued with herself round and round and round again.

If she was the one in control, if she was the one calling the shots and calling an end to it, then mightn't she be okay?

There had been no one before or after George. And she had last seen George over a year ago. A long year—which was probably why her desire for Ryan was so intense, right?

He'd said anything between them wouldn't impact on her job—how could she trust him on that? But he wasn't here permanently as her boss, was he? Just a couple of months while he oversaw the transition and recruited and trained a new manager. Then he'd be gone and she could keep working, keep studying.

One morning she could stand it no longer. She pulled on the jade blouse, her scarlet bra already fastened underneath, and matching knickers. She held her breath as he walked in. Saw his gaze flicker over her shirt. And then he looked at her computer rather than at her.

'I need some data from last week.' His frown was something else.

'Yes.'

'I want it on my desk before you go home tonight.'

'Yes, Ryan,' she said clearly, filled with desire and daring and a kind of defiance. *'Absolutely.'*

CHAPTER FIVE

HE HADN'T COME NEAR her all day—not even when she'd wrapped gifts in her lunch break. She'd sat at her desk all afternoon, growing colder by the minute, eventually frozen with humiliation as she pulled the data and assembled the figures. At ten past six, when the others had already left for the day, she knocked on the frame of his open door and walked right in. With a flick of her wrist the papers swooshed beside his keyboard.

'What's that?'

'The report. On your desk.'

He looked up then, and she gasped at the brilliance of his eyes—bright blue and blazing into her.

'It wasn't the *report* I wanted on my desk.' He stood.

Instinct made her take a small step back, but he followed—too fast.

'Yes,' he said crisply. 'Isn't that what you said to me earlier, *Ms Hall*? Or did I imagine that?'

'I—'

'Did you or did you not say *yes*?'

Oh, when his eyes were lit up like that there wasn't a woman in the world who wouldn't part her legs. 'Yes.' It was a whimper.

'And you know my feelings about that shirt.'

She could feel the heat as he stared at her breasts.

'Actually,' she said, her confidence firming at the same time as her nipples, 'I'm not sure I do.'

'Then allow me to show you.'

He walked with sure, determined steps. But to her immense disappointment he stepped around her. Then, to her intense excitement, he locked the door.

Desire, too long denied, rose. Slowly she turned and watched him return to her. 'This has to be on my terms, Ryan.'

'Name them.'

'Once only.' She had to set the rules while she could still think. 'Just once. Okay?'

'You're offering me a one-night stand?'

'It can't get complicated that way, right?'

His eyes met hers, dark now, solemn. 'Do you think once is going to be enough?'

'It has to be.'

He stopped right in her space and looked hard at her. 'I think that once will be enough to know.'

'Know what?'

'Whether once will be enough.' His smile had an edge to it.

Her heart was thudding louder than the drums in the Edinburgh Military Tattoo. 'What does that mean?'

He ignored her. 'Do you want me to touch you?'

'Yes. And…'

He leaned closer, spoke just as softly. 'And what?'

She whispered—the thinnest of threads detailing her deepest desire. 'I want to touch you.'

Slowly, so slowly, he stretched out his arm and touched her shoulder. The tips of his fingers glided down her silky sleeve until he caught her hand. He lifted it, still slowly, and pressed her palm to his jaw, turned his chin into it just a touch so he could kiss her. All the while watching her intensely, his eyes reflecting her own desire back at her.

She moved then—fast. Sliding her hand to the back of his neck, she pulled him home, capturing his mouth with hers.

Slow and sweet became fast and frantic as they stumbled together, passionately trying to get closer. His stubble chafed her cheeks, her lips—she loved it—kissed harder. He backed her up until she was against his desk, pushed papers aside. She sat on it, pulling him to follow. He did, pressing kisses down her throat to her open collar. His fingers worked fast to undo the top few buttons so he could kiss the top of her breast as it crested over the scarlet lace. She'd worn a skirt deliberately, and was now thrilled with her cunning. She wriggled her hips so he could push the material out of the way and slide his hand up her thigh. He stroked against her panties.

'Yes…' She sighed. If he touched her skin on skin she'd come. If he slid those fingers inside she'd… 'Hurry,' she urged. She'd waited for too long—wanted the pleasure now, so she could feel the relief and then be able to forget about it. *'Hurry!'*

'All efficiency, aren't you?' He lifted his hands off her.

'Why are you stopping?'

He'd placed his hands hard on the desk either side of her. His face was flushed, eyes glittering, breathing hard. 'One night, right?'

'Right.'

'Then I want *all* night. Not some one-minute quickie in my office. I want a good ten hours in my hotel room.'

She felt her eyes widen. 'You were the one who said you wanted me on your desk.'

He glanced down to her body. 'I changed my mind.' His fingers went back to her thigh, gently sweeping up the exposed curve of skin.

'But I don't think I can make it to your hotel,' she

wailed, as hot need washed through her. She couldn't say no. Not now. Not when she was so close.

His smile was beyond satisfied. 'I'll make it easy for you.' He scooped her off the desk and carried her to the door. In the lift he leaned her back against the wall, kissed her senseless.

It was only as the door opened and he set her on her feet that she remembered her shirt and managed to fumble her way into doing the buttons up. Somehow they got through the store. Her lips felt three times their usual size. Dazed, she supposed she was walking, but she felt as if she was floating.

The instant they were out of the building he had her hand in his again, and flagged a cab with the other. His hotel was only minutes away, and every one was spent in his arms. Still not close enough. In the lift again, he pressed against her so hard she could hardly breathe. She could hardly breathe anyway, so excited, so desperate as she kissed him back, already working the buttons free on his shirt.

'You're the most wonderful challenge, Imogen.' As the lift chimed, signalling his floor, he stepped back, looking almost cunning as he fished in his pocket for his key card.

'Why?' she asked, too mindless to be able to work him out.

'One night? You're sure that's all you want?'

'That's all.'

Determination deepened his reply as he opened the door. 'I wonder if that's what you'll say in the morning.'

She didn't get the chance to answer—even to think— as he locked her in his arms and backed her against the door to close it.

His kisses fired her until she was clinging and sighing, doing everything she could do make him take her *now*.

But he broke away. Stepping back a distance and staring at her, he took in a long, ragged breath. 'I want to slow down.'

'I don't.'

He laughed. 'No. I already figured that.'

He walked. She followed, watching as he pulled a bottle from the fridge. She seethed with frustration, focused on reading the label to try and hide just how much she didn't want to stop.

She lifted her brows. 'Your standard drink?'

He shook his head. 'I've had it in the fridge since you said you liked bubbles that night in the bar.'

'I said I like bubbles at *Christmas*.'

'But, Imogen,' he said, all innocent-like, 'this is better than Christmas.'

'You're very sure of yourself.'

He'd known this would happen.

'Optimistic.'

Inevitable. Her mood dimmed. She hated being a foregone conclusion. Had he already mapped out the rest of their affair? Undoubtedly. He was already betting there'd be more than one night. That made her even more determined not to follow his plan.

His grin didn't disappear, but it gentled. 'You can't deny it. You feel it. I feel it. And together we'll deal with it.'

He handed her a glass. She took a sip to soothe her dry throat. The bubbles hit the roof of her mouth and she closed her eyes, appreciating the sensation. Swallowing, she lifted the glass to have another mouthful—but he took it from her.

She looked at him.

'Uh-uh.' He shook his head and teased, 'Just a taste.

I don't want you blaming what's about to happen on the demon drink.'

'What's going to happen?'

'You're going to lose your head. We both are.'

'Maybe I already have.'

He chuckled at that. 'Not yet.'

'It feels like it. You make me feel…woolly.'

'Woolly?' He was really laughing now.

'In my head,' she said crossly.

'Stop thinking about your head,' he instructed. 'Stop thinking at all.'

In less than five seconds she'd done exactly that as he swept her close and kissed her deep. This time she wasn't letting him step away again. She ran her hands over his hard muscles, tested the breadth of his shoulders, and had his shirt off and his trousers down well before her own clothes were even undone.

He walked her backwards to the bedroom, stepping out of his clothes along the way, unzipping her skirt and opening her shirt buttons so she could do the same. He pushed her back onto the bed. He landed right on top of her and she arched against him, unable to wait any longer for that complete contact.

His laughter was muffled as he kissed along the line of her bra. 'Slow down, darling.'

Slow down? Was the man crazy? She didn't have time for slow. It felt as if she'd been burning for him for ever, and she was so close to fulfilment. She reached for him, stroking him, urging him.

But at that he gripped her wrists and firmly lifted them high above her head. 'Hold onto the pillow.'

She could feel something inside flare at his order. But a tiny sense of self-preservation made her resist. She tried to pull her hands free.

'No.' He pushed down hard, keeping her in place. 'Hold onto the pillow.'

He was kneeling astride her. All she could see were broad shoulders, hard abs tapering to those slim hips, and his thick erection arrowing right at her.

She shivered—tried to break free again. His dominance was a turn-on that she couldn't bring herself to acknowledge. 'Maybe I don't trust you.'

His laugh was short. 'If you don't trust me then you shouldn't be anywhere near this point.'

She stared up at him. She trusted him physically. It was the mental and emotional stuff that she was unsure of.

He was looking deep inside her again. He moved to hold both her hands in one of his and ran a finger down from her throat to her navel. 'Maybe you don't trust yourself.'

She shivered again. He wasn't going to let her get away with a quick thrill. He was asking for total response. The problem was the price that would be paid after. And she didn't know if she could afford it.

Her defence rose. 'You think you have me all figured out, don't you? You think I'm uptight.'

'Aren't you?'

'No.'

'Well, I guess this is your chance to prove it to me.'

Their stares clashed. Determination versus defiance. Temptation versus resistance.

But such determined temptation was impossible to resist. Her fingers curled into the soft pillow. But even as she surrendered, she challenged him. 'I *will* retaliate.'

'I wouldn't expect anything less.' He bent closer, whispered, 'But the thing is, Imogen, I want this to last more than five minutes, and if you keep touching me like that we won't even make it to two.'

She squeezed the pillow that bit tighter as pleasure rippled though her.

'Yes,' he said, approving as she flexed her hips. 'I want you that much. So we need to even out the score a little.'

She wanted him. She'd never wanted another man the way she wanted him. But he, as he'd promised, went slow. Trailing fingers, lingering kisses, gently stripping the scarlet lace from her body with teasing caresses. From top to toe he tasted and teased, eventually, finally—thankfully—settling between her thighs, from where he could reach up and toy with her breasts while tonguing her intimately.

Divine sensation. Mindless bliss.

Uncontrollably she thrust up, body rigid, right on the brink, wanting release so badly. But his fingers stilled and his mouth lifted.

'I won't let you be Ms Efficient in bed, Imogen.'

'Please.' She was frantic.

'Say my name. Say it.'

She did—chanting it over and over—begging, pleading, twisting beneath his fingers and mouth, desperate for the relief only he could give. Until finally, with just another tormenting silken suck, he let her crash over the edge.

Long moments later he blew on her face. She opened her eyes, saw him smiling at her. 'You are one delicious woman.'

Her glance skidded down his body. *He* was the delicious one.

He nudged her fingers as they slipped on the pillow.

'No point,' she mumbled. 'They're useless. I can't move anything.'

'Really?' He looked hard into her eyes. 'Answer me honestly, Imogen. Are you really that satisfied?'

No. As soon as the question was asked the answer

slammed into her and she wanted to shout it out. It was as if that orgasm, like an avalanche, had set a layer of snow free, revealing a deep chasm beneath—the need yawning wide within her. And he saw. With his vibrantly blue eyes, she knew he saw. And she also knew he had what it was that she needed—what she wanted.

It was that need that gave her strength, forcing her to move, to reach, to snare. Her fingers spread wide greedily. Her mouth parted and plundered. She couldn't get enough of him, wanted all of him.

She arched her neck, stretching that distance so her mouth could touch his. He caught hers full. That kiss was the ignition. Her body, rendered so useless only moments before, was now filled with strength and craving. She pushed, raking her hands down his body, touching, stroking, squeezing. Feeling his heat, testing his strength, his endurance.

He lay back, letting her straddle him, explore him, taste him with a hunger that only seemed to grow the more she had of him. Her sex was wet, aching with want, her breasts tight, her belly yearning and restless. She rocked, uncontrollably rubbing against him, all of her body, not just her mouth, wanting its fill.

The assertion of dominance changed again. She felt his muscles grow more tense, heard his hiss as her hands swept over him, felt his strength as he lifted her, rolling them both over, positioning her. His large hands were hard on her thighs, parting them so he could fit in between.

Mesmerised by the blue of his eyes, passion making them even more brilliant, she paused. Their mouths met again. Tongues curling intimately. Sealed. A merging of everything. Nothing held back. Giving everything, taking everything.

And in that moment he pushed inside her.

Her head flew back, breaking the seal of their lips as she gasped at the overwhelming sensation. 'Ryan!'

She sucked in another scalding breath as his stomach hit hers and he plunged in to the hilt.

'I'm here.' He took her hands, his fingers entwining with hers. 'I'm here.'

He thrust deep again, and that last remaining fragment of herself was shattered.

'Yes.' Her eyelids fluttered as she sighed, succumbing to the blinding pleasure.

Her body was humming. She was skinless, just sensation. Warmth and light and mingling with him. Surging forward, meeting him again and again, strength matching softness and merging into one. Her fingers were free now as his gripped her hips, holding her so he could push even closer. She ran the heel of her hands across his shoulders, followed down the vee of his body to his tight butt and pulled him into her as viciously as he was pushing.

It wasn't enough. It wasn't ever going to be enough.

She cried out at the realisation. *More.* She needed more.

Her eyes opened and she saw him looking at her with unbearable intensity, steely determination locking his jaw. He was utterly focused on her. She could feel him willing her to feel it.

'Yes,' he muttered.

She nearly nodded, maybe mumbled back, but at that point the goodness of it started to wash through her in an unstoppable wave. The sheer force of emotion had her gasping for air, screaming something, shuddering deeply as overwhelming pleasure racked her body. His arms were tight around her, holding her close as he buried deep two, three times more. His groan was so exquisite to her heightened hearing that tears burned at her eyes.

Her muscles quivered. A film of perspiration covered

her. She had never experienced anything so beautiful. She kept her face turned into his warm neck, panting as she breathed in his scent, not wanting to move from this weighted bliss. Even when he lifted his head and she knew he was looking at her she kept her eyes closed.

Her body was still trembling, her emotions threatening to wobble out of control altogether. She wanted to cry. It was too much. And she wanted to have him hold her close. More than anything she wanted to suspend this moment for as long as she could. She didn't want it to be over.

She was in trouble.

He lifted his weight from her chest, but his lower half still pressed onto hers. His fingers ran over her face lightly—her forehead, her cheek, her jaw—as if smoothing the frown that she'd determinedly tried to hide.

'It's okay, Imogen.' He didn't whisper. He knew she was only feigning sleep. He rolled onto his back and pulled her with him, so his chest cushioned her head. His arm encircled her, holding her close, and his other hand came to tilt her chin, lifting her face a little so he could kiss her forehead. 'It's okay.' He did whisper it that time. Then his fingers moved, stroking her hair, her upper arm. Light, warm touches that soothed her oversensitivity, calmed the fear clanging inside her.

He'd stripped her raw, taking every ounce of control from her, so she was utterly exposed to him, utterly vulnerable. Yet it was his arms that protected her now as the last of the tremors shook her. So gentle and comforting that some of those tears did escape. But by then she was so tired she barely noticed, and with a final sigh of exhaustion she capitulated completely and lost all consciousness.

HER HEAD ACHED. Correction—her whole body ached. No wonder. He'd not let her sleep long, had ruthlessly extracted that total, raw response again and then again, until all that was left of her was a quivering mass of nerves. He'd been right. She'd lost her head—body and mind— she'd given him everything.

Only now there was now—almost the morning after. Uppermost was her feeling of vulnerability. She'd told him she wasn't easy—what an absolute joke! She couldn't have been easier—falling into his arms, begging him with impatient, desperate, total surrender.

How could she have succumbed so completely and so quickly? And he was her *boss*. Had she learned nothing from George?

Any remaining high evaporated as unwanted memories dredged themselves up—the humiliation of George's betrayal, the loss of her job and the massive derailment of her career. She'd spent the last year working to reclaim it—how could she have been so stupid as to throw all that away for a few hours of physical fulfilment? Not only was Ryan her boss, he was also a guy who lived in a parallel world of untold wealth and an unreal lifestyle—one far more excessive than George's had been. And she knew that combination spelt trouble—in capitals all the way.

She screwed her eyes shut and denied her searing attraction to Ryan—blaming hormones for the physical ache that grew all the more painful as she contemplated pulling away from him. If she walked away now—if she *ran*—she might be able to stop this mess from worsening. But he was so close around her—such a sensual being that even in sleep he sought full contact. His jaw brushed her ear, his fingers rested lightly on her arm, his skin heated hers. She absorbed how relaxed he was—how frighteningly carefree.

How normal must this be for him?

Part of her wanted to submerge herself deep in his embrace. But it could only be a fleeting comfort. Mostly she wanted to cry. She clamped down on the wayward emotions—bit her lips. Tears stung anyway.

Don't get stupid, keep it simple—*one night.*

She couldn't be with him again—there'd be no early-morning frolic and a careless wave goodbye. Already she cared too much. Already her heart was breaking.

This one night had to be over this instant.

Hopefully it could be forgotten—by him at least. He'd move on quickly anyway. A guy like him would have no shortage of women keen to keep him company.

Whereas she? She would never forget. In fact, she had the sick feeling that she was going to leave behind a whole lot more than her head's impression on his pillow. Her heart was threatening to come right out of her chest and set up camp under his foot.

Slowly, carefully, she slid across the bed, inching her way out of his arms and onto the cold sheet. When free of him, she got right off the bed. They hadn't closed the curtains—even up on this floor of the hotel the street lights below sent a pale glow into the room.

She already had her underwear and skirt back on when she sensed his movement. She turned. He was sitting up and watching her with an expression so cold she froze.

The frown in his face echoed in his voice. 'Don't you *dare* tell me you regret it.'

CHAPTER SIX

'OKAY.' BUT IMOGEN'S whole body ached with regret. Regret about both entering and leaving his bed. She forced her arms through the sleeves of her wretched green shirt.

'What are you doing?' Eyes narrow, question direct.

'I have to go.'

'Why?'

Because if she stayed any longer she'd never want to leave. Because she couldn't do this anywhere near as well as she'd thought she could. Because she was sickly, hopelessly confused. But she couldn't bear to admit that—not to someone so in control and confident.

After too long a moment of silence he threw back the covers. 'Were you going to wake me before leaving?' He shook his head at her continued nil response. 'Unbelievable.'

He pulled on jeans with sharp jerks, not stopping for underwear, and then yanked on a long-sleeved tee. With stubble and tousled hair—hair *she'd* tousled—he was gorgeously, dangerously casual. Except there was nothing casual about the aggression emanating from him as he moved.

Her heart thudded and her belly heated.

More.

Desire wasn't whispering to her, it was shouting.

More, more, more!

Goaded by her body's flare to his magnetism, she raised her own voice. 'What are *you* doing?'

He kept stuffing his feet into socks and shoes. 'You don't think I'm going to let you walk out in the middle of the night and go home alone, do you? I'm seeing you to your door.'

'You don't have to—'

'You might be happy to treat me as a no-name one-night stand, but that's not how I'm going to treat *you*.'

'Ryan—'

'That's right. Ryan.' He rose, towering over her. 'That's my name. You breathed it, you *screamed* it, not that long ago. So what's changed?'

Alternating waves of heat and humiliation washed over her. She *had* screamed—and begged and pleaded and panted. Had been like a toy for him to handle however he pleased. And he'd pleased, all right—the most dynamic, delicious lover a woman could ever have the pleasure of knowing.

All too late she realised *she* couldn't handle *him*. How could she possibly admit to the fear and the overwhelming feelings burgeoning inside? How on earth could she say, *Hey, Ryan, you just made me fall for you—I don't just want an affair, I want the whole package.* She couldn't ask that of a man who'd have no idea of what that meant to someone like her.

'I made a mistake.'

'That was many things, but it wasn't a mistake.' He walked closer. 'Your mistake was thinking that we could get away with doing this just the once.'

He was right. Being with him had simply made her want more—from a man she couldn't possibly trust. He was George on steroids—more powerful, more moneyed, and much, much riskier. 'My mistake was in doing it at all.'

He shook his head. 'You'll be making a bigger mistake if you leave now.'

For the second time that night their stares clashed. Finality versus merciless magnetism.

'You don't want to enjoy what we have? You don't want to make the most of this incredible chemistry?'

In her head she shrieked her denial, but the sound refused to emerge from her mouth. It would be both truth and lie. She didn't want what she wanted more than her next breath. So she aimed for avoidance—scrambling for her shoes, trying to slip them on.

He was watching her all-thumbs clumsiness with an air of remote disbelief. 'You don't even want the rest of your one night?'

Chemistry. Sizzle. Va-va-voom attraction. That was what this was for him—a physical thrill.

Coward-like, she kept her gaze turned away as she forced an answer as firmly as she could. 'No.'

How could she have fallen for him? They'd known each other such a short time. They'd flirted then. They'd had sex now. They didn't then skip straight to for ever and ever. If she told him he'd laugh himself silly—then run a mile.

She was pathetic.

It took only a couple of minutes for a taxi to pull up in front of the hotel. Every interminable second shredded her insides.

'You don't have to—' She broke off. He'd already climbed in after her. There was no point saying it.

Her aches were worse now. She was regretting everything she'd said and done since waking up. So much of her wished she'd just snuggled into his arms for the rest of the night and let it happen. But better a little pain now than a lot of disaster later—and there'd be disaster for sure.

The silence hung heavy for the ten-minute ride. When the driver pulled up outside her tenement block she got out immediately, knowing there was no point in fighting Ryan over the fare.

She was at her door when she heard the car leave and his footsteps follow hers. Turning, she confronted him. 'Why did you send the cabbie away? Now you'll have to walk back to the hotel. You wouldn't let *me* walk home alone.'

'I'm a big guy. I think I'll be okay.' Short. Definitely ticked off.

'Ryan...' She hadn't meant for any of this to happen.

He stepped closer, his eyes big and blue and full of intent, and his hands lifted. She shrank back, bumping against the door, knowing her will would dissolve completely if he kissed her. She wanted to say no, but the nearer he got, the nearer she got to yes. But his hands bypassed her, pressed instead on the door behind her, on either side of her head. His face was shadowed as he looked down at her, as she fought to stand firm and not slither into that slimy pond of repetition.

You were supposed to learn from your mistakes, not make them again and again. She made herself remember that night with George—the accident and the aftermath. But Ryan leaned closer, and she could see nothing but him, and she had to press her lips together hard to stop herself saying anything—not least the wrong thing, like *yes, yes, yes* or *please, please, please.*

The longest of moments held them still as statues, both barely holding firm, until finally he pushed away. His eyes glittered with an emotion she couldn't interpret as he turned towards the street.

'Don't even *think* about calling me Mr Taylor tomorrow.'

RYAN STRODE, CONFUSION and frustration pushing his feet fast and far. He'd gone to sleep happier than he could ever remember being, having had the most incredible experience of his life. Only then he'd woken to find that the reason for his happiness was on the brink of slinking out of his room—as he suspected she would from his life if she could.

Why?

He paced the streets, replaying the night, trying to work out what it was that had made her take fright so completely. He couldn't come up with anything—hell, he'd never felt anything so *right* in his life. Their bodies were meant to move together. Hadn't she'd felt that too? They weren't on different planets, were they?

It wasn't supposed to be like this. It was supposed to have been fun and thrilling and the beginning of a fantastic fling. But instead of feeling tension-free, and thus able to concentrate properly for the first time in about two weeks, Ryan found himself feeling more tormented and distracted than ever. How annoying was that?

The next day she clearly had plans to avoid him as much as possible. Indeed she succeeded right through almost to the end of her lunch break. But just as Mommy was kissing Santa Claus for the sixth time that day, Ryan finally got to the front of the queue and dumped his present on the wrapping desk between them, determined to reclaim his ground.

'What's that?'

Wow, where had her customer service smile gone?

'A cactus. What else?'

He wasn't exactly Mr Friendly, either.

'I didn't know we sold cacti.'

'We don't. I bought it at another store.'

She lifted the pot, disdain written all over her.

'You think I'm abusing my position by getting you to wrap it for me?' he asked.

'Aren't you?'

He inhaled. Was that what she thought he was doing with her—taking advantage? Injustice seethed—*she'd* come to *him*. And he'd make her come to him again. He told himself to calm down and follow the only plan he'd thought of—to go a little slower, however much against the grain that was for him.

'The thing about this little cactus is that it's very rare. And even though it has big, sharp prickles, it's worth taking care of.'

'Oh, really?'

'Yes. Because when it flowers, it's the most beautiful thing.'

Her hands were working a little slower now, but she still wouldn't look at him.

'You want to know something else about this cactus?'

'Not particularly.'

He didn't believe her. Her fingers were trembling. 'It has medicinal properties.'

'Uh-huh?'

'That's right. It makes people feel good. In fact, this particular cactus knows how to make me feel *really* good.'

There was a short silence. Then, 'You can't take plants on a plane.'

'It's for a friend right here in Edinburgh.'

'Well, I hope he likes it.'

'I'm sure *she* will.'

Deliberately, slowly, he brushed his fingers across hers as he took the ribbon-wrapped plant. She flinched. She flushed. She wouldn't look him in the eye.

Only just did he quell the urge to vault the table and

haul her close. He *needed* to touch her—to find out what she was feeling. How could she have gone from *begging* him to take her, to freezing with something that looked a lot like fright? It didn't make sense. He kept his eyes locked on hers, willing, waiting...

Finally, she did it—looked at him properly. Her eyes were big and green, and she was pleading with him again—but for something he didn't want to see.

'Don't, Ryan.'

ONE MORE DAY DOWN. Only ninety-odd to go to get through the three months or so Ryan had remaining here full-time. It wasn't that impossible a task, was it?

Hell, yes. It was incredibly hard—especially when every moment she wasn't in lockdown mode her mind replayed scenes from that night—the way he'd held her, the way he'd felt. And her body felt them. The memories made her ache to move.

Bing Crosby had been asleep too long, because he was having yet another dream about a white Christmas. Imogen wished she could sleep without dreams—but every night Ryan came to her there.

She looked up at the next customer. It was him again.

Quickly she looked at the present. 'A child's fishing net?'

'Actually, it's a butterfly net. For my niece. She's eight.'

She felt him watching her closely, knew she looked paler than usual. 'Catching butterflies is cruel. What are you going to get her to do? Stick pins in them then kill them?'

'Catch one, look at it, let it go. Maybe it'll decide it likes it in her garden and it'll stay.'

'The net will damage its wings. You might as well just kill it.'

He sighed. 'Okay. Let's make it a fishing net.'

'Fishing is cruel.'

'Not with a net, it's not,' he said sharply. 'There are no hooks in the mouth and you can let them go.'

'I suppose. And even if you do damage it,' she said bitterly, 'there are plenty more in the sea—right?'

'I'm only interested in one fish,' he said, bitter right back. 'But this fish is probably so fickle it'll soon forget it was ever caught.'

Stung, she looked right at him. *Forget?* How could she forget that night?

If anything, he looked angrier. 'Do you always criticise your customers' purchases?'

'Only those who make unsubtle digs while I wrap.'

'Well, you're doing a hopeless job of wrapping it. Anyone could guess what it is.'

'Hide it behind some other presents.'

'That's a cop-out. I expected more from you.'

'You know I can't give it.'

'More like *won't*.'

'All right, then—*won't*.'

'And why is that?'

'Would you please excuse me? I have to—' She didn't bother even thinking of a reason, just left the desk and hurried across the shop floor to the staff stairwell, wanting to get back behind her desk—or cry in the ladies' room—or something.

'Imogen.'

He was right behind her.

'Imogen, stop.'

She did. She'd known this would happen—that it would affect her work. But worse than that, she couldn't look at him for fear he'd see the longing that just had to be written all over her in indelible ink.

'Talk to me. *Now.*' He climbed to the step below hers. 'You come to me, you say you want me, and so we—' He stopped, and then growled at her, 'I refuse to believe that what happened the other night was so awful you can't even look at me now.'

'No!' It took a couple of tries for her to say more. 'Of course it wasn't awful,' she mumbled, feeling terrible he'd thought that. 'It was…amazing.'

She heard his release of breath. Then his hand took hers. She closed her eyes—dumb move, because all the power of sense was transferred to touch, and she could feel him so much closer.

His fingers squeezed gently. 'Precisely why we should spend some more time together.'

He *was* closer. She could feel the length of his body— only a couple of inches away.

Trembling, she pulled her hand free. 'Precisely why we shouldn't.'

But he moved faster, hands gripping her upper arms, stopping her from climbing farther. 'All I want to do is get to know you better.'

His eyes were level with hers. She saw the light in them, chose to interpret it as one thing only. 'All you want to do is sleep with me.'

'You're making assumptions.' He gave her a small shake. 'You need to get to know me, too.'

For what purpose? What more was there to know that she didn't already? He was a fantastic lover, able to take her into another realm with just one touch. He was bright and funny and charming, and all too easy to fall in love with.

She knew that about him.

But she also knew that they held different priorities,

and had different views on what was precious in life. Ultimately they were on different trajectories—and he had the power to make her veer off course and crash. Her one other affair had done that. She couldn't let it happen again.

He lifted one hand from her arm, brushed the back of his fingers down her cheek. His blue eyes were intent on hers—so damn tempting.

'All that one night proved was that it wasn't enough. Not for me. And not for you.'

'But that was the agreement—one night.' She heard the desperate wobble in her voice, but had to try and hold fast anyway. 'You can't go back and renegotiate now.'

'The hell I can't,' he said softly. 'All's fair in love and war.'

'This isn't either of those things, Ryan.'

He didn't answer, just kept gazing deep into her eyes, as if he was searching for something right in her soul. She watched, shaking all over, until she could bear it no longer. She dropped her gaze to his mouth, so close to crumbling—knowing how good his kiss was, how close he was. It would only take the slightest step towards…

Suddenly she felt the pressure of his fingers on her arms tighten.

Had she swayed forward? Just the tiniest of millimetres? Surely not. She looked up to read his eyes.

His expression had lightened—he was almost twinkling, the corners of his mouth quirking up. With a lift of his brows he dropped his arms, turned and walked back down the stairs.

CHAPTER SEVEN

SOMEONE WAS PRESSING her buzzer and not letting it go. Half dozing on the sofa, the Saturday papers scattered around her, Imogen finally realised it wasn't a dream. She staggered to her feet, picked up the intercom handset by the door.

'What?' She'd had a rotten night's sleep and she was crabby now.

'It's Ryan. Come on out.'

'I'm not coming out.'

'If you don't come out, then I'm coming up. And if I come up you know what might happen. I think it's safer if you come out.'

She rested her head against the door. Damn, he was determined. He'd do it, too—break his way in if necessary—so he was right. It was much safer for her to go out there than let him come in here.

'Give me five minutes.'

Glancing at the clock, she saw it was after one o'clock—how had that happened? She pulled a woolly jumper on over her tee shirt and jeans, zipped up her boots. Swinging her hair back into a ponytail, she had a quick glance in the mirror and winced away from her reflection. Who needed make-up when Ryan was around? Thanks to the sensations just the thought of him inspired, she had colour in her cheeks, sparkles in her eyes, and lips redder than if she'd coated them with bright red stage make-up.

He was standing in the middle of the path, wearing a red roll-neck sweater over dark blue denim jeans. The sweater was fine wool and clung to his frame. Those muscles, that athletic body—wrapped in her favourite colour. It was a present she ached to unwrap. Instead she looked at the path ahead.

'How can I help?'

'Come for a walk with me.'

She hesitated.

'A walk, Imogen. Nothing dangerous.'

'Walking on these paths is always dangerous for me.'

'Good point.' He chuckled. 'I'd better hold your hand, then—help you balance.'

As he'd already taken her hand in his as he spoke, and started walking, she had little option but to go with him.

Trying not to enjoy it.

Trying not to want more.

They walked straight up to Princes Street and into the gardens. Lots of people were out walking—making the most of the rain-free afternoon. The Winter Wonderland and the outdoor ice rink were set up. They stood and watched the skaters for a while. He looked at her, his face all lit up with humour and a definite dare.

She shook her head, knowing what he was thinking.

'Come on—what have you got to lose?'

'An ankle? A leg?' *Dignity.* She hadn't skated in years, and she didn't want to fall flat on her face again. Not in front of him.

'It'll be fun.'

He made everything seem so simple. As they got nearer the rink, the sound of the blades as they scraped over the ice sent chills across her skin. Her fingers were numb as she pulled the rented skates on, and yet her cheeks felt hot.

He already had his skates on, able to stand on the thin blades of the boots with no problem, slipping his foot into place as if he'd done it a thousand times. She made him walk to the gate first, not wanting him to see the way she wobbled in the boots—and they weren't even on the ice yet.

She clutched the rail and gave him a baleful glare as he glided out a few metres—smooth and graceful as a swan. 'When did you last go skating?'

He grinned, winked, slid back towards her. 'Come on—I'll help you.'

She stared some more. He was a pro. 'Don't tell me,' she said sarcastically, as he took her hands and pulled her onto the ice. 'You did figure skating as a kid. Wore those tight leotard things and did triple axles or whatever.' She'd watched a few Winter Olympics. She knew good when she saw it.

He laughed. 'Ice hockey.'

Oh, great. Aggression on ice. 'Isn't that really violent?'

'It's challenging.' He was laughing. 'And great fun.'

She failed to see how sharp blades and flying pucks and big men going unstoppably fast could be fun. But she couldn't comment, could hardly keep her legs from splitting in opposite directions—and then they did, and her humour came bouncing back.

'It's like anything, Imogen. The more you work at it, the better you get.' He was containing his laughter. Just.

She didn't mind, was too busy giggling herself—giggling so hard, in fact, she lost control and sat with a bump.

'And when you fall down you get back up again.' He gave her a hand.

Like with the presents he'd brought her to wrap, she knew he wasn't just talking about skating.

'Sure, but you try not to make the same mistakes.' For example she knew she had to keep her legs *together* when near Ryan.

He gave her a sideways look. 'Are you in the habit of repeating your mistakes?'

'I'm trying not to.' Trying really hard. Only he was making it exceptionally difficult, and she was smiling too much to keep control of her emotions the way she should be.

He moved in front, skating backwards so he could face her.

'Okay.' She rolled her eyes. 'That's just showing off.'

'Skate with me, then. I won't let you fall.'

He went behind her, hands on her hips, locomotive style, pushing her gently but not too fast. 'See—you're getting it.'

'I haven't skated since I was a little kid.'

'Do you ice skate in New Zealand?'

'We have a few commercial rinks. We don't have many lakes that freeze, or anything. I went a few times—count 'em on one hand. But I did rollerblade.' And her balance was coming back now. Not enough to go super-fast, but enough to feel confident.

'Wearing hot pants?'

She laughed. 'Never.'

Once she had the rhythm he skated beside her, linking his arm through hers. He wasn't even watching where they were going. He was just watching her and smiling. 'Feel better?'

'You know I do.'

His smile deepened and he then looked ahead. 'There's nothing like fresh air to clear your head.'

She rubbed her nose. 'Very fresh air.'

'You got numb lips again?'

'No.' She wobbled. He chuckled.

They slowly went round the rink—again, and then again.

'Are you enjoying your studying?'

'Yes, I am. I never thought I would like studying that much, but actually it's great.' She'd found a job she was good at—and was determined to do even better. It was one thing she felt she could be sure of. Then she thought of *his* background and felt embarrassed. 'It's not like what you did, though—hardly Harvard.'

'I didn't go to Harvard.'

'You didn't?' She frowned. In that brief search she'd done she was sure she'd read that they all went to Harvard.

'My dad did, and my brother and sisters did. But I didn't want to.'

'What did you want to do?'

Now he looked a little embarrassed. 'I wanted to play ice hockey. So I did my undergrad degree in Canada—home of ice hockey.'

'Did you play?'

'Semi-pro.'

Wow. No wonder he was good at skating. But the no-to-Harvard was even more interesting. 'Did your dad mind?'

'For a while. He got over it.' He was quiet a moment. 'Once he saw how serious I was, he really came on board. He even built a rink at—'

'How come you ended up working for the family?'

He looked surprised at her interruption, but Imogen didn't want to hear about his money. Not, *Oh, I had a whim to play hockey, so Daddy built me my own stadium-sized rink* kind of money.

'I guess I didn't fall too far from the tree after all.' His smile was wide. 'I wanted to succeed in business, but I wanted to do it my own way. So I did my MBA at a school just outside Paris.'

'Paris?'

'Which was why doing French in Canada was helpful.'

Double-wow—a man of many talents. But then she'd known that already, hadn't she?

'And then I stayed on the Continent—away from the family empire until I was ready for it.'

'And you're ready now?'

'I think so.' He nodded. 'I'm determined to be.'

She glanced at him—that sounded a little as if Mr American-All-Star had the need to prove something. 'What happened to hockey?'

'A knee injury that kept me on the bench for most of my last season. A realisation that I did want to do other things.' He turned to her suddenly. 'What about you? How did you end up in Edinburgh? Why so far from home?'

Why indeed? She kept her focus on moving her skates. 'We all do it. Get a job for a while, earn some money, then go overseas and travel.'

'What job did you do?'

'Office admin in an accountancy firm.'

'Why didn't you do your studying with them?'

That would have been perfect—on-the-job experience in an accountancy firm. 'It didn't work out.'

'Why not?'

Because she'd been fool enough to sleep with her boss. Fool enough to think a guy like him could love a girl like her—as if their core values could ever harmonise.

'It just didn't.' Her legs wobbled. 'I like it here a lot. I love the store. It's a great environment. I love—'

'Mixing business and pleasure?'

She gave him a cool look. What exactly did he mean by that?

'Shopping.' He grinned. 'What woman doesn't like shopping? And you get to work *and* get qualified in one of the most exclusive stores in the country.'

He swapped position again, moved back behind her, only closer this time. He measured his legs to hers, matching the rhythm of her gliding, wrapped his arms around her waist.

'Are we ice dancing?' She couldn't get air to her lungs, and it wasn't because of the exercise.

'Just about.'

She really ought to move away. She really ought. But one more lap wouldn't hurt—would it?

One lap later she forced her flustered self to skate to the rail and jerk her head back to the rink. 'Show me how it's done properly.' She needed him to move away *now*, or she was in grave danger of moving his hands south into more intimate places. His body was harder than the ice they were skating on and burning hotter than the sun—despite their layers of clothing.

'You've accused me of showing off once already,' he protested, still deliciously close to her. 'I'm not risking that again.'

'I won't say that this time. Show me. I can feel you reining yourself in.'

'Oh, I am. But not about the skating.'

'Go burn some energy, then.'

He looked tempted.

'Go on. Go. It'll take me for ever to get these skates off anyway.'

'Okay, then. Just a couple of minutes.'

He went with her to the exit, made sure she was fine sitting on one of the benches and able to get her boots off. Laughing, she shooed him away. Watched him and promptly forgot about undoing her laces.

How could such a big guy look so graceful? How did he glide so smoothly like that? He was fast, fluid. She wasn't the only one watching him. Some kids were pointing him out to each other. Others on the ice moved, giving him a clean run on the outer edge of the rink.

His hair was wind-whipped, his eyes glowing. Colour tinged his cheeks, but best of all was the wide white smile and the sheer joy emanating from him. He seemed so in tune—with his body, with his place in the world. Confident, assured, capable, free—happy doing what he liked to do. Simple. He scared her. He really scared her. That carefree approach—enjoying every moment in life to its full and not worrying about tomorrow. But then, he'd never had to worry about tomorrow.

Sliding to a stop with a harsh scrape, he called over the barrier to her. 'What's that look for?'

'I'm feeling sorry for your mother. It must have been hell giving birth to you with those ice skates attached to your feet.'

He laughed.

She shook her head. 'Seriously. You're good.'

Seriously, he was gorgeous.

'You're not bad yourself.'

'Ha.'

THE WINTRY EDINBURGH afternoon sky was darkening. And she was having very bad thoughts of hot baths and even hotter bodies. 'I should get—'

'I'll walk with you.' He knew. 'Don't want you slipping and grazing your knee down the hill.'

'Thank you.' She was only slightly sarcastic.

'Means I get to hold your hand some more.'

'Uh-huh.'

'A man's got to take what he can get.'

'You think?'

'Hell, yes.'

She shivered, all hot and cold and going crazy.

He pulled her into the café at the bottom of the hill. 'I can think of a better way of warming you up from the inside out, but I think this is the only way you're going to let me today.'

Her reply was simply to order coffee.

Somehow another hour passed. An hour in which he shared jokes and bad ice hockey stories and had her laughing so hard that at one point tears were running down her cheeks. The skies outside completely darkened, and in the warm window of the café the lights from the fake Christmas tree in the corner flickered on his face. She was so nearly spellbound.

He didn't hold her hand as they walked the final stretch to her apartment in the tenement block. Imogen felt the tension rising between them. Neither of them was laughing now.

Partway up her path, he asked, 'Come out with me tonight?'

'Ryan, I can't.'

'You mean you won't? You won't even give us a chance?'

'We're co-workers. There is no *us*. We had one night.'

'Even then you didn't stick around 'til morning. Technically you owe me a few hours.'

'Ryan…' Was he joking? Couldn't he see how much of an edge she was on? A big, high, wide-open window ledge—and she was scared.

She heard his sigh. 'Don't worry, sweetheart. I'll claim them later.'

He turned, and she couldn't see anything at all any more as her vision blurred. Then she heard him mutter something else and he turned back.

'Damn it, I *am* going to take this.'

But he didn't take. His lips were warm and gentle as they teased over hers—inviting, invoking such delight that, helpless to resist, she opened for him, let him deepen the contact. Only then his kiss gave and offered too much—*promise*. Such sweet promise.

Every muscle inside her softened, aching to take the rest of him in, wanting him to take more. Reeling, she felt ready to give in, was longing to believe in him.

But she knotted her hands together to stop herself reaching for him. Digging her nails into her palms to keep that last part of her rational. She couldn't have him again—not now she knew his potency. She'd be addicted, she'd be *lost* to him—and all too soon he'd be finished with her and she would lose everything. Promises made were too easily broken.

He lifted his head, looking more sombre than she'd ever seen him. Gone was the usual smile in his eyes. Instead he studied her so seriously that she felt afraid.

'Whoever he was, he must have been one hell of a jerk.'

She pulled back, face on fire, her brain kicking her body as she remembered. 'He was.'

But Ryan stepped into her space, lifting her chin with his finger, forcing her to look him in the eye as he had the last word. 'I'm not him.'

CHAPTER EIGHT

RYAN HAD SPENT MANY long hours putting himself through punishing physical workouts, but he'd never felt the kind of complete pain he felt now as he walked. It was as if a vital part of him was slowly being pulled from his body with every step he took away from her. But he had to go. Understood that she needed time to trust him as well as want him. He sensed her capitulation to the latter had been close, but he didn't want her surrendering to his demands. He wanted her to come to him with her own demands. He wanted her to want him the way he wanted her, to be able to take as well as be taken—and not just sexually. Ultimately he wanted them to be *bound*.

Good grief. He was dreaming of being shackled—*wanting* it? Yes, wanting one woman, only the one, for evermore. And it was her. Shell-shocked, he found himself walking back through Princes Street Gardens and beyond, along the Royal Mile and down to Arthur's Seat—setting a punishing pace up the steep path and round the hill. Even so he felt he had energy to burn. His grandfather had said it would happen like this—with fast, total certainty. He hadn't believed him. But it had—just like that.

He'd loved her company today. Loved her teasing eyes, her dry comments, finding out just a touch about what had made her the way she was. There was so much more to discover, but he made himself breathe. There would be time. And for once he'd enjoyed talking about his life. She'd been interested, but she hadn't been dazzled. Hadn't wanted to know about the rink at their winter holiday home, or the luxury of the Taylor family compound— the Olympic-sized heated pool, the private cinema. She didn't know the half of it. And it seemed she didn't want to. As a result he'd shared more with her than he had with his closest teammates—which was saying something.

Eventually he trudged back to his hotel, had a long, long shower and then forced himself to dress in his tux. He had to go to this do—and it beat sitting in his hotel room being reminded of how she'd lain spread in his bed and screamed for him. Slow and steady was how he'd win her. He'd made ground today. He had to go and show his face tonight. It was too good a business opportunity to miss.

MONDAY MORNING HE SPENT in his hotel room, having a video conference with his siblings. His brother was keen to push the European expansion plans forward, which meant there was a ton more work and a ton more pressure on Ryan. They'd talk details over Christmas, so before then there would be no time for distraction. But as he walked to the store he found himself looking forward to seeing Imogen, working on her, all the more determined to win her—wholeheartedly.

He went straight up to the accountancy suite, but she wasn't at her desk. He glanced at the clock—lunchtime. He grinned and went back downstairs.

'Jingle Bells' was playing for the seventeen thousandth time. He put a wooden duck-head-handled umbrella on the table in front of her. She looked up, and her smile died. It didn't just die, it went nasty. Her green eyes burned bitter holes right through him.

'Imogen—'

'Who's this for?' Her voice was poisonous. 'Your Great-Aunt Agatha?'

Oh, my, she was feeling it today. So he gave her the truth. 'Actually, it's for me.' He gave her a meaningful look. 'Someone keeps raining on my parade.'

But she wasn't reading his less-than-subtle irony. 'It didn't look like you were too weatherbeaten on Saturday night. The way that woman was all over you, no rain could get near your skin.'

'Imogen—'

'And as this is for you—' she shoved the umbrella back at him '—you don't need it gift-wrapped, do you?'

He ignored the umbrella and grabbed hold of her arm instead. Firmly. 'My office,' he said softly. 'Now.'

'Actually, Mr Taylor, I'm on my lunch break.'

He moved around the desk, still holding her arm. 'Good. Because what I want to discuss is personal.'

'I don't want—'

'I don't want to do this in front of many of my employees and even more of my customers.' He walked. 'But I will if I have to.'

She walked with him—stalked, really—in complete silence up the staff stairs and into his office. He closed the door behind them. He could feel Shona watching, but he didn't care. Something had upset Imogen, and he needed to know what.

'Explain what you meant. What woman?'

'Saturday night. The casino,' she breezed. 'Don't think I care. It doesn't bother me at all.'

Ryan took a step back and leaned on the edge of his desk. Saturday night had been a commitment made before he'd even arrived in Edinburgh. A fundraiser at the casino with the who's who of Scottish society and all the media darlings out in full force. It had been a good opportunity to meet some local business people. He'd bumped into Saskia on the way in and helped her navigate the flashing bulbs. Looking at Imogen now, he couldn't help feeling both satisfied and sardonic—and couldn't quite hide either from his tone as he asked, 'It doesn't bother you?'

'Of course not.' She held her chin high, but wouldn't meet his gaze. 'But I don't want you flirting with me when you have other fish to fry.'

He waited until she did look up at him—albeit sort of sideways. 'Your eyes are looking very green today, Imogen.'

They flashed then—pure jealous fire.

He bit back his smile, knowing it would make her furious, but she must have seen it anyway because she took a sudden step forward. 'You have it too easy, Ryan Taylor. Women, work—everything.'

'Do I?' He wasn't finding *her* all that easy—quite the contrary.

'Guys like you.' She spat the words. 'You're born with more money than you could ever need, given the kind of privilege and power that can't help but corrupt—'

His humour fled the scene as he absorbed her vehemence. 'Tell me this, Imogen. What do you *think* you know about "guys like me"?' It was obvious she'd had a bad experience and he needed to understand it. 'Who was he? What did he do to you?'

'I'm not—'

'It's about time you talked. Come on—hit me with it. Let me know what I'm up against. Because your going off like this is way off base. So explain. *Now.*'

'You want the whole sordid story?' Her colour was high and her voice wobbled.

'Every last detail.'

So he could get rid of her baggage and get on with getting her to trust him.

IMOGEN'S FURY WAS A RAW beast that had been brewing for forty-eight hours—since she'd watched the late news on Saturday night and seen that model woman draped all over Ryan as they'd walked into the casino. Jealousy wasn't the word. She'd turned the rage on herself. Her stupid, foolish, soft-hearted self.

'His name was George. George Bailey-Jones Junior, to be precise.' She hated herself for the way she'd succumbed to his double-barrelled charm. 'He dazzled me, Ryan. He was smooth and fast and I was spinning. I couldn't believe that a guy like him could be that into me.'

'A guy like him?'

'Wealthy—from one of *the* families. Successful. Someone. Being with him elevated me, right?' She choked. 'What a thrill to be chased by him, to have him flirt with me. He was on his knees for me—or so he said. What I didn't know about was his gambling problem and his coke habit.'

'What happened?'

'He got in trouble—had several bad runs at the table. Hell, I've never even been inside a damn casino. I'm not interested. He came and picked me up late one night. I had no idea. Didn't know why he was so upset.'

'He was high?'

'In another universe.' She nodded. 'He crashed the car.'

'You were hurt?'

'A cut on the head. Nothing serious.'

There was a low grunt that might have been a snort.

'His family swung into action. They hired a brilliant

lawyer who got him off, smothered the scandal—including the fact that when they inspected his work discrepancies were found. And he'd got into my bank account and cleared out my pathetic savings.' She'd been taken for such a ride—literally. 'They repaid his debt, repaid me. But they didn't want me around. I lost my job and was shut out.'

'This was where you worked?'

'Oh, didn't I say?' She glared at him. 'He was my boss.'

He met her gaze coolly, waiting silently, until she could stand it no longer and the rest spewed out.

'I've never gambled, never done drugs, and yet somehow it was *me* who'd led him astray because I was a cheap chick from the 'burbs. The posh boy who'd had the expensive education wasn't to blame at *all*.' Despite all his flaws, *she* hadn't been good enough. She'd been a bit of fluff—fun for a while, but never anyone someone like him could be serious about. 'He lied to me, he stole from me, and then he said he'd never really cared for me. I'd meant nothing to him. I was fun to fool around with, and an easy supply of petty cash.'

'I'm sorry he did that to you.' Ryan stood with his legs wide, arms firm across his chest. 'But I really don't see what it has to do with me.'

'Oh, come on.' She threw him a withering look. '*Your* family background makes George look like he grew up on the streets.'

'*What?*'

Imogen tensed at the arctic tone his voice had taken.

'Are you suggesting that because I have more money, and supposedly more prestige and more privilege than him, I'm going to betray you even worse than he did?'

Imogen caught the anger in his eyes and trembled inside.

'How can you think so little of me? Trust me so little?' His step towards her was positively menacing. 'What do you think I've been doing these last ten years? Yes, I had more opportunities than most. But I'm not going to apologise for that. I'd have a lot more to apologise for if I hadn't taken them and worked as hard as I did. I earned my degrees on merit. I earned my spot in the team on merit. If you're not up to it on the ice you're going to be found out pretty quick, believe me. And I *worked* my way into this job, Imogen—I wasn't given it as my birthright. I know my field and I'm good at it. I don't need you thinking whatever small-minded rubbish it is you're thinking.'

She was thinking the truth—wasn't she? She wavered, thought about his business performance so far. Even she couldn't deny he knew what he was doing. So, okay, maybe he did have more integrity than George in a business sense. But how could she know if he had a stronger personal code?

'Why did you sleep with me?' He pressed on with his attack. 'Was I just some stud for the night?'

'I was trying to play it your way.' She'd tried to have a one-night stand—for the fun of it, the pure pleasure. But she'd been worse than an ostrich. Not content with putting her head in sand, she'd tried to put her whole body in ice. She'd refused to admit that her attraction to him was more than physical, that it couldn't be quenched by one wild night. He'd made her feel so much more, made her want so much more...and she was terrified.

'Which just goes to show you really have no clue about me. I wasn't playing with you, Imogen. I wanted you. I still want you. It's that simple.'

'It is *not* simple.' Sex like that could never be simple—not for her. Because it wasn't just sex.

'It is.'

'I don't want to be used by you.'

'Well, isn't that exactly what you're doing to me? I'm trying to get to know you, and you insist on treating me like a one-night stand.'

Because she couldn't afford not to. Not only was he her *boss*, he was so much the incredibly eligible bachelor he'd never want to settle—and certainly not with someone from as far over on the wrong side of the tracks as she was. He was the kind of man who'd enjoy savouring the flavours of a gilt-edged smorgasbord for ever.

'Leopards don't change their spots, Ryan.'

'And that's the whole *point*, Imogen. I'm not a leopard.'

Did he have to look so intent? 'Well, you're hardly a pussycat.'

'Maybe I'm an eagle.'

She frowned, not getting his point.

'We mate for life.'

All the blood left her brain. So did all the oxygen. Nearly catatonic, she whispered, 'You don't mean that.'

'Don't I? How do you know?'

He was doing that magic thing with his eyes again. Making them burn bright and mesmerising. She fought to stay sane. He was joking, wasn't he? No way would they want the same kind of things—they were light years apart in experience and lifestyle.

She shook her head. 'You move so fast, so decisively, so certain that everything is *simple*.' She stared, wishing she could believe in that glow of his. 'I need more time.'

'For what? What exactly is it you need to know? My favourite colour is green, my star sign is Capricorn. Is that enough? Or do you need to spend some quality time with me—is that it? Because *you* were the one who said no to that,' he growled. 'I'd be with you every night if I could.'

Every *night*.

'Quality time?'

'That's right. Every long, slow, wonderful minute.'

As she stared into his eyes her heart decided to beat at half its usual tempo as desire seeped into her skin and her bones and all the stuff in between. She hardly heard him talking now.

'Look at me, Imogen. Not my name or family or connections—just look at *me*.' His expression darkened. 'I thought you were different. I thought you weren't impressed by all the nonsense that people think about my background. And you weren't. You hate me for it, and you hate wanting me in spite of it.' He towered over her. 'Do you really think I'm like that guy? Am I worth the risk? You decide, and then let me know.'

Slowly she shook her head again. The only thing she was certain of was her uncertainty—and it made her deny herself and him. 'You expect too much from me.'

'And you don't expect enough from me,' he snapped, words flying, temper fraying. 'Look, we're either on or we're off. I'm not having any in-the-middle mess. I've got too much on my plate to be stewing over where I stand with you. If you want to know the truth, it's damn inconvenient to have met you right now, and I don't have the time to convince you. Here I am, thinking about how badly I want to get you naked instead of thinking about the store. You're the biggest distraction

I've ever had in my life. I've finally agreed to work with my family, and I refuse to stuff it up because of you.'

So it *was* just sex. He wanted her naked—to be his stress relief, not the cause of stress.

She retaliated rashly, her anger breaking her ability to reason. 'Fine. If I'm in the way, let me leave. I resign with immediate effect.'

'Don't be so childish.' He lost the last grip on his temper too. 'Didn't I say this would never affect your career here? Well, it won't. You don't have to resign. I'll stay well clear and never bother you again.'

CHAPTER NINE

HADN'T SHE GOT WHAT she wanted? He was not bothering her. Not even looking at her. Only commenting on work, and only when absolutely necessary. He closed his office door now—summoned Shona in when he needed her rather than coming out and chatting with his former relaxed style.

Every lunchtime she worked on the wrapping table, and for half an hour or more after her workday had ended. He never stopped by—no more ridiculous presents to verbally joust about. Instead, she chatted to the students on wrapping duty—got to know their names, what they were studying, what they wanted for Christmas.

What she wanted she couldn't have—and it was her own fault. She was realising she was the biggest fool on the planet. Why couldn't she just have taken whatever it was he had to offer? Why had she had to do the whole drama queen routine?

Because she was too scared. Too insecure. Too afraid of being hurt to follow through on a seasonal fling. And she'd held her defences, resisted him and rejected him.

So why was she hurting more now than when George had let her down? She'd been humiliated and used by him—yet she was more upset about the one little thing Ryan wasn't doing.

She just wished he'd look at her again.

'What are you doing for Christmas, Imogen?' Shona's smile was too kind, her eyes too astute.

Imogen's brain battled her muscles and stopped the wince. Christmas was only a few days away now, and she'd buried the lonely reality of it down deep. 'I'm having dinner with some other Kiwi orphan friends.' The lie was thin, but it came easily. 'We're having pavlova...a few drinks.' Making up some details to make it more credible. She could be doing exactly that if she'd bothered to hook up with the one person from New Zealand she knew in Edinburgh. But she hadn't.

'I didn't know you had Kiwi friends here.'

'A couple.' Really just that one, who she hadn't even e-mailed. She'd wanted a totally fresh start—wanted to forget her life in New Zealand—or the last few months of it at least.

She turned her head, catching something moving in the corner of her eye. Ryan was behind Shona, standing in his doorway, obviously listening in. His eyes were very bright, very blue. For a moment she was entranced as ever. Then she saw his frown—his eyes narrowing, brows lowering—and she knew he saw right through her. He didn't believe her.

'Well, if you'd like you could come to dinner at my place and have an authentic Scots Christmas.'

So Shona didn't believe her either. This was painful now. They were both looking at her with...*pity*.

Ugh. Why wouldn't he go away? She'd hardly seen him for days, and now he was standing like a statue, listening in on the one conversation that was mortifying.

'Oh, Shona—thank you, but no. I couldn't possibly impose.'

'No imposition. We always have too much food anyway.'

'Yes,' Imogen replied quickly, 'doesn't everyone? But really I'm looking forward to having my first Christmas away, not going with such a traditional day.'

Liar, liar—her pants should be hot ashes already. She loved tradition.

'Well, if you change your mind...'

'Thank you.'

It really was very sweet. But once again she wanted the ground to open up and snatch her away in one big bite. Please let this conversation be over. She chanced another glance at him. He was still looking at her, leaning against the doorjamb, papers in hand, legs too long and chest too strong for her not to start panting.

She twisted her mouth—almost smiling, but not quite able to. She wanted to say she was sorry. She wanted to talk to him. She wanted him to tease her again.

Instead he went back to his office. But he didn't shut the door.

As USUAL, AFTER HER official workday had ended, Imogen stayed on in the Christmas Shop. 'O Holy Night' was playing again. She focused on the wrap and the ribbon, and helping to make someone else's season that little bit special. Five customers into it, she saw him watching from where he stood by the forest of brightly lit trees in the corner. Jacketless, arms folded across his chest, showing off his wonderfully broad shoulders. Their eyes met and held—his as blue as ever.

Her heart beat faster and all her fingers suddenly seemed to have hard plaster casts on them. They wouldn't work properly. She tied a bow for the third time and looked down the queue at all the people waiting. Should she excuse herself after this customer? Ryan looked as if he might want to talk. She wanted to talk to him—to try again. Slower perhaps this time. She glanced at him again, felt the unstoppable upsurge of emotion—want and need and other things too scary to name. Maybe not so slow. Nerves and indecision and insecurity gave her hot and cold sweats.

But her current customer had four presents to be wrapped. And when she'd finally done the last Ryan had gone.

Later she went up to the office to pick up her coat—more than hopeful that he'd be there. But the lights were out and it was empty.

She walked home feeling more lonely than she ever had in all the eight months she'd lived in Edinburgh. Until he'd arrived she'd been fine—hadn't she? She'd put everything into her work and her study, forged a friendship with Shona, and been happy to settle for a safe, quiet life.

Only now she wasn't happy. Not at all. Ryan Taylor had made her want all kinds of things—things that she couldn't believe he could want to give her—things like love and commitment. There was only one thing to do. She pulled out her phone and dialled.

'Hello?'

'Hi, Mum, it's me.' Even just hearing her mother's voice gave her a lift.

'Imogen, love, how are you? It's *Imogen*!'

Imogen held the phone from her ear as her mother let her father and the rest of the neighbourhood know she'd rung. 'I'm fine, Mum—how are you?'

'Good, love, good.'

Imogen knew she'd left it too long between phone calls. Had blamed it on being busy, with working full-time and studying on top. In reality she'd isolated herself from her family and friends. She'd been so humiliated, so hurt. But had her own silly pride made her hurt more?

'Have you got everything organised?' She was eager to bond over day-to-day detail.

'Well, I can hardly shut the fridge, as usual—your father ordered a ham the size of Australia.'

Imogen smiled at the familiar mental image. 'Were you up all night making the pav?'

'Of course.' Her mother sighed. 'We have far too much food.'

'You'll burn it off playing cricket.'

'I suppose. Derek's mown a pitch in the park again. Don't know what the council will say.'

Imogen would have laughed then—if it hadn't been for the wistful ache in her body. 'They won't mind. It's Christmas.' Homesickness washed over her. Her family had fun traditions.

'It's going to be a good day. What about you, love? You got good plans?'

'Oh, yes,' she lied. 'I'm having dinner with some friends.'

'Did my parcel arrive?'

'Yes, and I promise I haven't opened it yet.' Although given her mother had dutifully named every item on the customs sticker on the outside of the box she knew exactly what it contained.

As she listened to her mother talk about their plans, she remembered the previous Christmas, and the shame she'd felt. Her parents had rallied round her, but all she'd done was get out of there as fast as possible. She'd let the nightmare of George make her feel as if she and her family weren't good enough—not even for a creep like him. She'd turned her back and run away. How could she have been so disloyal to them? Her parents worked hard and loved harder. She should be proud of them, and proud of where she'd come from. She'd been stupid in thinking she had nothing to offer. And she'd been even more stupid in laying George's failings onto Ryan. Ryan was more of a man than George could ever be—and he was honest. His accusation had been right—she'd been childish. She needed to grow up and grow some courage.

SHE GOT TO WORK LATER than usual the next day. She had frittered away time trying to think of a way she could fix things with Ryan. She'd been so scathing, so insulting, and he hadn't deserved it. She wanted to take a chance on him—but would he still want to give her one?

His office was empty and dark. She tried to relax, but was anxious all morning. Still he didn't arrive. At last she could take the agony no more.

'Shona, what time is Ryan getting in?'

'Oh, pet.' Shona looked up from her desk. 'He's gone back to the States for Christmas with his family. Left last night. Didn't you know?'

'Oh.' Imogen felt as if she was in a plane that had suddenly plunged two thousand feet. 'Of course.' Her stomach had been left up at cruising altitude while her body was hurtling to the ground.

'That reminds me.' Shona opened her drawer and pulled something from the top. 'He left everyone one of these.' She handed Imogen an envelope. 'Christmas card, I think. Who knows? Maybe it'll have a nice bonus in it.'

Imogen didn't want a bonus. She didn't want a card. She wanted to see him, and more than anything she wanted to touch him.

She waited for her somersaulting stomach to rejoin the rest of her before sliding a finger beneath the seal and pulling out the card. As she opened it, a red heart—scarlet red—fluttered to her desk. She picked it up, using the loop of gold thread at the top. In the centre of the heart another heart shape had been cut out—a smaller heart, hung by a gold thread in the space. A heart enclosed in another heart. As she hung it on her finger the heart swung and the smaller heart spun inside the larger one. Down near the bottom on one side he'd scrawled his name and the year.

He'd made a neat job of it, but it was undeniably, heart-breakingly home-made.

Imogen didn't think she'd ever received anything so precious in all her life. Now her stomach had tied itself into more kinds of knots than a round-the-world sailor could master.

'I don't think anyone else got one of those,' Shona said quietly, slyly.

Shona was no fool, but Imogen couldn't bear to talk to her about him. 'Do you mind if I go for a walk?'

'No. Take as long as you like.'

Imogen stood, determined to get out of there before she bawled—or threw up.

'He'll be back in the New Year,' said Shona. 'It's only a few days.'

But that felt like eons, and she needed to talk to him *now*—because she was more of a fool than the emperor with no clothes. *She* was the one not able to see what was right under her nose—until it was gone.

She walked along the busy street, barely noticing the Christmas crush and the cold of the wind through her shirt. She walked and walked, wanting to believe that there was so much more to his gesture than a simple Christmas decoration.

She got to the bridge where they'd kissed that first time. Even now she felt the passion of that moment burn.

She should have taken him then and held on tight. Why had she let one idiot ruin what was the most emotional experience of her life? Hadn't she let George do enough damage already?

She'd tried to bury it, to pretend that emotion didn't exist. Denied herself in the hope it would disappear. The stupid thing was that it hadn't worked anyway. That emotion was too strong, and now it threatened to overwhelm her.

She still had his Christmas card in her hand. She stopped halfway across the bridge and read it. It was a brief message in bold, black handwriting, wishing her a Merry Christmas. But it was the scrawl at the bottom—seemingly added in a rush at the end—that caught her attention.

'*Call me.*' There was a number alongside.

She got out her phone, dialled the number—and pressed the phone to her ear before she had the chance to think, chicken out or press the end button on the phone instead.

It rang and rang and rang. Then she heard his voice.

'Hi, it's…'

'Ryan, it's me. Imogen.'

But he was still talking.

'…can't take your call right now. Leave a message and I'll get back to you when I can.'

She took a deep breath. Waited ages for the beep—before realising the beep had already sounded and she was leaving a stalker silence and heavy breathing for him.

'Oh, I'm sorry, Ryan. It's Imogen. I didn't hear the beep. Um…' She cringed, breathed, ploughed on. 'I missed you today. I didn't get to say goodbye. But I got your card. And your… The heart. Ryan, I wish I could talk to you. I wish I could see you.' She was whispering now. 'I wanted to explain. You've always said this is simple, Ryan, and I've always said it isn't. But that's because I'm scared. It's hard admitting that, when *you're* so sure and confident in everything. I'm not sure about where this is going, and whether you really want what I want. But I went about it wrong and I pushed you away, and now you're gone, and the stupid thing is it's too late for me anyway. Because I do... I really have... fallen in lo—'

The beep was harsh, followed by another series of beeps signalling disconnection.

Imogen screwed up her face. Doubt and a sense of futility mounted. He'd probably forgotten her already. Worse, he might call her back and try to let her down gently—admitting that all he had wanted was a brief affair.

And then all her emotion erupted—hot rivers of rage and mortification and despair engulfed her. Long before she could think, she threw the phone over the railing.

It sank into the Water of Leith below.

CHAPTER TEN

'IMOGEN, WE NEED TO HAVE a meeting.'

Imogen looked up from where she'd been staring blankly at her computer screen. She wasn't quite crying into her coffee, but she wasn't far off.

'Now?'

'Yes. Let's go downstairs.'

Into the shop? Unable to muster the energy even to ask why, Imogen just stood and followed Shona. It was only when they went right to the basement and into the exclusive beauty salon there that she gave her manager a questioning look.

'It's a tradition of mine every Christmas Eve,' Shona said. 'I see no reason to change it.' She turned to the beautician. 'You have our appointments?'

'But Shona—'

Shona winked and followed the beautician to the big comfortable chairs behind the gleaming tables. 'Half an hour away isn't going to sink the books, Imogen. We've both been working very hard. I'll settle it with Ryan if there's any problem. But I'm sure there won't be.'

Imogen sat and studied her nails. It was the first time his name had come up between them since the day Shona had given her his card, and she still wasn't about to talk. Instead she gave herself over to the luxury of being pampered. Given how busy the in-store salon was at the best of times, Shona must have booked this months ago to get them in today.

Twenty minutes later, as she watched the beautician put on polish with skilled, sure strokes, she accepted the inevitable. She was going to have to leave. Everywhere she looked, just being in the store, she thought of him. And, as heartbreaking as the thought of leaving was, the thought of staying was devastating.

'What colour did you go with?' Shona asked from where she was seated at the table behind hers.

'Christmas red.' Actually, it was more like hussy red, but Imogen liked it and had decided to wear it on the outside for once—not just underneath. She had the jade shirt on—could pretend it was Christmas green. All she needed now was some light-up novelty earrings and, hey presto, season's greetings. If only she could jolly up her insides just as easily.

Hours later, some soprano was trilling her way through 'All I Want for Christmas', and there was an infinite queue of people wanting their last-minute presents wrapped. Imogen worked fast, glad of the business that kept her mind and body occupied. She didn't want the evening to end—didn't want the store to close. Because then she'd have to go home and face the reality of a lonely Christmas. So she kept her head down, folding paper and pulling ribbon, smiling hard as she handed each present over to each excited shopper.

Less than an hour to go and she was hot—and her happy day façade was starting to disintegrate.

'Excuse me, please.'

She jumped, eyes up, instantly alert. Had she just heard—?

Ryan?

She watched as he pushed his way to the front of the queue.

Weird how the music seemed to fade out and everyone around her seemed to stop still. Even Kristen, one of the not-spotty students, stopped wrapping and stood staring—as did her customer.

Only Ryan could have such an impact on the world. And Ryan looking like this was a force impossible to ignore.

She'd never seen him look so scruffy. Black jeans, a crumpled black tee shirt, rumpled hair. So damn gorgeous. So damn dangerous.

Because he made her heart stop. Then it slammed in her chest. She shuddered with the thud of it. Gripped the scissors as though determined to take them to the grave with her.

'Did you mean it?' He sounded as if he hadn't spoken in days, or maybe as if he'd done nothing but for months—his voice was worn out and raspy. 'Did you mean what you said?'

She looked into his face, saw past the travel stains and the sexy unshaved jaw to the tired eyes—the *vulnerable* eyes. She'd never seen any hint of uncertainty in him before, and she'd nearly missed it now.

Emotion clogged her throat. What an idiot she'd been. This guy was nothing like George. This guy was begging her to believe. Was there really that much hope hidden in there?

Suddenly she knew she had to repeat it, that most scary of things, in front of a store full of people. From somewhere she had to find courage. She gripped the scissors even harder. 'Actually, I didn't get to finish saying what I meant.'

'And what was that?'

No holding back. There was nothing more to lose. 'I love you.'

His lashes dropped, hiding his reaction from her. He cleared his throat. 'I have a present I'd like wrapped.'

'Did you hear what I said?'

'Yes. Can you wrap this, please?'

Imogen blinked. Felt her whole body toasting under the grill of humiliation. She wanted to evaporate, eviscerate—whatever, she wanted out of there. But she couldn't with all the world watching.

'It already is wrapped.'

'They didn't do such a good job. Can you do it again?'

With five bows? How humiliating. She ripped off the paper with rough jerks.

'It was done by one of those weird people who put the ribbon on the inside,' he said.

Sure enough, a deep red ribbon was underneath. She started to unwind it, quickly revealing a green and gold packet of chocolate-covered peppermint creams. She held the packet in one hand and stared at the ribbon in the other. Something was hanging on it:

'See—isn't it much more fun?'

She'd been too busy staring down to see that he'd moved around the table. Now he was right behind her. But she couldn't turn to look at him—couldn't take her eyes off—

'What?' Now it was her voice that was little more than a croak.

'Opening your presents on Christmas Eve,' he said in her ear. He took the ribbon from her shaking fingers, placed it over her head so it hung around her neck—and the gleaming square-cut diamond ring that was threaded on it rested between her breasts.

'We need to talk some more before you decide which finger to put that on.'

'Ryan—'

His hands were firm on her waist as he turned her around. 'But before we do that, we need to do this.'

He crushed her so close that it was a struggle to breathe, let alone raise her arms and cling. But somehow, eventually, despite kissing him back with the ferocity of a famished lioness, she managed. He smelt so good, tasted so good, felt so good. And she was so desperate to touch him that she shook with the fever of it. Next thing she knew he'd scooped her up and was striding somewhere—she didn't care where, because all that mattered was the way he was loving her with his lips.

Vaguely she figured that that the shrieking soprano's song must have been a live recording, because she could hear a lot of applause now. And then the noise died away and they were in the lift. Without breaking the searing kiss he managed to swipe his security card and press the button. Moments later his office door closed behind them, and he pinned her against the wall while he snibbed the lock.

'I can't wait for the hotel tonight,' he growled. 'It has to be the desk.'

'I've had a desk fantasy for weeks,' she admitted breathlessly.

The sudden blaze in his eyes was so wicked she'd have swooned if she'd had to be supporting her own weight. Instead she just leaned back as he placed her on the desk, and pulled his shirt to make him follow.

He didn't disappoint, raining kisses on her face and neck.

'I've missed you. Missed this. Longed for this.'

That rawness in his voice tugged deep in her heart.

'Ryan—'

'I love you. I fell in love with you that first day, when you tried to break into my hotel room—and afterwards, when you wouldn't look at me and were trying to prove how efficient you are.'

She shook her head. Still couldn't quite believe. 'But this is so fast. Who's to say you won't change your mind just as fast?'

He lifted his head from where he was kissing the base of her throat. Looked deep into her eyes. 'Have *you* ever felt this way with anyone else?'

She shook her head again. She could answer that honestly. She'd never felt so inside-out before.

'Then trust it, Imogen. Trust in me. Trust in us. Trust yourself.'

She wanted to—so much.

He smiled then—the sweetest, gentlest of smiles. 'It doesn't matter anyway. Because I have the rest of our lives to prove it to you.'

Her cry was smothered by his mouth.

'We'll be together, you can study—whatever. Do whatever. Just let me love you.' He kissed her. 'I've missed you too much.'

He was right. This was so right. Her hands went round his neck again, holding him tight so she could kiss him back. And in doing so she revealed everything—her need, her desire, but most of all her love.

'This is the real deal, sweetheart.'

With his words his love washed over her, destroying the last speck of her reserve. She wanted him—him and only him, and all of him—and now felt no need to fight it.

She unbuttoned her blouse, loving his groan as he saw her breasts. He bent his head, kissed them, and when he sucked her erect nipple into his mouth she was the one to groan. He spread his hand wide over her other begging breast and gently massaged it.

With firm fingers she pushed up his tee shirt, and he pulled away to wrench it over his head. She took the chance to unbutton his jeans. When she saw him she could wait no longer. She lay back, wriggling so she could slip off her knickers and pull up her skirt. He leaned over her, hands pressing into the desk either side of her, staring as if she was the most beautiful thing he'd ever seen.

She bent her knees, putting her feet wide on the edge of the desk so she was utterly open to his hot, hungry gaze. Wanton. Willing—so willing.

'Imogen, I—' Every muscle in his body was clenched hard.

'Please, Ryan,' she interrupted, arching towards him. 'I want you. I love you.'

He moved fast—holding her hips, lifting her to meet him, thrusting long and hard and full. Her cry of delight was utterly instinctive. He gritted his teeth and she saw determination flash in his face, but she held onto him, used her hands and her hips, driving him so there was no chance for either of them to regain control.

The desperate need that had been denied for days was unleashed. Frantic, they surged together again and again. Imogen felt wild freedom calling to her—the primal, almost animal joy that she could only get with him.

'Harder,' she begged him unnecessarily.

His eyes had gone cobalt, strain showed in the veins in his neck as he pumped with fast, fierce force.

For one long moment her body went rigid with the unbearable agony of anticipation, and then she collapsed, writhing in ecstasy, crying her satisfaction to him. Locked into her one last time, he, too, shouted, coming hard just after her.

His body crushed hers to the desk as they both lay panting.

'I knew you were efficient, but…hell!'

She smiled, an all-feminine sense of satisfaction flowing through her.

He must have sensed it, because he propped himself up on one elbow and smiled down at her. 'I won't always let you be efficient, you know.'

'I know. I'm looking forward to it.' She ran a hand over his rough jaw, saw up close the tiredness darkening his features. 'You're missing your family Christmas.'

'Yeah, but I've got some good plans for tomorrow.'

'Like what?'

'I'm going to get naked, place chocolate-covered peppermint creams all over my body and let you eat them off me.'

She giggled. 'That sounds like a plan. *I'm* going to spend the day wearing nothing but my new lacy knickers from Santa.'

'Another fine tradition is born.'

She hugged him close, turning her cheek to his. When she opened her eyes she saw all the presents she'd gift-wrapped for him piled against the wall behind his desk.

'Hey, isn't that your cousin Jodie's down jacket? Why didn't you take it back home with you?'

He lifted his head, looked behind him at the present mountain, and laughed. 'I made her up.'

'Uh-huh.' Just as she'd suspected.

His smiling eyes showed he knew she knew. 'I just wanted to talk to you. Wanted to get to you the way you were getting to me. Wanted to make it hard for you the way you were making it hard for me.'

'By getting me to wrap presents?'

'By making it difficult to wrap presents. And they were, right?'

'Yes,' she laughed. 'That's outrageous. What about Donna—did you make her up, too?'

'Actually, she's real. But she's about thirty-five now, and has no need for an abacus.' He laughed and leaned into her some more. 'There's more, you know. That I didn't get a chance to make you wrap.'

'No?'

'A broom. A small garden fountain. A rocking horse.'

'A garden fountain?'

'Yeah. It was the one thing I thought you couldn't possibly wrap. But it's really heavy. I don't think you could actually lift it, either.'

She ran her hand over his jaw, loving the way his body had hardened again, the way he was slowly moving inside her. 'You're crazy.'

'Yeah,' he grinned. 'Crazy about you.'

'I'm sorry I didn't trust you. Or me.'

'Sometimes trust takes time,' he murmured. 'You needed longer, and that's okay because I wanted for ever.'

He drew their foreplay out, making her suffer with his slowness this time. Teasing until they were both beyond teasing and all too serious and truly intense. She spoke his name, showing she loved him simply in the way she said it.

She floated with the feeling of tender, complete relief as she cradled him. The desk was hard under her back, but she wouldn't have had him move for all the world—in her heart she'd never felt more comfortable.

He toyed with the ribbon that still hung around her neck. 'I knew the minute I stepped on the plane that I'd made the wrong decision. I shouldn't have gone. Should have stayed here and sorted it out with you sooner. But as it turns out there was something I needed to get from home.' He followed the ribbon down to the ring. 'You know what I want to ask you, don't you?'

She needed to breathe—had gone all giddy. 'Too soon.'

'No,' he whispered. 'It happens. Let me tell you about this ring. It belonged to my grandmother. My grandfather proposed the day they met. She said he railroaded her into everything. He bought it with every cent of his savings. Said there was nothing worth investing in more than his relationship with her. So they married. And together they worked in the local store—she behind the counter, he did deliveries on his bike. Eventually they got the opportunity to buy into it, and then they expanded and the empire was born. They were together for fifty-two years, until she died. He died not long after her. He always said I was like him—going on instinct, determinedly doing my own thing. And he told me that when it happened it would be simple—for me at least. He wanted me to pass this on to the one woman I knew was for me.'

The diamond caught the light as he held it between them.

'I tried to call you from the plane, but I kept getting a no signal message from your phone company. So I called my folks, and they and an uncle, and my brother, both my nosy parker sisters and an even nosier cousin, drove all the way to the airport to meet me and bring me this ring. We had an hour together in the club lounge before I turned around and got on another plane.' He groaned. 'We're just normal people, Imogen. They said to say hi.'

Imogen's eyes filled. He reached into his desk drawer, pulled out scissors, cut the ribbon round her neck and pulled the ring free of it.

'You know you can choose which hand you want to wear this on, but there's something you need to understand. You're right. I'm decisive, and I'm very determined. I work on instinct and I'm rarely wrong. In this case I know I'm not wrong. I have never, ever felt this way about anyone. I know you're the woman I'm meant to spend my life with. You're the woman I'm meant to make babies with. You're the woman I'm going to marry.'

'I thought you said you were going to *ask* me.'

He held the ring up. 'I'm asking you now.' His eyes shone with love, compelling, wordlessly asking.

She held out her hand, the left one, and he took it gently in his. As the ring slid down, so did her tears.

He caught them with tender kisses. 'It can be two months or two years from now if you want. But when you're ready, you'll marry me.'

Eyes closed, lost to sensation, lost to love, she instinctively nodded. 'Absolutely I will marry you.'

It was one year. It was Christmas Eve. It was fabulous.

* * * * *

HARLEQUIN® A *Romance* FOR EVERY MOOD™

CLASSICS

Quintessential, modern love stories
that are romance at its finest.

Harlequin Presents®

Glamorous international settings…
unforgettable men…passionate
romances—Harlequin Presents
promises you the world!

Harlequin Presents® Extra

Meet more of your favorite Presents
heroes and travel to glamorous
international locations in our regular
monthly themed collections.

Harlequin® Romance

The anticipation, the thrill of the chase
and the sheer rush of falling in love!

Look for these and many other Harlequin and Silhouette
romance books wherever books are sold, including most
bookstores, supermarkets, drugstores and discount stores.

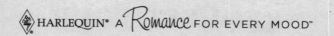

REQUEST YOUR FREE BOOKS!

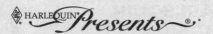 HARLEQUIN Presents®

PASSION GUARANTEED SEDUCTION

2 FREE NOVELS PLUS
2 FREE GIFTS!

YES! Please send me 2 FREE Harlequin Presents® novels and my 2 FREE gifts (gifts are worth about $10). After receiving them, if I don't wish to receive any more books, I can return the shipping statement marked "cancel." If I don't cancel, I will receive 6 brand-new novels every month and be billed just $4.05 per book in the U.S. or $4.74 per book in Canada. That's a saving of at least 15% off the cover price! It's quite a bargain! Shipping and handling is just 50¢ per book.* I understand that accepting the 2 free books and gifts places me under no obligation to buy anything. I can always return a shipment and cancel at any time. Even if I never buy another book, the two free books and gifts are mine to keep forever.

106/306 HDN E5M4

Name	(PLEASE PRINT)
Address	Apt. #
City State/Prov.	Zip/Postal Code

Signature (if under 18, a parent or guardian must sign)

Mail to the **Harlequin Reader Service:**
IN U.S.A.: P.O. Box 1867, Buffalo, NY 14240-1867
IN CANADA: P.O. Box 609, Fort Erie, Ontario L2A 5X3

Not valid for current subscribers to Harlequin Presents books.

Are you a current subscriber to Harlequin Presents books and want to receive the larger-print edition? Call 1-800-873-8635 today!

* Terms and prices subject to change without notice. Prices do not include applicable taxes. N.Y. residents add applicable sales tax. Canadian residents will be charged applicable provincial taxes and GST. Offer not valid in Quebec. This offer is limited to one order per household. All orders subject to approval. Credit or debit balances in a customer's account(s) may be offset by any other outstanding balance owed by or to the customer. Please allow 4 to 6 weeks for delivery. Offer available while quantities last.

Your Privacy: Harlequin Books is committed to protecting your privacy. Our Privacy Policy is available online at www.eHarlequin.com or upon request from the Reader Service. From time to time we make our lists of customers available to reputable third parties who may have a product or service of interest to you. If you would prefer we not share your name and address, please check here. ☐

Help us get it right—We strive for accurate, respectful and relevant communications. To clarify or modify your communication preferences, visit us at www.ReaderService.com/consumerschoice.

HP10R